MY
GHOST
STORIES

RICHARD PIRES

Pires Farm Media

"That guy looks familiar." Charlie was pointing at the broken-down man standing in the wind chill of around 5 degrees. Bundled up inside the café, on their ritual Tuesday breakfast outing before work, Charlie couldn't shake the guy's face. He knew him from somewhere. He had to be famous.

"The bum?" Martin responded pouring sugar into his coffee, still waiting to have their orders taken.

"Just because he looks like that don't mean bum. Remember Shaun? He used to sell cars at Mercedes? He said, talk to every guy walking on the lot, even if they were in sweats and a hoodie. He sold three cars accepting people for their derelict appearances. I bet you a hundred bucks he has thousands of dollars on him." Charlie couldn't let this go. He was burning all his synapses trying to recall this man outside.

"How would you even begin to figure you would win that bet? First off, you would have to walk over there and speak to him. If he wasn't a drunk or drug addict, he may swing at you due to mental issues. And on top of that, even if he had money, why would he let you know he had any on himself? He may just be a hobo riding the bus." Martin was lost in the menu now as he decided against waffles.

"Hobos rode on trains and had sack bundles on sticks. I think I know that guy." Charlie couldn't let this go.

"So, who is he?" Martin needed another coffee refill already.

"You remember the first ghost hunt show?"

"The Searcher?"

"No."

"The Ghoster?"

"That's not even a word."

"Hollywood invents words all the time."

"Ghost Seeker?" Charlie remembered.

"Ghost Seeker sounds familiar."

"That's him. That's the Ghost Seeker." Charlie was enthused.

"Did you watch that shit?" Martin now was looking at the same broken man at the bus stop.

"Yeah. Some one said he was kicked off the show because he was too fake. They had to bring in the team to take over."

"I heard they got rid of him because he really could see ghosts and it was too much for television. Like he was solving old cold cases or something."

"No, that's how he got the show in the first place. He solved some kid's murder it was like a decade old case. He went to the town, found the murder weapon and then they brought in the real murderers." Charlie was excited.

"He looks terrible, if that's him."

"Well, hell, that show was what? Twenty years ago? Time flies."

"Should we ask him if he is the Ghost Seeker?"

"It's too cold. I wouldn't walk across the street to meet John Wayne, dude." Martin waived over the waitress who had been busy doing nothing for ten minutes.

"John Wayne is dead. I'm going."

Before Martin could say anything, Charlie was out the door, heading to this possible former celebrity. Cold wind pierced his eyes immediately, the tears froze just as they formed. Charlie wrapped his head with his scarf, buried his hands in his pockets and walked across the dead street. If this was the Ghost Seeker, he was waiting for a bus that was always ten minutes late.

The broken man was shivering, but he didn't seem aware of it. His eyes were sad, for a moment Charlie believed this man may attack him as he got closer to him. Then, suddenly, the sad eyes disappeared, replaced by soft focused ones. As if he was awakened from a daydream.

"Can you do me a favor?" The broken man asked.

"What do you need?" Charlie was taken aback. He was supposed to be asking questions.

"Call my sister, her name is Casey Knight, used to be Claremont. Tell her Henry is at the McMahon House. She needs to come there. By the time she does, I don't know if I will be me anymore." He handed over a mashed piece of binder paper, scribbles danced around the number in the center.

"Hey, were you the Ghost Seeker?"

"Long time ago, now I am just a man heading towards an ending." The Ghost Seeker took out a wad of cash, it had to have been over five thousand dollars. "Take this for your troubles. Just please make that call for me. I don't think I can do it myself now."

Charlie didn't notice the bus had parked behind him opening its door to the Ghost Seeker. He limped on, leaving Charlie speechless. The hiss of the automatic gears sent Charlie jumping up a foot as the bus pulled off and sped down the road towards the interstate.

"Holy shit." Charlie walked back to the diner.

Martin had been watching the entire time.

"It was him." Charlie sat down.

"Cool."

"He also had a bunch of money on him."

"Glad I didn't make that bet."

Charlie dropped the wad of cash on the table. "Breakfast is on him."

"What?" Marin counted out the money, laughing.

"I have to make a phone call for him."

"Do it. Give him his moneys worth. Shit, I'll call too."

1

In the Beginning 1986

My name is Henry Claremont, in the year of our Lord, 1986, I developed the ability to see and talk to ghosts. I was ten years old. As kids my friends and I used to play around an old mine buried in the base of a mountain surrounded by a desert community. It was one of those ancient western towns Nevada forgot on the way to Las Vegas. Small but not tiny, we had an array of modern conveniences including an arcade, but very little else. My school was small but effective, the population was rounding out around three thousand, not too bad for a fledgling desert town that used to house bandits and brothels. We would get the left-over tourists from Vegas in the summer months, the losers Vegas created would lick their wounds out here, getting a decent trip for a decent price. Sometimes the local government would try to cash in on our status of being one of the most haunted cities in America. We tried to push Halloween parades and haunted hotels. The market wasn't quite there yet, but it provided enough interest to keep anyone living here their employment.

The hills that surrounded our town used to thrive in gold and silver at one point in the history of America, but now had all but dried out. The companies were long gone but their machines and carts and their tracks never left. Old crates laid about the landscape as if the horse drawn cart was coming up the mountain tomorrow, ready to take the contents to the steamship docked in the river port twenty miles away. We would hide amongst the antiques, firing at each other with our toy guns, protecting the natural resources inside the cave we never dared set foot into. However, all these precautionary measures we adopted to maintain a safe play zone yielded nothing. Unbeknownst to us, the children, running around a metal mesh secured over a deep chasm that led to the center of the mine below. Decades of dirt and rain and debris had coagulated on top, sealing the millimeter sized holes in the mesh which were slowly breaking up as the tiny feet of ten-year-old boys ran across it. This mesh screen was the launching pad for my destiny, my curse, my gift, my pain, my power, was delivered unto me.

The mesh did not give out beneath my feet. Above, was a pulley system, which brought up those crates from below. Ancient metal crisscrossed with ancient rope, both coated in layers of dirt that hardened both materials. We had always slammed against the poles holding the pulley system up, we had always yanked on the dangling ropes, swinging over the unseen mesh covering the chasm without an iota of worry. But, in that summer of 86, the pulley system snapped above my head, swinging with such a force that it struck my temple. I was flung across the grate, landing along its edge. It creaked, rocked, the dirt had finally fallen off revealing its truth: seventy-eight feet of blackness leading to solid rock.

Death was tipping in my direction as the grate teetered under the sudden increase of weight. My friends stumbled toward me, but stopped when they saw the grate's edge cracking, sending dust up. An unholy cry erupted over the sound of shouting and the ringing in my ears. I looked down into the dark void and saw a man, crawling along the sides of the hole. His face was so contorted with fear, sadness, and anger that it made me shake. I was pulled away within seconds as the metal barrier keeping the living from the dead creaked and folded within itself, falling into the chasm beneath.

I was breathing heavy, my head gushing blood, I tasted metal, dirt, and snot as I flew up off the ground. My friends gathered round me to make sure I was fine. We all stood still for what seemed like hours, gazing down the shaft. My head shrieked with constant drumming. I could feel my temples beating fast and hard as more blood pumped through the gashes in my head, all I could do was stare at the screaming man still climbing up from the bottom of the mine. My eyes rolled to the back of my head, I fainted, back to ground with such a thud I thought I was dead.

Two days in the hospital allowed me ample time to heal. I awoke to see several Transformers on my hospital bed side, and then passed out again. I figured I could wing another dozen or so action figures with the occasional moan and spasm. Grandma fell for it every time. Most of these memories focus on my grandmother, I wasn't given the ample time with her I wanted. She was short, stout, short hair, smoked More cigarettes and read romance novels that my grandfather called "titty touchers" due to the men or women casually seeming to rub the opposing nipple. I would tell her my own stories as an adolescent, usually one about a GI Joe character that wouldn't die. It was a totem that lasted hours if I wasn't stopped by a sane human being. She would laugh as I put stanza after stanza together describing the methods of death this GI Joe would experience. Each line ended with, "but he would not die."

My grandfather was more reserved and had a Catholic stoicism infused with a matriarchal need of the Mother Mary. He never had known his mother in real time. Only stories of what she used to be before he was born. He was lost before I ever knew him. My grandmother had an odd understanding of him, and they both made their marriage work all of forty-two years. I would catch them dancing together in the kitchen sometimes when I spent the night. I would always ask for eggs and bacon for dinner, and she would always cook it. So much grease splattered tile, I felt bad every time she wiped it down. She cooked me more eggs than most body builders eat today, this was the eighties mind you, the zenith of anti-egg propaganda. Now, looking back, maybe it was the added protein prompting the Second Sight.

I left the hospital one week later, the face of the man in the hole continued to haunt me throughout the healing process. I would wake up screaming, sweating, the stitches in my head split, forcing returns to the hospital. I was forced to speak to a specialist. He had a well-intentioned face, soft voice, one could fall asleep listening to him prattle on. His full name I never looked up, he was simply, Dr. Murphy to me. My parents were told he was an expert in neurology, my head had received such a hit most would have died from. For some reason, not only was I alive, but I had no effects reflecting any type of mental deficiency. No slurred speech, no vision issues, no lost memory. It was like I had developed a second layer of protection along the top of my brain.

"How is the noggin today, son?" Dr. Murphy asked checking my eyes with his trusty mini flashlight.

"Not bad. Not too many headaches. Just. I keep seeing stuff float."

"Float?"

"Like, hovers. I don't know what it is. Maybe I can see dust and molecules better than any human because of my head wound?" I was trying to see if the comic book trope of accidental event could equal superhuman powers. I was half right in the end.

"Probably just your eyes playing tricks on you. Perhaps the cornea was affected in the fall too? I just don't see it."

"Maybe it's nothing."

"Maybe. But let's double check."

"I was watching PBS on tv, and Carl Sagan was talking about black holes, dark matter, clouds of gases all over the universe, maybe I'm seeing that?" I asked hopefully.

"Doubtful, all that stuff exists billions upon billions of miles away. I don't think any of it is floating about with us. But you're a big space nut?" Doctor Murphy gave a clinical smile most pediatric professionals put on to soothe. Most kids know it's bunk.

"Not really. I like movies more."

"Neat. Maybe I will bring in the VCR and we can watch some classics. You like Westerns?"

"Sure. I just saw Outlaw Josey Wales two months ago. Dad rented it. Clint is pretty good."

"I'll show you The Searchers." Dr. Murphy no longer had that fake clinical smile. He was genuine in this small exchange.

Out of cautionary measures I was introduced to the MRI. Instead of seeing what he thought existed on my gray matter, we found something much worse. A new mystery for science to solve. Throughout my brain were pockets of black mass. As if I was carrying around pieces of Dark Matter, physically in the core of my mind. These masses would shift and pool in certain spots and then dissipate just as fast. A call went out to the hospitals around the country to see if they could figure out this new riddle my little brain spat out. I was featured in several medical magazines for a few weeks. I had an interview for one, but they cancelled last minute when the doctor said it might be too much. All the while the action figures continued to line up against my bedroom wall. Grandma and Grandpa felt they could keep me grounded to this plain of existence with plastic people. God bless them, they were on to something. As the stress mounted with my prognosis, my grandmother was failing health wise. All the worry and fear began to eat at her. First it was a mild fever, then a dizzy spell, then a faint. One day she just could not move at all. Her pain snaked across her back and sides. All her interior was beginning to wane as if the mortality clock was reaching its alarm. I did not notice at first because I was young and preoccupied with my own health issues. My father saw it and began to worry more about her than me.

Seeing the dead, at first, is disturbing.

Obviously.

I practically lived in the hospital as my brain was being explored by Dr. Murphy. It was a dour place for me. Children who were truly sick were stuck in their rooms as I got to roam the halls late at night with my father or mother holding my hand. One night, we had stumbled upon an empty room. I approached the open door, hearing a wheezing sound. My mother went to a nurse for some coffee, leaving me in her peripheral vision. Lights from the outside world danced along the walls from lowered blinds. The wheezing grew louder, as if whatever was making the sound had developed an irregular heartbeat. On this reflection, I realize, this ghost was far more afraid of me than I had any right to be afraid of her, but I was ten and still a child. A hand flew out in between the artificial light, looking to hook me to pull closer into an abyss of mundane hospital décor. I fell back, hitting the door shut behind me. My mother immediately dove for the closed door, but I hit the latch, locking it. I was frozen, watching the form of an old, corkscrew woman straightening up into a fully formed human shape. Her body shifted in the dark, I could see the different styles of clothes she wore during her time in life. Sometimes, a brief shot of her nude body in different stages of age. This was happening all at once. I was witnessing her life phasing in and out as she stretched out to me.

"Help me, boy…" Now her face contorted into the faces of her death rattles. Mouth open, teeth protruding out as if they were about to burst. Her tongue swelled so large; I could see all the imperfections of the muscle. Then she fell to her knees, the phasing slowly stopped, she rose, taking hold of a solid form for a full thirty seconds. This allowed me to see a single red Robin broach on her chest pocket of a nice black coat. This was the suit she was buried in. Diamonds for eyes, the red color of the bird was bright crimson, the black of the peak had a luster that took me off guard for a moment. This old woman, stood still, looking at me with such sadness.

"Help me, boy…" she repeated.

My mother came through the side door from a neighboring storage room, switching the light on. The old woman was short, we were eye to eye. Then she disappeared. I fell to the floor, passing out from the shock. I was rushed to my room, but the excitement stopped as soon as I woke up. I wasn't hyperventilating, I wasn't sweating profusely, I was calm. As if the whole incident was a dream.

"What happened in there, love?" Mother asked, still pale I wanted the doctor to check her out more than me.

"Nothing. Nothing. I just, I thought I saw something. I don't know." I couldn't tell the truth. I didn't want my mother worried about me eternally. I had to pretend this was an aftershock of the accident. I felt if I just ignored this along enough, normalcy would return.

The old woman with the Red Robin broach continued to find me as I went through my routine at the hospital. She maintained most of the form I last saw her in, but the phasing began to occur as I focused on her more. It was as if the more I concentrated the more life returned to her. When I had my MRI, she would appear, sticking her head where my feet stood out. As I lay motionless, she smiled and uttered:

"I do apologize for my appearance. I just didn't know how to express my confusion. My name is Minerva. And I think I'm dead."

That's how it began. Minerva introduced herself with a soft voice that had the power to soothe and melt one's own heart. Minerva would tell me bedtime stories she had remembered as a child. Minerva was my first experimentation with speaking to the dead. At first, I was too obvious, I spoke loudly as if everyone could see her, making me look incredibly psychotic. Having black matter floating around my brain tissue calmed the fear however as my doctor was quick to remind me.

"You are not seeing dead people, Henry. Your brain is experiencing spasms, probably more frequently as time goes on. You are seeing these things in your mind. They are not real. They do not respond to your speaking to them out loud."

"They respond. When you hear me talk to air, aren't there breaks?"

"I don't like to ease drop on people. But, yes, I do notice those pauses. Though, again, you are hearing their responses in your mind. Reality is muddled as your brain slowly heals itself. The swelling is going down, the black masses are subsiding. I think soon you can go home."

"Can you see black holes from here?" I asked smugly.

"No."

"Then how do you know they're there. Just because you don't see something doesn't mean someone else can. Eyes can be like a telescope with infrared, Dr. Murphy. Carl Sagan had a special on astronomy last night."

"We need to watch more John Wayne." Dr. Murphy smiled.

"I think we should watch more John Ford." I liked the directors more than the stars in the golden age of Hollywood.

"Touché. I have seen this reported before. In the most extreme cases of head trauma there are side effects that can really produce damage to the psyche. I just hope these illusions you're having doesn't complicate your healing or your life." Dr, Murphy wrote in his notebook, an exercise he was participating in more and more dealing with me. He had written three articles already. Little did I know he was making a fortune off me with seminars around the country, one even in France. "Oh, and if you want to watch a real western by a true master, I will have to introduce you to the maestro: Sergio Leone."

"I think I heard of him."

"Oh, you will love this guy." Dr. Murphy smiled again, breaking that clinical wall. I was beginning to think of him as a friend. A great tutor of film, he was opening my eyes to the classics as Minerva was opening my mind to the dead.

"I would say you need to learn how to listen more closely and communicate stealthier." Minerva said inspecting my row of action figures lining the window.

"Stealthier?" I asked loudly, a nurse poked her head through the door.

"You need something, honey?"

"I'm fine, thank you."

I saw Minerva shake her head. "You see. Therefore, we should practice speaking quietly. You will be seen less as a freak show and more like an oddity."

"That doesn't sound much better."

"It will in the long run. Trust me. I died old. I have flashes of what I used to be. A teacher, I believe. I remember having summers off and reading creative writing with truly little creativity in the spring. English teacher, I have no doubt." Minerva continually shifted as she spoke to me. Making my equilibrium twist and churn. I had to close my eyes in these early encounters to maintain a balance. As I got older, I became used to the shifting.

"My dad likes to listen to old radio shows. One of them is called Edgar Bergman and Charlie McCarthy. He's a *ventrilogust*." I said it incorrectly, unable to make that '*ist*' sound.

★ 9 ★

"Ventriloquist. Throwing your voice isn't quite what I was thinking, but in this case, it might be worth considering. Try speaking to me under your breath."

I began to speak low with Minerva in the hospital, developing a shorthand speech pattern. A to the point sentencing in a low register. I could've been a ventriloquist if I put more effort in it, I could've headlined in Vegas. Even the nurses couldn't hear me after a while. I remember Minerva smiling, listening to me speak to her as the nurse checked all the boxes on their clipboards. None of them ever once noticed.

"You're getting better and better every day, Henry. I believe you won't be needing me much longer." Minerva said, staring out at the window a full moon was offering a lit-up cityscape. She would always lose herself at the view. Something she saw bothered her. Often, she was drawn to it only to jerk away, shaking off whatever she was witnessing.

"What is it?" I asked, desperately wanting to know what she continually rejected.

"I don't know. Sometimes it's the city I grew up in. I see the newspaper stand on that very corner, the same boy with the new edition in hand offering it up. I would walk down fifth street to collect the paper for my father. He would always give me a penny for my troubles." Minerva exhaled, falling into a sadness. "It only lasts so long. Then the whole city shifts, and I see what I assume is today. Other times it is entirely unrelatable. A massive city, lines of cars stuck in traffic, people rushing across the street in shabby clothes. There's a building surrounded by cars, the words, Starbuck hang along the awnings. Strange."

"Maybe you see the future?"

"If that's the future, then I am glad I had my time." Minerva was visibly shaken, like she saw a ghost. I caught Minerva losing what control she had maintained. She would lose herself in mid speech, gazing toward something I couldn't see. I watched fear creep into the stoic teacher façade. "There's something else too. It's been gnawing at me since I realized I was dead." She stopped herself not wanting to confess.

"Minerva, tell me, what's wrong?"

"A door? I don't understand it. I just keep seeing it. A door that I remember when I was a little girl. It was my grandmother's room. I read every book in her library growing up and right here, right now, it appears to me."

"Shouldn't that be a comfort?"

"You'd think so."

"Then why are you so afraid?"

"It makes me want to leave here. It makes me want to leave you. But I am not done here. I need to finish what we started. I need you to be okay."

"Don't stay on my account. I think I figured out how to speak low. How to maneuver this ability. You can go on home." I don't know why I said home. It seemed to fit the occasion. In my youth, home was more important than any other place I knew. It was safety, it was unity, it was security. I feel the tears grow as I remember the simplicity, the warmth of the fire in the winter, the cool hose water in the summer. The hills engulfing the sun as it laid down to sleep on the horizon. I had these moments to myself for years, never understanding their true meaning. Now with nostalgia, I weep for the past. My memories of life before the ghosts grow dimmer and dimmer every year. Some days I yearn for my door to take shape in the distance, allowing me to swallow back the emotions and let out the tears I keep to myself. To be free of this and to go home. Home is the only word I could think of every time the door is mentioned. Home is what all life needs, but not always guarantees. Perhaps that was the reason the ghosts always questioned it.

"Home?" Minerva walked across the small hospital room,

pantomimed opening an invisible door. As soon as she motioned the action, a gust of wind burst from the void only she could see. Electrical spasms erupted from anything plugged into the walls. Alarms sounded, machines wailed, sparks erupted. Nurses and doctors rushed in to check on me, their hair raised erratically due to the static electrical signals in the air. Most of the doors I encountered never erupted this violently. I always wondered why. Perhaps it was a way to convince the doctor and myself that I wasn't crazy. Maybe the door was too close to electrical currents and people. The door seemed to feed off energy or absorb it. As if the brief opening broke through the black matter in between reality and the beyond.

"What the hell happened in here?" Dr. Murphy shouted, noticing the hairstyle changes of the entire staff.

"If I told you, you would just put me back into the machine." I said pushing my hair down.

I had a chat with Dr. Murphy in his office telling him what I had experienced with Minerva. He wrote in his book, he listened intensively, his face going back forth from skeptic to believer.

"Minerva?" Dr. Murphy wrote into his book again.

"She was as real as you are. She just went in and out."

"In and out?"

"She would be in different clothes. They would come and go. A flicker. You know, like a film reel. Twenty-four frames a second. That's what it was like."

"And when the energy release happened? You said she went through a physical door?" Dr. Murphy used his fingers to pantomime a person walking. It almost made me laugh out loud.

"No. I didn't see it. Only she saw it. She said it was her grandmother's door."

"Interesting."

"Am I crazy?" I truly meant it.

"No, no. Honestly, Henry, if it was in your mind how do you

explain the sudden sound and fury that erupted? There are some things in the living world that have few explanations. This episode is one for the books, I can guarantee that. I am terribly excited."

"Why?"

"You could have answers to questions we have been asking for thousands of years. Or you could be an anomaly. Either way, worth exploring. Worth investigating."

"So, more tests?"

"None will be evasive. They will be simple. No tubes. Just sticky cups around your noggin and some wires. No pain. I just need two more weeks to explore an idea I have."

"You're the doctor." I glumly stated.

"I will put in a good word to your grandmother and grandfather for some Masters Of The Universe figures. Maybe even the Castle Greyskull." He smiled.

"I like how you do research." I smiled.

The two weeks turned into six. I was being probed every way one could be that was legal. Dr. Murphy was trying to catch my brain in a flux as I spoke to the dead. Unfortunately, in these last weeks I hadn't come across a spirit. I was alone in a sterile hospital ward where few people ever died let alone visited. My parents were growing concerned as the time spent in the hospital meant expenses they weren't counting on. We all came together for a meeting with Dr. Murphy to keep me here few months longer. I was too tired to speak as I sat in between my father and mother.

"I understand the fears, but I can assure you both that the expenses will be covered with grant money I have secured to no extra cost to you. Your son is experiencing a type of phenomenon that needs to be studied. I need more time with him to ensure his life will be as normal as it can be." Dr. Murphy laid out his case.

"He had head trauma sustained from the hit, but he has healed from that, right?" My mother asked.

"His brain is developing a growth that as of now has no abnormalities effecting his health. But as time goes on, it may develop into something worse. Or it may not. I just want to be sure." Dr. Murphy explained.

"Dr. Murphy, we do appreciate the extra care you have provided, we just don't think another six months is truly necessary. Henry has already lost a lot of time in school. We don't want to hold him back any further. Is there a way he can come back to you if he notices any discomfort?" My father asked.

"Of course. But, in this time, it is developing. In six months without observation, I am not confident that what is occurring will subside naturally. I fear what he is experiencing may get more pronounced and if that happens there might not be a way back." Dr. Murphy brought out the pictures of my brain displaying a black cloud surrounding most of my grey matter.

"Is it cancer?" My mother asked.

"No. It isn't affecting his brain, but it is affecting his vision. More to the point he says that he can see ghosts. And there is evidence to support his claim."

"You're serious?" My father was beginning to back away from Dr. Murphy's assessment. "I can't believe this is where you are taking this."

"I wouldn't have believed it myself, yet here I am trying to explain to you both the possibilities. And I have evidence from other medical resources that back up my assessment. I hope you understand I have the best interest for Henry in mind."

"If this ever came out, he would be a freak show, Dr. Murphy. We don't know how to handle something like this. Especially right now, with my mother being in the hospital. I just don't know if I, well, we, could put this on top of all else at this moment in time." My father was being honest, and I didn't blame him. This is something no parent could ever consider in a realistic way.

"I understand. But if this persists, I implore you, let me help me. I can at least try to understand what is going on. In the future there may be other cases matching Henrys. I just want to be sure as to what exactly is going on in his brain." Dr. Murphy knew he already lost the argument.

"We will be in touch, Dr. Murphy. We thank you for all you have done up until now." My mother ended the conversation.

Grandmother was in the hospital. She had collapsed at home. My father was in a tailspin, my mother was trying to catch up. I had no compass to guide me as I began to see what lurked in the shadows of the express way ramps and highway over passes. I saw so many souls walking in circles, tired of being ignored. I kept my eyes to the floor of the car as we stopped amongst the traffic lights. Any time I moved my head and opened my eyes to the ones I knew were dead they noticed my attention. Some would run full force to the window, screaming inaudible curses and pleads. I saw their wide eyes, drooping faces, caught in a far worse mask than Edvard Munch's portrait. All these screams were lost in the black hole of the living. But I heard them. I buried my ears into the headphones of my audiocassette Walkman, losing myself to the sounds of mid-eighties new wave. The hospital was much worse. Every room had a ghost. No one noticed them as I kept my eyes to the floor. No one noticed me either, only the dead seemed to care about me. I was waiting on the plastic chair in the hallway as father and mother spoke to the doctors about grandma.

Hospitals were littered with ghosts due to the obvious mortality rate hospitals keep. Most of them linger for a few moments then discover their doors. Others got lost on the way. When I was young, I didn't understand the concept of memory, it affects everyone differently. When you're young, you are living moment to moment, not looking back at anything, you have no reference. In later years you began to realize the moments were so fast because you weren't paying attention. You weren't taking notes of what was happening around you, you were just living. The dead didn't have that quality anymore. All they had were half remembered dreams of what they used to be. Time was different to ghosts, a point I would later learn and understand. I just wish now, looking back, I took the time to take in my surroundings and how my parents loved me in these moments. Every year, now, I lose more and more of them to old age. Soon, I may never truly have anything left of them. But this isn't the time to dwell on that part, yet.

"Come on, honey. Let us see grandma." Mother was lost in emotion. I could tell the news was far from good. I knew my grandmother had little time left.

"Okay." Was all I could muster as the ghosts clinging to the door frames clawed at me. Some were old people. Others were younger with bullet wounds, stab wounds or burnt husks from the fires that consumed their physical forms. Some were children. All with the same violent phase shift that cursed them.

"I need my bear. I can't find my bear." This little girl was begging from the entrance of the Children's Wing. Every time the automatic doors opened; I saw the rows of children all seemingly needing the same thing. Doctors and nurses doing their rounds, walked past the myriad of specters.

"Do you think there's ghosts here?" I asked my mother as we approached the room. From afar I could hear the machines breathing for my grandma.

"There are no ghosts in this world, honey. That's in the movies. Now, be careful saying hi to grandma."

My father stood with my grandfather sitting in the sole chair in the room. The blinds were closed, the buzzing and soft hisses of the breathing machines and read outs gave the room it's only personality. At first, I didn't recognize her. Her skin had yellowed, green rashes snaked across some of her exposed skin, her hair was wet, slicked back tight against her retreating skin against the skull which was growing more prominent as death was nearing. Looking at her, I felt nothing. At this moment, I realized this is where all of us end up. Lying in bed, those left around you, crying or thinking of the past. Meanwhile, you, the husk of flesh waiting to shed the physical for the next outfit, can only moan in pain or indifference as the time you understood begins to slow. The dead must have a whole new set of unknown rules to learn. All of it you must face alone. That's what I took from the hospital room that night. The loneliness death creates is one you must prepare for because we are all alone at the end of the road.

No adult has an answer for you, if you broke down to speak of what you were seeing they ignore you then dismiss you just as quickly. On average, ghosts present themselves as incredibly passive. Their physical description varies, some are holding their wounds that killed them. Others have an eerie glow, reminiscent of a translucent plastic caught in the dim light of a bulb. Some are just pathetic, lost with sunken eyes, filled with this unwanted knowledge. I believe that the damned were the most graphically maligned, forced to hold on to their wounds based on their deeds in the past life. Hospitals had many of them, roaming the hallways. The damned always had something following them. I couldn't see them as a youth, it was as if a beast existed under the foundation of reality, like a shark in the water. You could make out a shape but no detail. Only an audible growl followed, forcing me to look away.

The weeks went by, the nights got better. This allowed me time to reflect. Being ten years old, reflection was not something I under-stood. Though the time to myself in these weeks allowed me time to adapt to the coming powers. One night, as I tried to sleep in my bed at home, I felt a slight nudge against my elbow, as if someone were waking me up on purpose. I slowly opened my eyes to see my grandma. She smiled at me and spoke with such a low voice I had to sit up and lean against her to hear.

"Food for thought, I think you stumbled onto something important when you hit your noodle. And not just the ability to get more action toys." Granma spoke in a fading pattern; some words audible others weren't. But I could follow what she said. She always called action figures action toys because not all figures were figures, some were robots, some were aliens. Not figures. But all action. She had a funny way about her, but I never got to know more.

This was my last night with her.

"I love you, a bushel, and a peck. A bushel and a peck. And a hug around the neck. With a barrel full of heap. And I am talking in my sleep, about you. About you."

It was her song to any baby growing up. She sang it to my dad too. It was a tradition that died with her I have never heard it since. Her form wasn't shifting either. She was whole. Perhaps the door she opened was to my bedroom. In the hope I would be up to say goodbye because I was the only one who could reciprocate.

"Does it hurt?" I asked timidly.

"No. It's like the universe makes peace with only you and everything washes away."

"But I don't want you to go." My lip quivered tears began to fall.

"I wanted you to know that you didn't have to be afraid anymore. The dead need you sometimes to aid them. Now, you can save so many. Try to save as many as you can. Open yourself to them. Never fear the dead. Fear the living." My grandmother began to shift. My last moments were ending.

"I love you." Was all I could tell her before she smiled back at me.

"We will all be at the same table one day. As if no time has passed."

Then she was gone.

I tried to reach for her, but the door opened sending a blast of light into my room, engulfing my view of her. As my eyes focused back to the door frame it was my father standing there. He was sad but hadn't shed a tear, yet.

"Hey, buddy. Granma is in heaven now. She passed away tonight." He said it with no emotion. It was pap, a note card for a parent who didn't want to open more. He wasn't an emotional man but how could he be with an eleven-year-old. I never hated him for being cold. He didn't understand all I needed was someone to pay attention. I didn't care if they knew the answers. I just wanted to know he was present. But fathers are not always present. They are miles away with their worries and fears. Their ultimate mistakes haunt them like the spirits haunt me.

"You okay, buddy?" He came to my bedside and pushed my hair away from my face. I didn't tell him what happened. In my head I already knew. It didn't scare me this time. In fact, it changed me.

"I'm fine. Did she suffer?"

This pushed my father away. "Suffer? No, she just went in her sleep. She's gone now. No suffering. Thank God." He kissed my forehead and tucked me back in.

"I know she's okay now, daddy." I said back to him as he walked away.

"You 're absolutely right, son, absolutely right." He closed the door slowly.

I confided in my mother the next day, telling her what happened to me the night before. My mother was taken aback, knowing what had happened to me in the hospital, knowing the reports of Dr, Murphy. I think that was when the schism started. It scared her. I saw it in her eyes when I mentioned the singing.

"You shouldn't tell your father this. Just keep it to yourself." Mother went back to the kitchen, looking for something to focus on other than me. "Just keep some things to yourself. People will look at you differently if they know too much."

"But he should feel good about it, right? She's in heaven."

"Stop!" She shouted.

"I'm sorry."

"Don't be sorry. Just be quiet." She turned the radio on, blasting the Top 40.

After the funeral, I told my grandfather the truth. I felt it would help him more than telling my dad. Grandfather was an old-world type of fellow. He read more into what I was saying than my father. He took me aside and pulled me close.

"You saw her? She was happy?" His eyes swelled with tears.

"Yeah. She said there was more to my noodle than everyone thought. Sang me our song and told me she loved me. Then she was gone."

"Blessed be God forever." He said to himself. He seemed to melt away. As if my reporting of what happened was enough for him to move on. In fact, within six months he too passed away. My father had lost both his parents in the span of a year, it changed him. No longer did he come to my bedroom at night to say goodnight. No longer did he tuck me in. Instead, my parents began to shift most of their attention to my sister, Casey. She was six showing signs of intelligence beyond her years. Casey had the future I couldn't have. My curse was established, forcing them to let me go at an early age. It was out of fear, maybe shame. What I could do, no one should be able to do. I was a freak, and my sister was salvation. She could be the one to bring them out of their doldrums and broken dreams. I was the Albatross.

My mother must have told father what I revealed to her. I am sure it scared him. It scared me to tell her, but I didn't know what else to do. Normal people aren't allowed the time to ponder, they need to work a nine to five job, maintain a routine. Normal people aren't built for dead men's tales. I was becoming more able to deal with it. Minerva gave me the skill; my grandmother gave me the strength. Maybe I had to find another ghost to see if I could send them on their way. If I couldn't comfort my father or mother, perhaps I could save a lost soul.

2

An Arsonist, an Old Bandit, Gangsters and the FBI

I was out of school for a while as I healed. My mother had maintained a curriculum within the school's perimeters allowing me to keep up with the class. When I spent the first full day back in the classroom, I realized I was three weeks ahead. Being bored allowed me to focus on a corner. Suddenly, the form of a child appeared in the classroom. His clothes were obviously from another era but soaked in ointment. I couldn't smell it, but it looked thick. Not water, but maybe grease? Oil? Once the boy was fully formed, his head was lowered, eyes blank, as if he were caught doing something wrong. Then, suddenly, the clothes changed like Minerva's did. All the clothes he wore in life fluttered across his being, allowing me a disjointed fashion show. I looked away, feeling a tinge of guilt. I had to know more about who this kid was. I had to do research.

I ventured into the library, figuring the school librarian would know something about this school's history. I was wrong. She was twenty-six and had just graduated Graduate School to be a librarian. Good money, so I was told. But nary an iota of history degree in her pedigree. I was given the address to Mr. Samuel Harmon, the local historian who had been desperately trying for years to open a local museum in town. Various mayors and city council members have always applauded the idea, but when it came down to cutting a check their zeal was removed and the lack of fundraising was always the excuse. However, Mr. Harmon carried on, keeping thousands of documents in an insanely ordered system he designed after spending fifty years as a librarian and archivist. The digital age was around the corner, but not quite available in my hometown currently. So, Mr. Harmon literally had a house held together by documents.

"What are you asking me?" He was a curt older man.

"I was curious if my school has a history of tragedy. Did a kid ever die in the school? A fire? A flood? Something cataclysmic?" I was being specific as I knew a fire was the best choice looking at the sad kid's image.

"Johnny Kerosene," Mr. Harmon exhaled tiredly. "I was there that morning. 1934, they took his body out of the school when the smoke cleared. Then they took out two more bodies. Mr. Cutterwick, the janitor and Mrs. Salmanstern, the childless old maid who lived in the school out of duty."

"She lived in the school?"

"That was an exaggeration, of course she didn't live at the school. She was a slave to it. One of the most oppressive teachers a child could ever meet. I rather have had a nun. But it was a tragedy, of course. She was napping in the lounge when the smoke got her."

"What about the janitor?"

"Passed out drunk in his sleep closet. Burnt up quicker due to the jars of moonshine."

"Wasn't prohibition over by then?" I was serious in asking this because I had just watched a documentary on Public Access.

"Yes, good memory on you." Mr. Harmon smiled, but immediately switched back to curmudgeon. "He still made moonshine; old habits die hard."

"So, Johnny Kerosene was his name?"

"Nick name. He was a pyromaniac. Liked the smell of kerosene and the flicker of fire. He lit up more than he could manage and burnt up in the fire."

"Poor guy." I said this to myself, but Mr. Harmon took it to heart.

"He was a weirdo. Shouldn't play with fire, you die. A tough lesson."

"That it is, Mr. Harmon. Thanks for your help."

"That was all? You have no other questions? You know the mine where you fell around was a place for outlaws back in the 1880's."

"I might come back to ask about that one too. School project, maybe."

"I'm always here, my boy. Just knock."

I waited until lunch recess to head into the classroom. Not one teacher was in sight, it was Friday before a three-day weekend, so most of the teachers were halfway out the door already. I assumed they were smoking in the lounge, the married teachers discussed where they were taking their families on a camping trip, the un-married teachers were talking about what bar trash they might take home, and the gay teachers were all taking a trip to the city where the clubs were welcoming.

I stood at the door, creeping my head out to check the hall, not a soul. Suddenly, my eyes noticed the nebulous shape began to churn. Within seconds it was the same boy. This time I knew his name.

"Johnny?"

He stopped and turned his whole body wet. In his clenched fist was a small box of matches. "Hi. You know my name? Did my mom send you?"

His face shined for a second saying the word mom. He began to take notice of the room we were in. Its décor didn't match the one he knew fifty years ago. Then his being began to shift again.

"Where am I?"

"At school. We just had to remodel. After the fire." I said the last part fast, not thinking if it would cause him to snap or curse or fidget like some mad man on the streets. But nothing stirred out of him. He just nodded his head.

"That was my fault. I didn't mean to start it. I thought… I had a bucket of water, but I spilt it too fast. My mom and dad must hate me. God too. I just wish someone could tell them all, I am sorry. I didn't mean to start it. I just liked burning my paper towns. The kerosene made it funner."

"I don't think anyone hates you. It's been a long time. I think your mom and dad and God want you to go home."

"Really? They said that?" His shoulders propped up, his eyes were turning blue, his grey skin returned to its original peach hue. Johnny was returning to what he was before the fire. A transformation that took seconds to conclude. Even his clothes stopped shifting allowing a new set of colors to emerge, he was whole now, then he smiled at me. "Should I use the door?"

I shrugged my shoulder and told him, "Why not. If it opens for you, use it."

He was off like a shot, stopped, then opened an invisible door, like a mime performing only for me.

"Good luck, Johnny!" As I shouted this, the bells rang and the kids and teachers rushed into the halls, Johnny was churned like a towel in a washing machine. But as he got to the door he turned around, looking straight at me in this sea of elementary school students, each one running through his image. Then the energy release erupted into the hallway. Papers fluttered into the sky; back packs were pulled slightly toward the vacuum of energy. Static electricity danced around every man, woman, and child in the hallway. Ever one started laughing, feeling a sudden joy only children feel on Christmas morning. Within moments it was over, the electrical fields had ceased, the children and adults dismissed the event with nary a wink. I stood in the middle of it all, laughing, forcing everyone to look at me with curiosity. I wasn't afraid anymore. I wanted to know more. I wanted to see more.

The police had blocked off most of the mine with yellow tape that was not enough to keep the other kids away. I had heard everyone was spelunking down with harnesses and ropes, trying to find if there was any gold down here. As I approached, I heard the scrapping, the clawing, and the screaming rise from it. As if on cue, it grew louder the closer I approached.

"Okay, cool it, man!" I shouted like Shaft, which was on Cable before I came out to the mine. It was close to midnight; I had snuck out of my room to head up here.

"Cool it?" The disgusting voice croaked. It was filled with mucous and spittle as if he could never spit that glob out. It rolled around the tongue and stuck in the opened wet mouth in a never popping saliva bubble. "You seem to hear me, boy?"

"I hear you clear as day. But you got to spit that stuff out, maybe you'll feel better."

The man plopped out of the hole, crawled toward me in a distorted version of a human with a broken back. He stood up for the first time in a hundred years, his face shifting from decay to human. It was as if the moon was fixing his posture and face. Bringing him out of the death mask and back into the image he used to exist in.

"You know how long it has been since I've seen the moon?"

"Hundred years?"

"You got it."

The ghost sat Indian style in front of me. He looked up at me with an incredible curiosity. As if I was not real. His form wasn't still. His arms, legs, chest, even head, had sporadic changes. One millisecond this man had a long sleeve shirt on, then in another he was bare, in another he had a black winter coat over it. Same with the legs, several variations of pants and bare leg fluttered like a flag caught in the wind. It took me a few seconds to get over it. But as soon as he spoke, the cloth change slowed but remained as if the timeline of their life was rolling over them like shadow sucking up sunlight.

"Well, what's your deal?' I asked.

He furrowed his brow and spit. He looked around and stood up again, standing about six feet six inches tall. A massive figure that was more paternal than supernatural.

"I don't know. I feel like I was screaming before I came up here, but now I don't seem to remember shit. I remember the moon though. It was full when I looked up from the shaft. Marcus went to get Helen, but he didn't know I fell." His eyes were moving back and forth as if there was a physical brain searching out the recall of memory.

"Helen your wife?" I asked genuinely interested.

"Whore. But she was close to a wife. I wanted to marry her, but I fell down this here hole and that was the end of that idea."

"Did you find gold?"

He looked back at the hole noticing the new ropes and harnesses snaking along the sides and down the chasm. He circled around the hole keeping his eyes on the neon green ropes and reinforced straps.

"Shit, I only used one rope to back and forth. What the hell is all this nonsense?" He asked with a disgusted tone.

"Well, lots of people are into safety now. That is probably the reason you died. Lack of safety."

He furrowed his brow and spit, gave another look to the green straps and ropes. "Good point."

"My name is Henry Clermont."

"My name is Frank Grant. Glad to meet you. And no, we never found gold here. Shit, this was just a scam me and the fellas came up with to cover our robbing of government coaches. We would steal from heavy land barons tied to the federal government, they were always hauling silver and gold pieces across the states. So, we would steal them, then melt them down and say we found them in this here hole. Come to think of it, the government taxed us on our findings too. So, they robbed us right back!" Frank Grant laughed, slapping his knee like a stereotypical miner from 1849.

"How long you do that for?" I asked with sincere curiosity, now sitting Indian style looking up at this wonderful specter.

"Got away with it for round six years. I think because I went down neck first into that hole, roughly, during winter. We started round five winters prior… I hope my buddies came out alright. And Helen. Shit, I hope she turned out okay."

"You got their last names? I can look them up, maybe. See if there is any history on them. I can check with Mr. Harmon, he's the local historian, knows everything."

"Helen Cain, Marcus Toll, Sammy Camster and Snake Monroe. Those were my friends. Let me know what happened. I will be out here. I think." Frank lost himself to the vista down the hill. He saw the new city below, but then he saw other things. As his clothes continued to shift so did his expressions.

"What's wrong?" I asked, snapping him out of his glaze state.

"I don't know. It was as if suddenly I saw the times of all my years flutter in a moment. As if I was standing over the clock of the world, seeing all its modern workings and stone age beginnings. Then when I close my eyes, it all seems to slow down. And the world is back in this moment."

"Time is different to ghosts, I guess." I stated not understanding the implications that statement would conjure up. "Do you sleep?" I asked really wanting to know. This talking to a ghost thing was a revelation.

"I think I nap. It's like I twist and turn then I wake up when I hear something specific. With you, it was like a cock doodling to the rising sun. It was distinct, but familiar. Like I was supposed to respond to this noise as opposed to the others."

"Frequency stuff." I said to just myself, he had no idea what the hell I just said.

"Do me that favor, son. Find out about my friends. Then maybe, I can get you a nice little token of gratitude."

The next day, I rushed to Mr. Harmon's house, spitting out the names as quickly as I could, "Helen Cain, Marcus Toll, Sammy Camster and Snake Monroe?"

Mr. Harmon looked up from his stacks of papers on his dining table. "You can write those names down and I could research them in a timely fashion, but luckily for you, you have breached my favorite time of the town. You find these names at school or something?"

"Yep. I read about them in some pamphlet at school. I think they were criminals. If that helps?" I asked, trying to see how this archive system worked. Mr. Harmon kept his hand over the interior of his book as if I were trying to copy his answers. Answers to what question? No clue, but if you took this much time to audit local history, you had to have a few screws loose.

"Helen Cain was a local legend. She cleaned up a lot of the town back in 1887. Took down several saloons and whore houses. She became a Temperance Leader early on, essentially leading to several woman's groups growing to political power in the state. Not a bad record." Mr. Harmon smiled reading over her achievements.

"Was she a hooker at any point in her life?" I asked, knowing full well she was at the beginning. Hell, most people must be sinners before they become saints.

"Hooker?" Mr. Harmon scanned the pages. "None I can see here. But the records are vague prior to 1880. Hmm, Marcus Toll was hung in 1882, says here, he was a bandit. Murdered two Federal Marshals."

"That's all it says?"

"That's all I got in the records. Seems to be one of the earliest newspaper articles. The Local Herald, started up in 1882, the fall, he was hung round winter, Christmas time." Mr. Harmon nodded his head. "I wonder if the city hall has older records?"

"I thought you had all the records?"

"I do. But Mayor Hershal, back in 84 took an interest in the earlier history. I never understood it. This could be a great excuse to finally discover why." Mr. Harmon was incredibly excited. "You realize I have spent twenty years trying to produce a concise history of this town and the surrounding area?"

"I did not know this, sir." I added the sir to be profound, but he rolled his eyes.

"Mayor Hershal knew something. Now it's time to figure out what."

Mr. Harmon began his search without me. He told me to come back in a week. I went back to the mine, only to hear the same old screaming and hawking of snot. It was like a rerun, every noise recounted, every broken breathing repeated. It became less and less scary every time you heard it.

"Hey Frank Grant!" I shouted as he crawled out of the hole.

The ghost schtick ended immediately, "Hey, buddy."

"So, I got some information on Helen and your buddy Marcus."

"Yup?"

"Looks like Helen cleaned out the saloons and whore houses and Marcus was hung in 1892 for killing two Federal Marshals."

"Damn. That's doubly disappointing."

"The local historian is checking up on the older stuff at city hall. Something about Mayor Hershal he must check up on--"

"HERSHAL?" Frank screamed an unholy cry that would shake the walls of Hell. "What the shit is Hershal still around here for?"

"Well, he was mayor. Not anymore. I think he's retired."

"Hershal blood line never retires. That son of a bitch was after us way back when, probably the reason Marcus got hanged. Why Helen changed her ways too. Herbert Hershal was running things then, what is the new guy's name?"

"I don't know his first name. And I told you, he isn't mayor anymore. He retired."

"Trust me, son. A Hershal keeps his finger in every pie. Hundred years later don't make no difference." Frank walked over to the edge of the cliff overlooking the major hub of the city. Main Street wasn't very impressive then, it took another ten years to get a nationwide auto part store. But this did not stop Frank from guffawing out of wonderment. "Would you take a look at that?"

"It's okay. We don't have a movie theater. We must go to Oaksquare for that. Like a twenty-minute drive."

"Drive? You don't ride?"

"Never learned."

"Hell, what you guys doing down there for fun now?"

"Arcade is cool."

"Arcade? I wonder if I can go down there." Before Frank could finish, he placed a foot out against the sky, leaning toward the gradual slope of the hill leading to a gas station. His foot began to disintegrate. He pulled off from his current trajectory, allowing his foot to return to normal.

"I guess you can't leave this place."

"That's a bunch of bull shit."

"I wonder if that's how you get into heaven?"

"Heaven?" Frank was shocked.

"What?"

"I don't know if I was good enough for heaven. Seeing your own foot fall apart like that puts things in perspective." Frank walked back to the shaft. He traced his steps from the left side of the hole. Marching twenty steps he came to a boulder.

I walked along with Frank watching his recollection take shape. "What are you doing?" I asked gazing at the boulder.

"You think you can push this rock a good five feet?"

"It looks heavy."

"The exact point when using a boulder." Frank tried to move his hands around it yet couldn't make contact. His hands seemed to float amongst the surface.

"What's under there?"

"A bag full of coins. I never got around to smelting them. But they're all yours if you want them. I got no use for them now."

"Gold coins?"

"What else kind of coin is there?"

Suddenly, my strength doubled as I put my whole body into the boulder. My legs dug into the dirt, kicking up mounds behind my heels, the hundred years of dirt and dust slowly began to crack, allowing gravity to take its toll. Frank was beaming with paternal pride as the boulder moved across the dirt. The ratty bag become visible, through the holed in the tattered sack, gold shined through like ten mini suns breaking their way through a galactic abyss.

"Holy shit." T'was the first time I ever cursed out loud.

"Indeed. Now, I would keep this to myself if I were you. If I know people, and I like to think I do, anyone who sees this or hears about it will come after you and make your life miserable or end it coldly." Frank knelt beside me and looked into my eyes to make sure I was paying attention. In his peepers were moving particles, like swirling nebulas hanging against a backdrop of tinted blue gemstones. The tendrils that floated around his being echoed a harmonic buzz, almost like a musical tune, though I couldn't compare it to any song. His whole aura was alive, floating against the backdrop of my reality.

"I won't tell anyone." I began to lift the bag, but the weight of gold tore it apart. "You got a wooden box around here?"

"I got a sled."

When I was eleven years old, I ran down a hill with thirty-five million dollars' worth of gold coins at my back. The sled had a wooden box nailed to it properly, perfectly allowing the strain of the added weight of the sloshing gold. It was heavy as all hell. We put a tarp over it and added a few bricks to disguise it more. This added to the weight, but the hill allowed me an incline taking much of the weight off. No one saw me heading back home, no one noticed the sled being dragged against the black top of the street. It was as if this were all a show for me, but in the back of my mind, I knew these gold coins would never see the resurrection into green bills.

I took the sled to our garage connected to the alley, removed from the main street. I was sweating profusely, I took a few coins to my pocket, wanting to keep a few to myself, I felt I deserved it.

When I showed my father, he exploded in joy. He hugged me tightly and lifted me up, spinning me around like some family mov-ie where the dog spoke English. My mother was hesitant, worrying about the too good to be true scenario, always the realist, her curse. Though, when my father began to sing happily it broke down her demeanor.

"Where did you get this?" My father was counting the coins, each one bringing a brighter luster across his face.

"The mine shaft." My father was taken aback, but the gold con-tinued to blind any type of sense he might have had left. "I told you to stay away from there. You hurt yourself, badly. You shouldn't go back there."

"Sorry."

"It's fine. If you learn from your mistakes. And bring gold home, all is forgiven." He smiled down on me and I smiled back, never loving him more. In the euphoria, my father failed to realize that a moment like this should be kept quiet. No one should know about this situation because it is a one-in-a-million type of event. But what my father didn't realize was that gold tends to bring out the worst in people. And the worst was coming soon.

Meanwhile, Mr. Harmon was buried deep in the sheets of public documents. Most of the land documents were held by a Landowner named, Herbert Hershal, he had essentially bought the town with murder and chaos. This was the preferred method of getting ahead when all you had to do was kill your competition. Hershal had created a monopoly on murder and theft. One man seemed to stand up to him through land purchases backed by real money, not lead. Hershal couldn't compete with real businessmen who went straight to the lawyers and government officials with trunks of gold ready for the purchase. Frank Grant had amassed a fortune of stolen gold, though that was not known at the time. The scheme worked; The Grant Gang would rob the government coaches carrying money across the state lines into the uncharted west. Taking the government gold, they smelted it into bars, then placed a mark onto it signifying the Grant family crest, even all involved were not related. Hershal suspected a nefarious angle, because he was indeed, nefarious. Patience was a skill Hershal developed in his long career. Sometimes a farmer or landowner would change their mind when a stack of cash was plopped on their table. They were even more malleable when you threw in a local whore, sweetening the deal. All one needed was a signed document in those days, simple to the point legally sealed deed to land that would be invaluable to this day. Hershal couldn't sway all that way; he especially couldn't sway Frank Grant that way.

Frank Grant had amassed seven thousand acres in the Oak Square Valley. Grant used to live where the multiplex stood in present day. He had wanted to build a farm with an enclosed grazing lot. He had started to buy cattle before he was thrown down a shaft. Hershal was never able to find that last stash of gold which was going to make that dream a reality. Frank put under that stone, where I took it up and gave it to my father, which ended up being the biggest mistake.

The newspaper reported the whole event, verbatim, from my father's mouth, making the front page the very next day. Within three days we were featured in the local good morning news program, the type of show you watch getting ready for school early in the seven-morning timeslot because they ceased airing cartoons. After that, the story went nationwide. We were never featured in the Network channel news segments because they were the type of fluff piece the real news ended on:

EXAMPLE

PETER JENNINGS

Dateline, small town USA. A lucky local, finds a bag of Wild Wild West loot worth north of 30 million dollars. Not a bad day's work, if you can get it. Haha, till tomorrow, America. Good night. (Shuffle Papers)

My uncle loved Peter Jennings, thus the example.

What no one knew at this time was why Mayor Hershal had re-tired. Behind the scenes he had been searching the local mine shafts for years. Apparently, his grandfather told him about Grant's loot when he was a boy. He also told him how to rule the best, with fear and violence. Mayor Hershal evolved to a modern-day land baron, no murder that you could see, no theft that you could understand after his lawyers ran through your property finding numerous is-sues with the land that would be confiscated by the government if you didn't have the right local officials in your pocket. He would then buy the land that was abandoned by the original owner for pen-nies on the dollar. If anyone ever questioned the why and who of the backward deals, a hole would open in the desert and questions stopped being asked.

In the months leading to the campaign win of Mayor Hershal, he had a Campaign Manager named Earl Jost, a slime ball of the highest order, slippery little bastard who would sell out your mom then his mom to prove he was being fair. Earl Jost was an amateur spelunker and explorer. Using his local historical knowledge uncovered with the aid of Mr. Harmon, Earl Jost discovered that one of the local caves was in fact the cave belonging to the Frank Grant Gang back in the days of Hershal's grandfather. Mayor Hershal was reaching a ripe old age of 68 by this time and knew he was approaching the launching pad of the mortal coil; he knew through the stories of his grandfather what could be in these caves. He had no proof that there was any gold, but he did have a hunch. Hunches were psychic sonic booms for the Hershal family. Problem was they skipped generations. This generation was not about to let the possibility of finding millions of dollars' worth of gold in a cave float away. Earl Jost was the key to his problems. One day the two went into the mountains of the town, but only one came out. Hershal testified to only being with Jost with one-night camping in the mountains it was a ritual they had participated in since they were kids, so said Hershal. However, Earl Jost was twelve years younger than Hershal, but no body no crime. The local police didn't want to press the matter as no one was asking about Jost too much. He didn't have any living relatives or children by one of his many hooker friends. Peter Hershal surrounded himself with people who didn't have people. His grandfather made that a personal rule to follow and Peter followed it closer than Jesuits following the Ten Commandments. But the pressure emanating from Earl Jost's disappearance become too much, Hershal stepped down from the mayor's office. He then disappeared himself. Within ten months, the case lost steam and the locals forgot too.

Mr. Harmon had collected stack upon stack of evidence to prove the nefarious nature of the town's early founder. However, who would listen? The reality of history is covered in blood, no one doubts this anymore, but the consequence of their legacies is either forgotten or so mired in slime that no one genuinely cares about the truth anyway. Mr. Harmon felt that it was his place to dispel the truth. He was a beacon. If anyone wanted to translate this little town, he could be their Rosetta Stone. He was fearless, he was meticulous, and he was a pain in the side of Peter Hershal, the grandson of our town's former Mayor. Peter Hershal had been ostracized from the community due to his father's gambling debts. Most of the luster the Hershal name had had turned to a mossy patina. No one wanted to do business with a failure and the son of a failure didn't ease any investor's pain. However, this didn't stop Peter Hershal from returning to his homeland. This was his birth right. This town was his and his grandfather built it not to have it squandered away in one generation. Peter was to be the savior of the Hershal name. His father was going to be the lone footnote of failure.

By the third week of our media exposure, Peter Hershal made his way back to his hometown. Long removed from the people, not one person noticed his giant Cadillac, painted black with tinted windows, followed closely by two others when he pulled into the main street. I could imagine his disgust with the town. It hadn't grown an iota in the years since he had left. The possibilities for it were monumental, since we were roughly thirty miles from Vegas. Rumor had it that he bought twenty miles of desert between here and Vegas, waiting the day where the BOOM would hit. I think he was off by twenty years. It was coming, but he was just too much of a Visionary to make it work in his own time.

"Pull up to the newspaper office." He spoke with a slight accent that seemed soft Cajun. Or maybe it was a show. A slow way to speak to make anyone scared feel at ease. He had a way with his movements. Once he was out of the car he danced around the curb of the street, as if the record store still had an opened window with music playing. That place closed right after he left. He pointed it out to the driver, who looked to be hired from friends from Jersey, translation, Mafia. "Used to be a record shop right there. A nice piece of music used to play from that window every day. People would just sit and tap their shoes. Spit their chew, smoke their cigars, cigarettes, kids with ice cream cones. That made me smile. Now, no one on the street. Looks like most kids are playing at that fucking arcade."

Down the street was the arcade, filled with the local kids jamming quarters into any slot they could find. Hershal spit, shaking his head.

"Ah, hell. I should have invested in that. Daddy's weakness falls into my veins sometimes. Never had an eye for what kids would spend money on. I guess kids with quarters is just as good as a miner with a pan." Hershal smiled at the driver.

"Fucking kids." The driver responded lighting up a cigarette.

"Give me a few minutes in here. If you boys want to look around, knock yourself out. There is a lot of history on this thoroughfare."

Peter Hershal's form blocked the dimming sundown the front entrance of the newspaper office. Bud Clark, the head editor, the local reporter, the secretary, the founder, and the printer, stood up with his ham sandwich in his hand.

"Mr. Hershal?" Bud sputtered out as he choked back the ham.

"Mr. Clark, I knew you would remember me. In fact, that article you wrote about my sudden departure was such an enduring example of local news papering that I almost teared up in the rose dust of nostalgia."

"Thank you." Bud said still in a daze as the Jersey Driver came in, staying behind in the small waiting room.

"I have to ask, what is the name of the boy who found that bag of gold? I know the father's name. All I see is that fool. I want to see the child who discovered the bag. And want to ask him, how he did it?" Hershal walked around Bud and sat in his chair.

"I want to know the name of the boy who found that gold. Not the father, he is useless to me. I want the boy. Give me his name. Now."

Within two hours of being in town, the former mayor found me walking towards the arcade. The last few days of television and radio interviews bored me to tears. Why I never mentioned them. It was a lot of running to a room, being given a free soda then laughed at, then told how exciting it must be to find something like that. *Blah, blah, blah*, then the blatant morning zoo whistle would alarm, and the local traffic would be discussed then the top three songs of the morning then the intern pointing to the exit door that led to the back of the building not the front. We had to walk around the entire radio station just to get back to our car. But they gave me a free t-shirt, so I guess I succeeded. The television stations gave me dick. Not a single t-shirt or soda. Their green room consisted of TAB and diet drinks, a mediocre fruit basket with no cheese, and a prepackaged shrimp tray. A disgusting display below the framed glossy of the news crew, only the weather girl had anything going on. Those moments were fleeting, they mostly spoke to my father, who wouldn't shut up about the luck he had. No one asked him serious questions about it. No one cared about the history around it. No one asked me a god damn thing either. I felt the stigma of the ordinary. Certain people have a look, a way about themselves, an aura. They call IT the IT FACTOR, and I apparently did not possess it. I possessed a power unlike any human on Earth, but when you are just a pudgy kid looking off to the side of television stage, fidgeting due to nerves, they dismiss you. When I laid my eyes on Peter Hershal, he didn't see those things. He saw money. He saw his future. He saw retribution.

Peter Hershal gave me a look reserved for heads of state. He took me in carefully, trying to gauge me, trying to analyze me. He was very handsome, clean, stoic, very lean too. His shoulders were broad, his forearms rippled, he had worked with his hands for years and you could tell. In his eyes was a man tired of being a working man. He was roughly, sixty-four when he met me. He was ready to be a Titan in a small pond. This town was small, and his ego could easily wrap around it to satisfy his needs.

"My grandfather was many things. But the one thing I took away was his blatant honesty. He wouldn't lie about the things he did. He took pride in his schemes. In the men he killed to get what he wanted. My grandfather embraced his sins and tossed away their shame. He didn't like killing his enemies or competition; however, he saw the necessity of it. Better to be feared. Then no one would question you when you arrived with an envelope filled with cash. Granted, it was much less than the true value, but it wasn't cold thievery. My grandfather knew man's need for cold cash as opposed to bank letters and deeds. Cash is king in the real world. You could fool a man with a stack of bills easily. But gold. Gold is something else."

He stopped to make this point hang.

"Your father should've kept his mouth shut. He got too excited by the shine of gold. See, a stack of bills sedates that. Gold pushes common sense out the window. He spoke to the local paper, who will speak to the local news station, which will spill out into the major city market, which leads to the national news media. And then the watchers see it from above. The IRS, the Federal Government. The big bad true thieves of this modern era. They do what my grandfather did, only, they hide behind the legal language of the educated. Their bloody hands are washed clean with such ferocity that you or I would never see one speck of red and I know where to look. These new bandits will ride into town in black SUV's, armed to the teeth with military hardware and briefcases filled with legal papers that will protect themselves from any thing you can throw at them in a court room. They will sit you down at your own table, tell you how that gold is theirs and they will take it to protect you from any audits that maybe coming to you soon."

"Audit is a tax thing, right?" I asked.

He smiled. "You get it. I figured you would. Now, can you take me to where you found the gold?"

I shrugged my shoulder, never really understanding the situation. "Sure, I guess."

I told the Cadillac driver to head towards the entrance of the mine at the top of the hill. Hershal twitched back with a quizzical look on his face.

"Why the top? You weren't in the caves?"

"No. I found the gold above the shaft."

Peter Hershal laughed to himself. "That explains a lot."

"You've been here before, haven't you?" I began to put the pieces together.

"Oh, just in the caves. A friend of mine told me if anyone were to hide gold, it would be inside the cave. So, I never ventured beyond his advice. My mistake." Peter Hershal laughed to himself again, he shook his head and under his breath said, "sorry Jost,"

The car pulled alongside the trail leading up to the top of the shaft. I could see the outline of my sled ride down the hill, wishing it were someone else's journey. The driver of the car opened our doors and closely followed us up the incline. It was hot as hell and his suit was black. Glint of gun metal protruded from his coat as the sun hit it as it flopped in his shoulder holster. Peter Hershal was armed with a smile, but I could tell he had a gun too. Marching to the top, he looked down to the town below and frowned.

"So much wasted time. I was going to make this a stop before Vegas. Malls, large, gated estates with lagoons filled with blue water. I just did not have the time or the money to see it happen. Too many problems get in the way."

"Your dream?" I asked, almost feeling sorry for him.

"Yes. I always believed that small towns could evolve into the greatest places on earth. And the real estate would triple in a decade. Me, with all the deeds going forward. But I will settle with the gold that may be around."

"I don't think there isn't much left." I said, knowing full well Frank gave me everything.

"This is just a walk over. I will be taking the gold from your dad, in exchange for you, of course. My other friends in the big Cadillac will be bringing him out here soon."

Peter Hershal spoke so plainly, never frightening me. My life was literally in the hands of a mad man and yet I had no idea. So, I never broke a sweat. Naivety can be a strength sometimes.

"You talked to him already?"

"No. My friends of ours is doing the talking." I never understood the reference until years later. "Show me where you found it?" He removed the gun from his holster, holding it gently never aiming it at me. It just stood in his hand, limp to the side. The man in black never removed his gun. I do not think he was enjoying this moment in the sun.

"Right here." I lead them to the boulder. Again, I saw the lines in the dirt where the rock moved. Peter Hershal went to his knees, examining the dirt, seeing the dark moist ground that once hid a heavy sack with millions of dollars of gold coins.

"Holy shit." He dug into the ground, discovering a loose gold coin. He pulled it up and tossed it to his black suit friend. "Take that to the boss. He'll believe me now."

He took the coin with no excitement placing it in his pocket. The shoulder holster remained untouched as he looked for something to sit on. He settled for a rock with a smooth top.

Frank Grant began making his ghostly noise, rising from the shaft. I saw him straighten up, his face immediately twisting into shock and awe staring at Peter Hershal the spitting image of his grandfather.

"Holy shit!" Frank yelled. "Hal Hershal in the flesh! Son of a bitch." He lunged at Hershal, but nothing happened. Hershal floated away from Frank's grasp much like when he tried to help with the boulder. Frank seemed to merge into the stomach of Hershal, his stumbling forced him to face plant into the dirt if he was physical. Frank seemed to float over the ground, then he pulled himself up and stood straight, his face contorted into an array of frustration.

"You feel that?" Peter Hershal was surprised. His hand rubbing his stomach as if he had been hit with a sudden gas pinch.

"What?" I was asking for Frank more than myself. Then the pinch hit me all at once.

"A tremor? Is this ground stable? We are over a shaft?" His brow was beginning to display sweat.

The friend from Jersey stood up from the boulder, putting his hand to the ground, trying to sense if there was a shallow center beneath us. It was funny to watch if the circumstances were not dire.

"Did I do something?" Frank asked. He stood in front of Hershal, inspecting his eyes. "I think I did do something."

"Did you fall through that hole? Or were there others?" Peter asked with fear prickling through his stoic nature. The gun drooped to his side as the nausea erupted through him again.

When it hit him, it hit me all at once again. I was about to stop Frank, but the nausea kept my mouth shut.

"Let me try something." Frank slowly put his hand through his chest, then kept it steady for a few brief seconds.

Peter Hershal jerked down, his abdomen twisted, and he dry heaved. He was on his knees now, trying to throw up the phantom fist. Frank removed his hand and backed away. With a sudden jolt of energy, Peter leaped back up and screamed.

"What the fuck is happening to me?"

"Are there fumes up here?" The friend from Jersey asked seriously.

In the distance, the other black Cadillac was approaching. Dust trail cutting through the quiet desert backdrop. I fell to my knees with Peter Hershal, we both were in the same position gazing at each other. His eyes darted back and forth trying to understand what was happening as I saw Frank continuing to churn his hands inside his enemy's belly.

"Fuck it! They are bringing his father. We will take the gold and be done with this bull shit." Peter Hershal spit a wad of bile and so did I.

"Frank! It's hurting me too!" I shouted not caring who would look down on me for seeming insane.

"Frank?! Grant?" Peter Hershal was beginning to put the unbelievable pieces together. "You can see him? You see him!" Peter raised his gun, pointing it at me. He stood up, backing away to aim the gun. "You're a piece of work, kid. But I'm sorry I have just come too far for this not to work."

Frank leaped to the back of Peter thrusting both hands into his head.

We both saw a bright white light take over our vision. Blood shot out of Peter Hershal's eyes, ears, and nose. The gun fell out of his hand as his entire body went limp, falling backwards into the soft, mesh metal covering the top of the shaft. His body easily crashed through it.

The friend from Jersey was in shock, witnessing the sudden death of Peter Hershal. Frank Grant rushed to my side as the Black Cadillac made it to the base of the mine.

"You okay, buddy?"

"I'm good. Wow. I think I don't want to do that again."

"Wonder what happened?"

"Everything you did to him, I felt it."

At this point, when we were questioning the whys of the moment, something much worse came over us. Darkness descended unto the top of the hill. The friend from Jersey was frozen, his hand was in his holster, reaching for his piece. I rushed to the side of the hill, checking to see the Cadillac beneath us also frozen, my father being pushed out of the car at gun point. I looked up to see the sun blazing, but the heat and the light was stifled by invisible forces.

"What the hell is happening now?" Frank asked.

"I'm sure it's not good."

As I turned to look back at the shaft, the ground around it shifted, cracks ripped open along the edges, black tendrils poured out, it reminded me of oil blasting through cracks under the ocean. A rotten smell fell over us. A howl burst through these new fissures, it had the vocal elements of animal and human. Frank was the first to see what was coming out.

"Look away, boy! Please for all God's creations, close your eyes now!"

I did as Frank asked.

I felt hot breath against my face, a tinge of spittle hit my nose, I could not manage to wipe it off. My eyes were burning, I wanted to open them, but Frank kept repeating: "Don't look." When the air around me became crisp I opened my eyes seeing the ass end of Hell's collectors. They had a perverted humanity to them; their bodies were contorted to a degree where their arms and hands were where the back feet of a dog would be. An inverted creature more human than any quadrupeds. Their arms were legs, dragging elephantine testicles much larger than their entire body. They dragged on the dirt, I could hear them scream in pain, a mixture of human moan and wolf wail. One sensed my eyes upon it and turned its head, filling me with such dread that I was going to say an Our Father every day until the day I died. It had the face of a woman, one eye was shut with moist puss, the other enlarged and red. Its lips were shredded due to the jagged teeth from the maw, so much larger than normal that it too dragged on the ground. This beast winked at me right before it jumped down into the shaft.

"What was that?" I was breathless.

"Death Birthers. They take the damned. Indians talked about them when I was young. Never believed in them. Now I fear I might be too late to be asking God for forgiveness." Frank sadly sat on the ground.

Over the silent black sky, the Earth stopped, we heard the Death Birthers rip apart the soul of Peter Hershal. I didn't see what they did to him. I would not know their true horror until years later. You will want to know what they do. You will be driven mad with curiosity. Then when all is told, you will be ashamed and fearful that Death Birthers might come for you one day.

"You saved my life, Frank. I think God might give you a break." I sat next to him, feeling the dizziness and nausea drift away. "Isn't forgiveness a big deal with him?"

"Christ, yes. God? I don't know. Hopefully, Christ gets to speak up from time to time. How you feeling?"

"Better."

The sun moved again, the Friend from Jersey snapped out of the frozen stance, seeming lost and drunk. The men from the bottom of the hill were making their presence known:

"Hersh!" A thick New York accent made it up before my father.

"What the fuck happened?" Another New York accent asked keeping his gun trained on my father.

The Friend from Jersey threw his hands up. "One moment, Pete was here, the next thing I see is him flying over backwards into the fucking shaft! Then there was an earthquake and shit, did you feel that?"

"Earthquake? No! We were in the car!" The New Yorker with the gun put it away and my father rushed to my side.

"You okay, buddy?" He was more confused than scared.

"Yeah, dad. I don't know what happened."

"Did you at least get the gold?" The Friend from Jersey asked.

"Yeah, yeah. Right here." The other New Yorker lifted the satchel heavy enough to hold that hefty amount. "Now what do we do?"

"I don't know. Take the shit and leave." New Yorker who had the gun suggested.

"What about them?" Friend from Jersey asked.

"Don't give two shits. Let them go. I just want to get back to Vegas. I want to try that buffet."

"Which one?" My dad asked.

"Breakfast at the Suntaur?"

"Oh, no, you don't want that one. The Circus Tropicana has the best breakfast buffet." My father informed him.

"How much is that one?"

"I think it's cheaper, actually."

"See, you got to ask the locals where the eating places are. They would know." He exhaled and started heading back down the hill, the other two followed.

"What are we going to tell the boss?" Friend from Jersey asked.

"Just tell him Hersh fell down a shaft. He never liked him anyway."

Within the second of their laughter rose the thunderclap of blades of a helicopter exploding out of the sky. Sirens erupted next, then the sounds of crackling feedback of a bullhorn escaping the plastic speaker strapped to the bottom of the FBI helicopter.

"PUT YOUR GUNS DOWN! AND DROP TO YOUR KNEES!" The tone of the agent was profoundly authoritative, dripping with a morality dyed in the wool of the colors of the American flag. It made me feel safe.

The New Yorkers and Friend from Jersey immediately fell to the ground, they were experts at doing what the law told them. My father and I did the same, not really knowing why.

The helicopter landed as the other agents ran up the hill, rifles and pistols raised. Quite a gathering for a trio of mobsters. Within seconds they collected the Friends of Ours and then turned their attention to my father and I still on the ground.

"Mr. Clermont?" The agent from the helicopter spoke with the same tenor of power in his voice. He was a testament to the power of Langley. His stance was carved out of discipline. Not an iota of fat on this guy. His hair was jet black, eyes piercing blue, teeth the purest alabaster I had ever seen.

"That would be me." My father rose shaking hands with the agent. "Thanks for the rescue."

"That's part of the job. But the other part of the job is confiscation of government property. Do you have the gold discovered on this hill in your possession?"

"We got it here, chief." One of the agents picked up the satchel my father brought up the hill. He opened it, doing a quick count. "Looks good from here."

"You guys came for the gold?" I asked now.

"No. We have been after Peter Hershal for a few years now. Your discovery smoked him out for us. Looks like we are going to have to have the meat wagon driven out here to clean up old Hershal. But the gold found by you was property of the US Government. And thus, we must confiscate the full amount of the gold discovered. "

My father went back to the ground, the wind knocked out of him.

"So, you guys are taking the gold?" I asked.

"Yes, son. Nice job finding it. I'm sure the senator will send you nice letter of gratitude. This money will help the state greatly. I'm sure." He seemed to smirk at the last part. I don't think I was old enough to understand the joke.

"Oh. Well, okay. Thanks. I guess." I was confused yet still enthralled by his voice.

"Thank you, gentlemen. We will be in contact in a few days' time if anything comes up." He jumped back on the helicopter with the bag of gold. Within moments the Feds had disappeared leaving me, my father, and Frank, staring out at the waning sun heading down into the mountains.

"They didn't even offer us a ride."

"No point in sticking around here. Let's go home." My father took my hand and led me to the trail downhill. We saw the Criminal Investigation Van coming up down the desert road. Two more vans followed suit. I wanted to see how they worked but my father had a rough day, losing thirty-two million dollars in gold would do that to a person. Myself, I had my three pieces locked up under my bed, the value was not the important thing, it was the memory. These three pieces of gold were to be a reminder of what was given and what was taken away. I became a Libertarian overnight.

Frank Grant stayed within his perch on the hill, waiving at us as we made it down the trail. The CSI teams began to rope off the area, setting up their tents and equipment to begin the investigation. Frank laughed at all the attention.

"This is the most action up here in one hundred twenty years. All because of some kid. You got quite the future."

I waived back at Frank, "thank you!"

"They can't hear you from here, son." Father told me holding my hand as we gently walked downhill.

"It's nice to try." I saw Frank smile knowing he heard me.

The Federal Government visited us two weeks later to put the dots on the I's and cross the T's. We signed tons of paperwork to ensure that we wouldn't fight for money that we though belonged to us. We agreed to keep the silence regarding what happened to Hershal within the media, which was tough because they offered some decent money for our inside story. But apparently Hershal was one cog in a criminal machine the Feds were after in the Midwest. Due to the untimely death of Peter Hershal, most of the proposed ideas the mob had in developing a small community within driving distance of both Vegas, Los Angeles and San Diego went kaput. The Feds gave us a little medal and a few gift certificates to some eateries but the thirty-two million dollars in gold was long gone.

After we hate spent the gift certificates, I went to see Frank on the hill. He was out of the shaft hole, gazing toward the town which began construction on a slew of projects. Peter Hershal was right about the location but was dead before he could partake in the construction grant given to the county. I assumed half of the gold was given back to the community, so in a way, my father, with his big mouth created a boom of economic growth. Which we saw none of because we were moving out of town. I wanted to see Frank to say goodbye.

"Well, maybe it's my time to go as well. You know I have been looking at that door for what seems like a week." Frank said pointing to air.

"What door?" I asked, perturbed not seeing what Frank saw.

"You don't see it? I don't know if I should be happy or scared shitless about that."

"Well, if you see it, it must be just for you."

"Kind of a letdown, ain't it? The great beyond is a door?"

"Life is simple, why can't death?" I said this not realizing how deep that phrase could go. Profundity didn't enter my mind; I was still angry that I couldn't see it. "You should open it, don't cross it. Just crack it open, look."

"If I see a tentacle reaching for me or a hand of the devil, you'll know it, grab me." Frank put his hand on the invisible knob.

"Okay, do it." I extended my hand to be within inches of his hand, just in case a unholy vortex or Devil Dog was waiting on the other side.

Frank turned the knob, his face broke open in a full giddy smile. He fell to his knees and began to sob.

"I don't deserve this place." He kept his eyes closed, his chin and cheek appeared to be pressed by an invisible hand. When he opened his eyes again the tears were free flowing. "Oh, my beauty. How I missed you." He rose to be eye to eye with an invisible beauty.

"What is it, Frank?"

"All that I loved, all that I lost. I can't be any clearer. Be careful out there, Henry. The world is what it is. Cruel, dangerous, blind, and cold. It is up to you to find the warmth and the love hidden inside. It may take a lifetime, but it's worth the pain." Frank stepped across the threshold of the invisible door and disappeared as the wind came up. The soft hum of nature covered up the gears of mortality taking hold of one more soul.

"So long, Frank. Thanks for all the government gift certificates." I said to the empty world around me.

3

HIGH SCHOOL: GHOSTS OF GROWING UP 1991

Years went by after the FBI raid, with little an eventual ghost story to tell. I was dealing with the pangs of puberty, blood shooting through the penis, giving one the awkward hard on, forcing one to experience shame on a whole new level. I was more than just gangly in appearance or in social circles, I was starting to realize kids pick tribes and I was beginning to lose several friends I thought I would have past college. But here we are, me at 15, still seeing the occasional dead human not realizing that they should go into the light and that bull shit, I never ever said something that dramatic. I never saw a light. Remember, all the ghosts saw invisible doors to the other side. No light. I was not allowed to see the door. I thought I would be more special. But I was just me and I didn't know how to handle that.

High school started and I was not heading in the direction of the elites. Most of the kids in my school were on their way to colleges and prebuilt futures already in place. The stones to their brighter world were laid out in front of them. Most of them came from established families, self-made men, and their brood as well as the occasional scholarship winner. I was one of the scholarship winners. I had written an in-depth dissertation on the power of faith and Catholicism facing the modern world at large.

Well, I ghost wrote the piece, utilizing an amazing connection I made in the public library one day. He was a former Jesuit Priest who had lost his faith in the years leading to his death. He had so many things to say to a person who had an ear. My ear was good enough for him, so he spoke and spoke and spoke. I had not asked for this diatribe, but he delivered unto me as if he was mandated to. The Jesuit was convinced this was the reason for his being. To help someone like me reach that next step into the larger world. Exceedingly kind man, but almost too eloquent. The original essay I wrote was thirty-seven pages with Latin phrases and Aramaic break downs. A little too intense for a kid just trying to garner a five-thousand-dollar scholarship for the local private high school. Hell, I was barely a Catholic. I had taken First Communion but had checked out before Confirmation. My Jesuit connection relayed all the information I needed to fast track the process of becoming an adult in the church. Most of the mysteries of religion could be solved by writing out of a check to any Priest willing to bend the rules. Come to find it that was every Priest he had known.

I wrote a few letters to the names given and within six weeks I was brought into the grace of the church just as I was about to enter the scholarship game. I was accepted with open arms and curious gazes. I was a borderline genius who exhibited extraordinarily little shrewdness or complications a genius would produce. But the checks from the Foundation Scholarship always cleared, so no one investigated.

August days began to hit, the last vestige of the summer before high school was peeling away as if timed with a digital clock. So many minutes and hours rushed by that I forgot I was just fifteen, not old enough to understand teenage foolery but young enough to be excited for it. I thought I was going to discover so much about life in the upcoming four years, however the first three months did not seem to be leading to adventurous times and sticky situations with girls in the back seats of cars. I was not a jock, not a nerd, not a goth, not quite anything really. Just normal and forgettable, lost in the sea of the average pimple marked bad haircut with a book bag drone, walking to the classroom where I would daydream about getting out of high school to walk amongst the adults. Always looking ahead, never at where I was. This is the true curse of human existence. When you know there is a life beyond death the biggest questions that remain are what is life going to offer me? That is a selfish way of thinking, but when you're fifteen, you don't know shit.

I had three friends from grade school stick with me, Joey, Ray, and Marc. Always eating in the main luncheon area. Picnic tables set up along the edge of the back-parking lot, where the seniors and juniors parked. We would watch the seniors drive out the back, heading to the various drive-thru palaces of forbidden fruits. What we would have given to be able to attain a fast-food meal combo in these early days. It was not to be until we reached that seminal time of Seniority. For now, we settled with the picnic tables and rough menu items offered by the school. Due to the private school acumen, we were free to have a broad menu of awfully bad food. Everything fried: from burritos, French fries, onion rings, mozzarella sticks, and the occasional ta-quito. Burgers wrapped in tin foil, if you were lucky and early in line you could grab a bacon cheeseburger. I had three in my lunchroom lifetime, in hindsight, I think I saved myself stints in my heart.

Often, we would hang out, discussing the nonsense of our age. I can barely remember anything concrete we talked about. Most of these days are blurry. Though the food I remember, the lunch time rush of doing homework due next period I remember mainly due to the anxiety created because of lack of discipline for homework All these things are nothing compared to the one thing I do remember during this period, her name was Samantha.

Drama class was the one thing I was looking forward to the most. I was wanting to explore acting, playwriting, storytelling, stage crafting such as building sets and setting up marketing for such plays to be held on the main stage of some auditorium which we didn't have since this school spent every dime on their money-making football team. I was imaging after school events and hanging out with other kids that liked the movies I did and wanted to have something to do with them. I got none of those things. The class subsisted of thirty, half of which were seniors forced into taking an art class to pad their college entrance resumes. I tried to discuss Orson Welles with one of them all I received in return was a look of disgust and pity. We did one play in the classroom in March, we had to open the partitions between our class and the geometry class next door to set up the makeshift auditorium seating which were raised platforms with school chairs. We were able to shove forty people into this fire hazard. All of which were the parents and families of the class members. We did three performances and shuttered the raised platforms in one week. You will ask what was the play? At least something provocative, like a Patrick Marber play. Or go old world with Shakespeare? No, we went middle of the road with Fame. I wasn't even given a main part. I was the uncle in one scene. But I made him Swedish because I could.

In my disappointment with Drama, one would think I would transfer out. Samantha was the one thing that kept me seated in that classroom for that year. The first time I saw her she seemed to strut. Cool, collected, smart, cute. No one was hot at my school, so to discover a cute girl with a sense of humor was striking blood diamonds with no slave labor. She sat next to me in the first week. At first, timid, looking at me through the side of her face, not knowing what to think of me. I had already accumulated five o' clock shadow at an early age suggesting that I was older than I appeared.

"You a sub?" She asked cocking her head to side.

"Undercover drug enforcement officer." I responded.

"A NARC?" She hid her initial crack of a smile.

"Yes. My wife hates me doing it."

"What about your kids?"

"They graduated last year. I got to pay for tuition somehow."

"Crooked?"

"Straight as the Eagle Scout. And I have a master's degree in philosophy."

Her snort laugh broke my heart.

"My name is Henry."

"Samantha." She took me in totally this time, her head went up three inches realizing something. "You're the kid who found that gold few years back."

I rolled my eyes, I had hoped no one would know that since we had moved roughly two hundred miles from that location.

"I'm sorry, I just never met a celebrity before."

"More sucker than celebrity. Government took the money from us since we did not technically own it. And it was stolen hundred twenty or so years prior. I guess the moral of the story was, don't tell anyone about anything worth north of twenty million dollars."

"I would say so. Did you keep some of it? Come on, you can tell me." She hit my arm, sending me into sexual torment land.

"I kept, like, five pieces."

"No shit! I would love to see that someday." She smiled so brightly and genuinely it was hard not to fall in love with her right there.

"Maybe one day. But not around these peasants."

"Absolutely not!"

We were told to be quite as the teacher began discussing the next festival to raise money for the Drama Club, yet to be created due to lack of funds. Then she mentioned the plans of building a haunted classroom for Halloween. This perked me up immediately and I noticed Samantha had a deep interest as well.

"What is your go to horror movie?" She asked under her breath as the teacher prattled on about everything other than theater.

"I would say, Poltergeist."

"Nice choice."

"You?"

"I have rented Silence of the Lambs ten times since it's been out. It better win every Academy Award out there." Samantha released a dead pan impression of Tony Hopkins as Hannibal. "Your bleeding has stopped."

"You're sick."

"Yep."

"I think I know what we could do for Halloween."

"Lay it on me, Clarice." She smiled again, the smile that still haunts my dreams on the occasional flashback.

"I have to show it to you, for you to get the full effect of it."

"So mysterious. You better bring it tomorrow."

"Oh, just you wait, Buffalo Bill."

"Wasn't she a big fat person?" Samantha was gifted.

The next day I promptly removed my Michael Myer mask, which was the William Shatner Don Post mask I spray painted white. Almost movie accurate. She went wide eyed and geeky.

"That is so amazing. We will do a throat slice. I will lay on the table, you cut my throat with a big knife. I have a makeup effect I want to try out. And I will let out the worst scream you can imagine." Samantha was thinking out her costume, lifting her finger to her mouth, eyes moving to the image playing out in her mind. "I'm thinking a man's shirt with jeans to wear if we can wear jeans that day. (Private School Dress Code) Give it a college girl babysitter chic."

"Sounds good. I wonder who's going to come through here?"

Kindergarten through senior class walked through our classroom of terror that Halloween day. I felt bad scarring the 5- to 7-year-old children, all of whom seemed to tense back as I gazed at them with dead eyes under the Michael Myer's mask, slicing Samantha's throat. My ability to see ghosts never scared me as much as I scared them, Samantha loved it. Her scream was so ear piercing she was told to knock it off halfway through the showing. Granted it was borderline psychotic to be this good at being pretend murdered, but she was talented.

Samantha and I would walk with each other after school to the front driveway to be picked up by our parents. This was a passing nuisance as next year most of us would be driving with our new license tucked into our wallets. When she was absent, I felt it. When I was absent, she mingled with a dozen or so others because she had that ability. During this time, I had managed to forget about my curse. Not one ghost had manifested itself to me in months. The new house was just that, new. The school itself was thirty years old with no dead kids roaming the halls. No suicide teacher hanging from the rafters. Just brick and mortar and the promise of a new gym in twenty years due to fundraising. It was as if she was the one thing that brought me closer to be human again.

As the weeks went by, we got closer as friends. Never romantic. Platonic asexual robot I was and would always be. Though in all honesty, it didn't bother me. I just wanted to be around her. All the other kids snickered behind my back, knowing full well I wasn't getting shit out of this relationship. A guy who could see ghosts can detect pointed mockery. Again, I didn't care. If I leaned in for a kiss, forcing her to jerk away it would have killed all the times we had. I didn't want that to happen. I was fine being an asexual platonic robot. Making her laugh was enough.

"Her mom is as crazy as cat shit, you know." Joey said taking out his burrito from its gold foil wrapper. "Hand me those fries, I want to shove a few in here."

I handed my fries over to Joey, watching him shove four of the longest potato spears into the center of his molten hot bean and cheese mess. "I've never heard that."

"You didn't go to elementary school here. Martin did. He's in my English class, he said, her mom used to come into the school yard without a bra and white shirt in the rain, showing off her big titties." He took a chomp out of the burrito and spat it out due to the heat of Prometheus.

"How is that crazy? I would love to see that." Ray added, picking the tomatoes out of his home-made sandwich.

"I would too, but she was shouting something about aliens and a bomb at the time."

"I just don't believe that." I spoke.

"Ask her." Joey said dead seriously,

"Did you finish Habeeb's Algebra chapter? I need the answers." I took out my homework, checking the clock.

"I will if you ask her."

"Fine." I took his homework and copied with all the fury of the finest delinquent.

Samantha met me at the tree in front of the chapel which took up the direct center of the driveway. It had a nice rotunda, the saints and Mother Mary adorning each point of the hexagon design. A single cross stood in the center where the stained-glass window over the altar stood. I felt like jumping on it to get out of this situation.

"I got to get home fast today, Henry. Sorry. I'll see you later." Samantha threw her backpack around her front, holding it like a very pregnant woman would her forming baby. "Hold on. Let me give you, my number. We can talk later that way."

I almost hit the cross backing away from this sudden notion. A phone number to her directly? Was this a way of asking me out? No, it was just convenience due to my amazing being. Right?

"Your number?" I blankly asked.

"Yeah, don't get too excited. I do my homework, so don't constantly call." She hid a smile writing the number on a piece of paper. She handed it over and launched ahead toward the minivan her dad drove every day to pick her up. He gave me a hateful gaze but suddenly smiled and waved as Samantha said something to him. I waved back as they took off, my eyes going to her number, my grin was so big I'm sure she noticed as they sped off.

"Phone number?" Joey looked at the paper. "You know she likes Steven Jerrel. And they've been all over each other in English."

Ray nodded his head. "I heard he finger banged her too."

"But does he have her phone number?" I asked.

"He has her stink." Marc said.

"You guys are disgusting."

"You're an asexual robot." Ray spoke the truth.

"I am not. I just... Why can't a girl and a guy be friends?"

"Then you're a gay asexual robot." Joey added.

"Oh, for fuck sakes."

"I suggest you ask her out. When you call her, ask to come over to her place. If she says no, you will know right away that she wants it. If she says yes, then you'll defiantly know she wants nothing to do with you sexually." Joey took my fries again dumping them into his burrito.

"Does that add any flavor?" I asked.

"I think it absorbs the heat. Also, the carbs. I need more carbs."

"It's a burrito. It's all carbs."

"I need to gain weight."

"If I ask her out and she invites me over to her house, how is that not something special?" I ask.

"One, she lives by the school, you could literally walk there from here in ten minutes. Two, her dad picks her up because he wants to get away from the house and his crazy as cat shit wife." Ray retorted, taking a swig of his bottle of cheap soda. The private high school forbade name brand sodas to enter their machines. They were leased by a local company that provided the worst drink choices this side of Mogadishu.

"Still unsubstantiated! Plus, what would that have to do with it?" I plead.

"Three! Her mother is at the said home. If she cared about getting down, she would not want to have her mother intrude. And she would not want to expose a future boyfriend to a crazy momma. It wouldn't be prudent. In fact, it would be a downright boner kill. And if that were her goal, to get to your boner, she would not risk the almost certain boner death coming face to face with insanity itself." Ray finished tossing the empty soda bottle into the recyclable bin.

"Can I get your Algebra homework?" I finished our lunch conversation.

I didn't call Samantha until two weeks later. I figured it was a suave move. Shows that I am interested but not too interested. When she answered the phone the first time, she sounded exhausted. As if she had been in a screaming match with someone. I was hoping she had gotten in a fight with Steven, allowing me time to swoop in and save the day. But that was immediately dashed when she spoke the words I never wanted to hear.

"Do you think Steven would go out with me?" She was being honest, wanting me to be the equalizer. I had to make the choice for her. Why? She was fully capable of going or not going out with him. It felt like a knife in my kidney when she asked in a soft, defeated voice.

"Absolutely." I assured her instantly with such an excited octave that she thought my dream was to go out with Steven.

"You think so?" Her defeated tone echoed in my ear, making me feel so much worse. Something just had happened to her, and here I am bugging her about nothing. I should have never called.

"I'm glad you called. I was wondering if you ever were." I imagined her smile creeping over that cute face, any tears forming in her eyes were dried out. All things were beginning to churn in her direction. My eyes were tearing, my rudder ripped out of the boat and tossed into the river. I was spinning in a circle, and no one gave two flips.

"I didn't want to bug you."

"You can't bug me. You're too good of a friend." Samantha sounded happier in an instant.

"That's what I am here for." To be an asexual robot for your programming.

"Should I call him?"

"Shouldn't he do that? I mean that's the way things go traditionally?"

"We are friends, that is far from traditional. Currently, I think I can ask anyone I want to out. This isn't the 50's." Samantha smiled.

"You're right. Should you give it two weeks? I feel that is the appropriate length of time. And I don't think the 50's were the 50's either."

"You're insane."

"Think about it."

"I am going to call him now."

"Now?"

"Absolutely."

"Get it, girl." I was having heart palpitations.

"Okay! Wish me luck, you're too good to me." Her defeated voice was replaced by the sheer excitement of simply dialing a number to someone else. My eyes were getting heavy, my teeth gnashing against each other. She abruptly hung up leaving me clenching my chest. Being fifteen, I wasn't dying or having a panic attack. I was simply keeping my heart from ripping open. It hurt so much that I couldn't speak for roughly twenty minutes. I remember my mother giving a strange look but shook it off when dad rushed into the house with dinner.

I was alone in this situation. But then again, it wasn't the first time I was alone. Being able to speak to spirits forces one to be a tad eccentric. Not many people understood me. My parents were kind and loving but a deep conversation was not in the cards. The last thing I needed to be was honest with them. I am sure they thought I was on pot those four years of high school. I wish I were that cool. I ate dinner forcing a smile on my face to detour their worry. When I went to bed, I cried. I went through half a box of tissues, for God's sakes. I am embarrassed to look back on this. I should have been happy for her. It's not every day you see someone start a long-lasting relationship in life. But for now, being fifteen and angry and bitter, things would have to get worse before they would be completely forgotten anyway.

Weeks went by and the two seem to take off splendidly. I watched them eat lunch together from afar, I saw them walk with each other after their shared classes in the halls, holding hands. Her laughter from everything Steven said made my stomach turn. I hated seeing two people falling in love. My end of the day walks with her were over too. I stood by myself at the chapel, watching her walk home with Steven. I could feel the snickers behind my back. Everyone gave a passing look at me when I stood next to Mary the Mother of God. I would sit down, looking up at her alabaster face, seeking a comfort from the Holy Mother only receiving the cold expressionless cuts of a bored sculptor. So many days spent under that veneer of piety always watching the cars coming and going. I missed our talks. I missed her laughs. I missed what time I had. Simple things that were never really mine.

December came and the winter was rough. Rain poured for most of the month, suggesting a deluge, I wish building an ark was mandated by a higher power because I was beginning to get more perturbed sitting next to Samantha in Drama class speaking about what Steve and she did the previous night and day. Nothing salacious, it was pure *Leave it to Beaver* simplicity. She was excited and wanted to share it with someone. Other girls didn't seem to care for her, I noticed that as time went on. Steven was the one true Messiah at this private school. And she was the Mary Magdalene, even given the whore title. None of that was going on, obviously. She was just a simple girl with a simple guy both discovering a sweet, simple innocent relationship. I was envious, beyond all hell. Hearing her speak about those moments with Steve would break me as I would change the subject.

"You're right. It's just, I don't have a friend to talk to, really. Steve and I talk about other stuff. But, you know, I am sorry. You want to see a movie this week?" Samantha asked with a crack of a smile that broke my heart so wide I couldn't begin to fill it with hate. This fissure in my heart was earned and her smile was enough to make me forgive all those blushed filled recounts of the previous night with Steven. I was quick to oblige her request and we planned to go to the new theater in town.

Steven was with her. I was the third wheel. This was not discussed, and I was not happy. I was visibly perturbed and even Steven had the sanity to keep his distance. He even rejected Samantha's hand as she tried to wrap her fingers around his.

"Hey, Henry. What's up?" Steven extended his hand; I was quick to shake so there would be hint of bitterness. "Samantha said you would be down with my choice of movie. I am a little embarrassed by it."

"We aren't watching a Swedish Nude picture, are we?" I joked.

"No, I wanted to see, and actually, I am really excited to see, Star Trek The Undiscovered Country." Steven was a Trekkie. The high school football captain was a fucking Trekkie.

"Umm, that was my number one holiday movie this year. Don't tell me you liked The Final Frontier?"

"Oh hell no. What does God need with a starship? I was so pissed." Steven immediately became a friend. "You watch the Next Generation? I think it's finally found its footing; it was rough for a minute there."

"Two seasons of rough." I admitted.

"Roddenberry had to let it go. I hate to say it, but I am glad he's dead." Steven winced, "I know I shouldn't say that. But shit."

"I like the way you think." I really did. "You guys get the tickets. I'll go and get the food?"

"Sure. I got some money." Steven dove into his pocket removing a wad of tens.

"Jesus, are you a drug dealer?" I asked, making them both laugh.

"My family has a stand at the local fair. We usually have tens left over for some reason. I get paid cash. I don't mind it. I heard you had a few million dollars once?" Steven was serious in his interest.

"Oh, did Samantha tell you about that?"

"Yeah. That was cool."

"Let me tell you about it, Steven. After I get us the sweets."

"Large popcorn! I want the refill after the movie." Samantha said.

"As you wish." I went to the line and discovered their reflection in the massive poster case advertising *The Prince of Tides* coming soon. I saw the two sneak a kiss, her hand squeezed his in a tender moment only lovers share. I wanted to leave suddenly. But I swallowed back bile, throwing myself into ordering our snacks.

After the movie, we walked to the parking structure waiting

for our parents to come pick us up. Samantha cradled the popcorn as if she were the Cinemark Pieta. As her dad's lights caught her in a faint smile, I noticed Samantha became truly anxious. We had a fun night that was coming to an end, I saw her face transform into deep depression like a Lon Chaney Jr. werewolf metamorphosis. Steven noticed it too, rubbing her shoulders causing her loose sweater to bunch up past her elbow exposing a series of bruises. Samantha rejected his comfort, pushing her shirt down quickly, hoping I didn't see what I just saw. In this sudden revelation I recalled all the days I was smitten by her. Samantha always wore baggy clothes. Most of her clothes were long sleeves or layered, covering most of her skin. I figured she was just modest. As the winter began to fade away into spring the clothes remained the same. I was in short sleeve collared shirt with khaki pants due to the school's dress code. A female student was allowed skirts below the knee and short sleeve sheer blouses which still killed any budding sexuality in a teen. Samantha never utilized that look. She kept her conservative cape adornments even when the temperature is reaching over eighty-two degrees.

"Are you okay?" I asked her one March afternoon on an unseasonably hot day.

"Sure. What is your deal?" She asked with a tinge of anger.

"It's hot."

"So?"

"I mean you could get away with wearing a skimpy airy blouse. I would wear one instead of this cotton neck strangler."

"Lose weight." She was abrupt and unable to gleam the comedy from my previous remark.

"Good advice." I returned a curt response, almost taking her hit as an insult.

"What do you care about how I dress? I don't have to dress anyway for you. You are not anything worth thinking about." Those words came out like a geyser, she didn't mean to say it but she didn't apologize either.

"Forget I asked." Was all I could muster.

Samantha snorted then adjusted her seat inching away from me.

"She's on the rag, bro." Joey said assuredly, with a homemade lunch for once.

"I'm just stupid." I said weakly.

"No, you just care too much. She wants nothing to do with you so drop the bitch." Ray said with his bacon cheeseburger in hand, a once in a lunch time grab as they always sold out in three minutes.

"That's a little mean."

"Not at all. One of these days you're going to have to learn about friend zone limitation. In your future, I can sense years of rising sexual tension and sealed prostate valves." A clinical Ray emerged from between bites of horrible food.

"Sealed prostate valves?" I repeated not still believing a fellow fifteen-year-old could come up with that.

"I worry about you. You have potential. We all do." Joey added.

"Maybe you guys do." I said accepting the current position of friend zone fatality.

Weeks went by, Samantha didn't speak to me as much as she used to. I would bump into Steven a few times but never brought it up. He would be pleasant with me, never pushing the fact that he won her, and I didn't. Spring dance was upon us, and he was wondering where the best flower shops were.

"I don't have a fucking clue." I responded.

"I didn't mean to ask like you would know. I was simply curious." Steven was being nice.

"Sorry. I just don't know any cause I'm not going to the dance. No one to ask."

"What about Amy? Melissa? Chandra? Meryl? Cristina? Mary?"

"I know none of those people."

"Maybe I can provide a word."

"Oh, don't worry about that. I just have no interest in wasting money on a dance that's not Prom." I said this thinking by the time Prom would come I could get a date.

"Okay, well if you do think of one let me know." Steven walked away heading to the herd he called friends. Some of them looked down on me from afar, others snickered. I didn't care that much. I had enough friends that were living even more that were dead.

I used to walk around the neighborhood when I was depressed, which was most of the week. These little interludes were the reason I was always copying math homework. Looking for any lost souls that needed a point in the right direction provided me with a bigger reason to exist than homework. Honestly, I was lazy and couldn't bear doing any kind of number work when I could search the streets of mystery. On further reflection, I went on these walks to not think about Samantha. When she stopped talking to me, I was in a stupor. I knew she didn't care about me, but in youth you tend to just accept those facts and move on. I wasn't going to allow myself to focus on the heart ache because it was selfish to think just about my pain. Samantha was with a good guy, a guy that treated me with respect and dignity, unlike many of his followers. I think when some broken hearts hit their twenties, truly insidious machinations begin to form. I had met a ghost of a twenty-five-year-old mechanic on one of my first walks. His name was Gary Simmons, he was a gear head to the extreme, a living encyclopedia of engine parts and car specs. Yet he always brought up Gloria.

"That fucking bitch, Gloria. She used to spread her legs to all those guys with money and Jaguars. I used to work on those small cock cars, seeing all the bull shit behind them. I wish I would've cut brake lines when I was alive. Then it would have made a difference. I wish I would've cut her lines. Maybe she would have burned up in a crash." He took a drag out of a cigarette that wasn't there. It was habit.

"Did you ever talk to her?" I asked, carefully.

Gary spit the invisible butt out of his mouth and screamed, "fucking whore couldn't talk!"

"Why her? Out of all the girls out there? Why her?"

"Because she was perfect. Just a dim wit. Never saw me, though. Never saw me. Even after she married me. Never saw me."

Yes. This was his wife he was talking about. He must have had strong anxiety over her. I never knew if it was real or in his head. Being dead allowed for short term memory loss and long-term memory gains. It was a type of Alzheimer's Disease I would discover in more than a few ghosts. What I noticed in many cases was that if the emotional connection to another was intense, the outcome of not being able to be with them or an abrupt end, forced them to marinate in this stew of bile and anger. Most were angry, focusing the hate on the former partner. Their lover would be their enemy. What kind of death is that? A horrifying idea. Being trapped by your own web of anxiety over a rumor you never knew the truth about. It went all the way to death's door. I didn't want that to be inside me over Samantha. I didn't want to hate her for finding someone else or losing patience with me. I just wanted her to laugh at me again, to smile at me again. Even if it was out of a sibling relationship. We were two close people being ripped apart by an unknown force that still perplexed me. I wanted to know what was going on with her. I wanted to see if I could help her. But how the hell could I do it at fifteen? Gary was twenty-five, full of hate so much he couldn't admit he loved his own wife based on his own conjecture out of jealousy.

"You see that door again?" I brought up the door anytime Gary seemed tense. Which was every time I spoke to him.

"Yeah. It's right behind you."

I put my hand behind my back to try to feel it. Nothing but air. "Really? Am I on it?"

"You're close. You want me to open the fucking thing? Get your curiosity satiated?" He leaned into me, forcing me to jerk away then stopped. His hand was at the invisible knob. Gary wasn't moving. He jerked up as a spasm rushed through his ghostly form.

"Well?" I asked.

"Shut up, kid. I don't think I should. I never liked the look of this thing from day one."

"When was day one?"

"I don't know. What the hell question is that? Day one, is day one. I've been hanging around here for, what? Few days. Shit." Gary was utterly confused.

"Do you want me to tell you the year?" I said it delicately, I noticed the fear rise in him wondering how long it truly was.

"I can tell you that. Shit, it's 1963."

"Okay."

"Gloria used to doll herself up and walk around like a fucking peacock. Teasing me, I never thought she would let me touch her again. We were married you know. But she would've left me for a hobo off the rail if she had the chance."

"I don't believe it." I was adamant in my denial.

Gary would've slapped me if he could. But he was a ghost, couldn't do shit and you could see the dismay on his face.

"Fuck you, kid. What do you know? Women cheat. They leave you to die and move on when they find a guy with dollars coming out his ass."

"I don't believe it." I repeated.

"You, little shit. What do you want from me? You can talk to me and see me? Good fucking deal for you."

"Open the door, Gary. Open it and see what you miss." I

remembered Frank's face when he saw behind the invisible door. How lost in emotion he was. All his sins forgiven; I believe. Maybe the shock of what was on the other side was enough to break any stoicism, any hardness. Gary could be broken by it enough to be forgiven by it.

"I don't want to."

"Let it go, Gary. Just go home. You don't need to work on any cars in this garage anymore."

Gary told me more than a few times how he died. He was checking the oil of a Jaguar, seething with such anger because Gloria was sitting with her back to him in the waiting room. She had been wearing a black polka dotted dress, showing off her perfect tits and round ass. Cotton panties hanging off her form, begging to be removed with teeth. This was all from Gary. I didn't have that descriptive creativity. His head began to ache, then he felt tightening in his chest. He tasted burnt toast and had a spasm sending him down to the concrete floor, headfirst. He remembers feeling his forehead split open and blood fill his eyes before going dark. Then he woke up and saw Gloria over his body, her white polka dot dress covered in blood as she tried to lift Gary up. He said that she cried over his body. Gary said that moment broke him more than all of life up to there. Gloria might have loved him after all, but his memory of her was so full of hate he seemed to forget this. Ghosts exist in their last moment, but the most intense feelings override their current being. Ghosts didn't have minds, couldn't remember substantial events. They could only remember the anger, the hate, the pain or the love and the brightness of the past.

Frank was different. I couldn't figure it out. Maybe it was due to the lack of human contact for years. As kids we were the only other breathing entities to come across him. Perhaps if there were miners and other spelunkers constantly invading the area, he would have forgotten most of who he was. Always seeing the modern world presented forced him to forget the past, much like Gary who died in his garage which still stood in the middle of an ancient street. The garage was derelict, long abandoned. Many people suggested it was haunted, which forced me to check it out. I spent a few months there, seeing Gary. His day-to-day Gloria bashing was a lot to take in at first. In the garage, I came across a few framed photos on the wall. I took it down and cut through the grime and dirt caked on it. Gary was leaning on a Jaguar, throwing a towel at a laughing Gloria. Under it was a note card with the caption: ME AND GLO, OPENING DAY.

I brought the picture to Gary.

His eyes were wet, his face contorted in a silent scream of sorrow. It was more frightening than any Halloween mask.

"I want to go home." Gary mourned.

"You can now."

He gazed at the picture then the invisible door.

Gary provided a pantomime of a man opening a door. His face morphed into a younger, reassured version of himself. He smiled, he laughed, the first time I ever saw that in these weeks with him.

"You got to go home now, Gary." I said to him, giving the permission he needed.

"I loved you. I missed you. Tell me you forgive me?" He stepped through nothing and within a flash he was nothing more in this world but my memory.

"Hey! What the hell you doing in there?" A phlegm filled voice erupted over the empty garage, followed by a heavy wet spittle.

"Sorry, I was just walking around. Bored." I walked out with the picture. "You know these people?"

The phlegm man was old and broken. He seemed to be twisted by age, his jaundice skin was yanked over a frail skeleton wearing suspenders and a belt.

"The hell you doing in there. You can't be walking around in there."

"Sorry. You know them?" I handed him the frame photograph.

"Holy shit. I didn't know that was in there." He never got out of his car, the top down, his body sucking up the UV Rays providing a Vitamin D refill. "That was my mother. That was her first husband."

"Gary?" I was shocked.

"How the hell you know that?" He was more shocked.

"It's on the back."

The old man turned the frame over, seeing the post card. He smiled.

"This your place?"

"No. Well, yes. But I never wanted it. It was where my mom spent her early years. Her fun years she would say. Her first husband was a mechanic. They were married young, but she had money and he had a gift. Apparently, a genius with any car. They were here for about ten years. This was before I was born mind you. Okay? So, Gary died suddenly, and my mom remarried my dad and never really got over Gary. I inherited this when she died, and I never cared one way or another about it."

"Interesting." I was talking to myself more than to phlegm man.

"Who are you?"

"My name is Henry. I was just walking by."

"I've been told some kid been milling around here. You that kid?"

"No. This is my first time here. I live up the street. Just walking."

Phlegm man gave me a good look over and spit another wad of death juice. "Well, keep out of here. I am going to be tearing this place down next week. Getting a Dollar General built here."

"Good job." I spoke. "Have a good day."

"Right. Thanks, by the way. For the picture. I never saw this before and I have been in there so many times. It's been a long time since I've seen my mom like this. Funny." His eyes went glassy, but the spit rose harder and rougher.

"Right place, right time, I guess."

"Yeah. Destiny."

"Maybe… Gloria was your mom?"

"She was. I, I forgot what she was like. She's been dead for twenty-five years. My dad died two years before that. He always said she was the love of his life. I never thought that. I think she loved Gary more than anything. My dad said he saw her across the street when they first opened this place. Gary didn't appreciate her but took care of her well enough. My father was jealous but didn't start anything. I think he flirted with her for years before Gary died. Must have pissed Gary off bad. Now, what's left of that moment is going to get smoothed over with a new foundation and store front."

"Good investment." I managed to say, never breaking his gaze from the picture.

"You and I found each other in such an odd moment. I feel like this is all closed now. I feel like, you're the reason."

"First time here. I was just passing by."

"Take it easy, kid. Don't let little things get to you. There's so much bull shit in between, it's not worth the effort to pine over shit you can't change."

I couldn't grasp the full moral of this moment, but I took enough of it with me as I walked to Samantha's house. I was going to apologize. Open to her as friend, a confidant. Not a wannabe boyfriend. Friend zone meant nothing to me. Her personality was too wonderful to be discarded over jealousy. I wanted nothing but the best for her and the future she could have. I was so excited with my decision that I didn't realize how fast I walked to her front door. Now I was facing my own invisible door.

I knocked.

Nothing.

I was checking out the neighborhood street, way more money

here than mine. Forcing me to think about the gold the Feds took back. Bastards.

I went for the doorbell this time.

A few seconds then the lock cracked free, the door swung open, and I was face to face with Samantha's mother. Her breasts were heaving out of her low-cut lacey blouse, her skirt was ripped, askew from sudden tampering. Her hair was up in a giant frizzy bun, circles under her eyes suggesting zero sleep in weeks. Her fingers on her free hand danced around as if she was trying to wake them from numbness. She was breathing heavily, forcing her massive breasts to heave with a ferocious sexuality, I was entranced by them, hard not to look away when you're fifteen in the throes of puberty.

"You looking for Samantha? Or are you looking for me?" She spoke with a smoky accent that sent tremors down your back. This was the set up to so many fantasies one couldn't possibly believe they were real but here I was.

"I was looking for Samantha."

"She's upstairs doing homework and shit. You want to come in? I can call her down here. I can summon her. I can summon things. I am a summoning being." She laughed keeping the joke to herself. "My husband isn't here, off fucking some tight little thing. Or his secretary. Or the nurse. Or the teachers at the school. One of them is getting fucked. I ain't."

To say I was uncomfortable would be an understatement. My face was beat red as she explained to me the possible ways her husband was cheating on her.

"I don't think he does that. He seems okay to me." I didn't realize you never question a woman with mental illness. You are supposed to agree and listen. Not enter a negative.

"The fuck you know. You're a man too. All you got is a cock and a hard on. Everything else is a dream. No heroes. No knights. Just cocks. And they're all hard."

The house was clean, pristine. I couldn't believe it. I would think the state of mind would match the interior of the domicile. This was a reversal. I knew now what Samantha dealt with. I could see her on her knees cleaning the stains off the carpet of whatever her mother spilt. Bleach spray on every white surface, as if the disinfect would kill the madness in her mother too. My heart ached for her in that moment. I saw her crying as her mother gazed out into nothing as she did at this moment with me. Pill bottles littered the end tables, as if the mother were kept in this room and no other. She had to have her view of the outside world from the living room. I saw a small cot in the corner, tossed apart like it was the victim of a fever dream. The curtains had streaks of black fingerprints polka dotting the white fabric. How many times had this woman clung to the curtains, thinking her husband was cheating on her every waking moment.

"What are you doing here?" Samantha spoke from the stairs. She was dressed in pajamas, which featured her curves, making it hard for me not to stare. She was so beautiful standing with her arms out.

"I wanted to see how you were. I wanted to apologize."

"You picked a fucking bad time to do that." She marched down the stairs, her mother reached out for her and grabbed her hand bringing it to her forehead.

"Do I have a fever? Love? Do I feel warm?" Her mother was sweating profusely now.

"You just need to put the fan on, mom. It's hot down here." Samantha clicked on the portable fan; the high setting hit her mother immediately giving her a shock. She closed her eyes and took in the cold breeze.

"Thank you, love. Thank you."

Samantha led me to the door and took me outside.

"I didn't know." I said as soon as we hit the patio.

"Now you do. Now you get it. This is what my dad and I deal with every day."

"What's the issue?"

"She has a hard case of schizophrenia. She has her good days and bad days. My dad is getting a refill on her meds so she can stop acting like a fucking porn star."

"Your bruises?"

"She sometimes holds me too hard. It's not like she does this on purpose. She just can't help herself." Samantha sat on the patio chair but stood up within a nanosecond. "You shouldn't be here. I gave you my number, not my address, okay? Boundaries, dude. Fuck."

"Again, sorry. I didn't know."

"Now you do. So, don't tell anyone about what you saw. Last thing I need is more bitches giving me shit about my mother. I get enough of that being with Steven."

"Does he know?"

"Of course, he knows. He saves me. He keeps me from losing it. But that's his duty, not yours. You are not my savior."

"I know. I'll go. I'm sorry." I hated being told I couldn't save her. I wanted to be the one to do it. I wish I were the man she desired. I was just another footnote in her life story.

"Just get out of here. Before my dad comes back. I don't want him to see you here."

"If you need anything, call me, okay?" I said walking away.

She stayed on the patio watching me walk into the dark of the street. As soon as I hit the streetlight she was gone. Inside to sedate her mother as I started to cry. The living was beginning to weigh me down. I could talk back to the dead without any fear, yet with Samantha I was on eggs shells. I didn't want her to hate me, but now I knew it was too late. I saw her true life. When one sees the truth of another it's worse. No more hiding behind laughter. No more smiles to detract. No more long sleeves to hide physical bruises. I saw them all now and she could never cover them again. Samantha wanted me to be a funny character on this stage, and I rejected her wish by trying to be the leading man. How stupid I was. I wish I were able to turn the clock back and be her clown. It was too late now. I was just a reminder of her pain.

Steven approached me the next day. It was early. He was alone on the benches, the cars were beginning to drop off the freshmen in the parking lot, the older classmen pulled up in their own cars. Steven was quick because he didn't want anyone to hear what he was about to tell me.

"I'm sorry you had to see her mom. Samantha is so ashamed, but also, she understands it's a sickness. Her mother doesn't have a choice in this. It's just life, you know. Samantha must deal with it all the time and I try to distance her away from it as much as I can. You did that too, for a while. She told me you were helping her for a long time. You made me jealous."

"That's funny." I laughed.

Steven shrugged his shoulders. "It's true. I was intimidated by your ability to make her laugh. I try to do it, but she doesn't give me the same smile she gives you."

"Steven, why are you not like what you're supposed to be?"

"How am I supposed to be?"

"The jock, the dick. The guy who gets laid and trips the nerd with his foot in the hallway."

"I can just be me."

"I need to stop watching movies."

"No, don't do that. Everyone has secrets and everyone is not what you think. I don't think you're a weirdo."

"Who says that?"

"Everyone."

"Oh."

"I don't think that. I know you."

"Just tell her, I'm sorry."

"You already told her that. The rest is on her now. I'll put in a good word, though." Steven got up from the bench and headed to his locker as the football team morphed out of the halls embracing him as they would in a high school movie.

I was on the outside looking in at the fake reality high school produced. Steven was right, though, everyone has secrets, and everyone is not what you think. They called me weirdo because I was distant with most people. Sometimes kids from school saw me on my walks, talking to air. They didn't know I was talking to a ghost, but shit, if I told them that it would be much worse. Secrets were wrong to have. They were wrong to keep. I think if I were to be embraced by Samantha again, I would have to be honest. I needed to show her what I could do. I had to tell her I could talk to ghost. I had to prove it to her so she could understand me completely. Hell, maybe I would become more interesting.

This was not to be. In the end, the last weeks of Freshmen year prompted several changes to occur. I lost Ray to the new high school opening in the fall on the other side of town. Samantha's father got a new job in New Mexico forcing them to move away. Steven was stolen by Downey High School football, where he excelled, garnering college after college program begging for him. I heard he stayed in contact with Samantha, maintaining a long-distance relationship. I remember hearing they were engaged before he took off for college. I heard they married two years later. I saw Steven on ESPN cheering with his playoff team. I saw Samantha in the stands crying when he won and went to the championship only to lose. They were two of the best people I knew at fifteen.

Never ran into them again.

I just continued.

4

Junior College and the Lost Souls Along the Way 1995

Nothing much happened in the subsequent years. I passed through the halls of Sophomore, Junior, and Senior without any major event occurring. It was a boring time. A normal time. How I would wish they never ended. No ghosts, no lost souls begging for help, just the end of the day bells and the occasional school dance I never went to. Schooling was never an interest or practice I excelled at. Most of my grades were in the mid C category with the lone A grade prompting up the ever-sliding grade point average. Most colleges never looked at me, nor did I apply. I knew better. I decided to head off to state college, most would call it the 13th grade. Though this program was one of the better ones in the country, so I liked my odds of moving on to a decent college after the obligatory two years.

The problem with this decision was not realizing the school sat on historical land mass stretching back hundreds of years. My first class was labored by the musings of Manuel Perez, former football player who had died from alcoholic poisoning. It was controversial in 1978, he was a star athlete on his way to a real college when he had a binger on a Friday night after the championship game. Coach Stallwell, a reported pervert but winner of five consecutive championships, so, local hero, gave him twenty shots of Jack Daniels and a Patron chaser.

"Well, the Patron chaser was the whole bottle of Patron. I didn't feel anything off it because I was dead already. Didn't know it yet, too. Now I do. Which sucks." Manuel Perez informed me as I was trying to map out my ten-page creative writing assignment.

"Don't be offended. I am listening to you, but I can't look like I am listening to you." I said under my breath. I scanned the room checking for any ease droppers

"Oh, I get it. You can hear me and talk to me. I appreciate it. You know how long I've been floating around here, bored to tears? Shit. I am so glad I can now at least have a halfway decent conversation. Did you see Star Wars? I was going to catch it Saturday, but shit happens."

"It's good."

"Yeah? I heard they made more?"

"Yes. Three of them."

"Oh, man." He was visibly perturbed. "Well, then I got it spoiled. I've been overhearing people talking about it, here and there."

"That movie came out twenty years ago."

"Holy shit." Manuel Perez shook his head. "Really? I thought I was only removed like a few years. Not twenty."

"You see a door at any time you roam?" I whispered, catching a cute girl with gorgeous green eyes catch me speaking to air next to me. She gave me a look of utter horror, but I quickly gave a hacking cough, filled with phlegm, I spat out into the neighboring garbage can, forcing her to spin around in disgust now.

"A door? Yeah. Sometimes right in the middle of the hallway. Kids running through and shit. I never thought of opening it. What if it's a black hole or something. I open it, the school gets sucked into a vortex, killing everyone in in here plus half the town. I'd feel bad with that on my conscience."

Some days walking through the halls I would see Manuel, he would get excited then began to talk about the same thing we talked about the first time we ever met. A constant rewind I noticed. I think the problem stemmed from my lack of retort. Hard to do with fifty kids roaming around. Lack of reciprocating dialogue creates a lull in the memory of a ghost. In these moments, I began to jot down notes. Some ghosts were different, though there was a single connecting thread, they knew they were dead.

"You ever move anything out of frustration?" I asked him, thinking back to Frank, the bandit who saved my life when Hershal came 'a calling.

"Frustration? You mean, like when I get mad, I can throw stuff off a wall and shit?" Manuel ran across the hallway, trying to knock the posted flyers off, two were caught in a windstorm of his movements, sending the two sheets of paper fluttering around madly. Manuel smiled, pointing to the only papers heading to the ground.

"See. I can get a small amount. Wasn't even upset too. If I was really mad, I think I could blast all the papers off. But I don't want to spook nobody."

I wrote in my notebook detailing this experiment. "Do you think you could ever hit someone physically? Not to hurt them, just to get their attention."

"I never thought of it. You think I could hit someone?"

"I have seen it before."

"Really? Crazy, man. What happened?"

"Well, this ghost killed a guy. But it was self-defense, he was going to kill me first."

"Damn, kid, you've been around. I don't want to hurt nobody."

"I know. It's not to hurt them, I just want to see if any ghost could do it. If not, why was Frank able to do it?"

"Maybe God allowed it. You weren't supposed to be there to begin with, maybe. How did you get this gift?" Manuel sat down next to me and gazed into my eyes, trying to see if I was connected to the actual halls of heaven. When he said God, he lit up, I don't think he had thought about the actual concept of the afterlife until that moment.

"I was hit in the head when I was ten, ever since, I've been able to do this."

"Had no control over it?" Manuel kept his eyes focused on mine.

"No." I tried to look deeper in his eyes, only to see an empty void. No life in these eyes because that was extinguished so long ago.

"Everything happens for a reason." Manuel said this to himself.

"I guess." I said less enthused.

"I see the door, again." He pushed past my eyes, coming to the invisible door behind me. "You said, it's only for me?"

"I would say so, yes. I never see them."

"If I don't go now, I'll never go. And right now, there's no kids in the hallway. Just you and me. And you can't see it, so I guess it won't hurt you if it exploded."

"It won't explode."

"Black hole might implode then. I don't want to hurt you if that happened."

"I can without a doubt tell you this one thing, the door is not a black hole. It won't explode."

"Implode?"

"It won't do that too."

"Okay. Okay." Manuel rose, he headed for the door, reaching out for where a knob would be. He turned the empty air and laughed out loud. I couldn't help but smile seeing his expression. He was so happy. He was so lost in what he was looking at.

"What is it, Manuel? What do you see?"

"I can't say. But you'll get it when it's your turn. You're right, it's not a black hole." He smiled and jogged to the end of the empty hallway. "I've always wanted to see if I could make a wind tunnel with all this paper. Let's see if I can do it on my way home!" Manuel

RICHARD PIRES

began to run with all his speed, all his athletic prowess on display in an ethereal glow that grew brighter the closer he got to the invisible door. I couldn't keep my eyes off of him as his smile grew so wide, I thought I would begin to spill tears of absolute joy. Papers flew off the walls, dozens of flyers, test results, ads for guitar lessons, play audition notices, and the occasional tutor advertisements all in the eye of a spiritual hurricane. Manuel leaped through the invisible door, disappearing into the next steps of his journey beyond us.

"Son of a bitch." I said aloud as the papers began to slowly fall to the ground.

"So, I take it Manuel is gone?" A voice spoke out behind me forcing me to turn a sharp about face. It was bespectacled tall man with a stack of laserdiscs in bis hands.

"How did you know?"

"I could hear you talking the whole time. My door was slightly ajar. And I have seen you speaking to air for the last few weeks too. I just put two and two together." He spoke nonchalantly, never mocking me.

"Oh." It was the only way to respond to this.

"Come inside my classroom. I have some questions."

I immediately saw a kindred spirit. On the walls were dozens of movie posters, old black and white classics, post war delights, best films of the late sixties and most of the seventies strewn about with such care. His stack of movies in his hand were some of the greatest ever made all Criterion too. I was amazed.

"Is this a film class?" I asked.

"Trying to get it going, yeah. You like movies?"

"Yes, sir. I've been wanting to take a class like this since I was a freshman."

"Well, it's a developing idea. I think the board cringes at the idea of film history. You're Henry Clermont, aren't you?"

"Yes. How did you know?"

"I heard about that time you found millions of dollars in gold coins and the government got you."

"Yeah, I seem to be a celebrity for all the wrong reasons. It wasn't just the gold, there was a guy named Peter Hershal, tried to kill me for it."

"I read that too."

"So, how long have you been noticing me and Manuel speaking?"

"Couple weeks now. Lots of teachers always talked about the presence." He used his fingers to air quote, PRESENCE. "Papers flying off desks around these halls, off walls, but not much else. I guess they built the new building over the old football stadium parking lot where poor old Manuel drunk himself to death. I just put two and two together and it equaled you." He put the laserdiscs down on the desk. "Which ones are worth the showing?"

Michael had laid out some major titles: Citizen Kane, 400 Blows, The Third Man, Seven Samurai, Duck, You Sucker, or Once Upon a Revolution, for you true Cinephiles.

"Leoni is always a good way to go. Westerns need to come back." I said checking out the back of the package. "I almost bought this set too. Damn."

"I'll let you borrow it. I think I am going to go the easy route with Kane. Simple to the point and if the students can't stand that one then they have no future here."

"I never read about a film history class."

"That's because it's still in the experimental period. I've been pushing for this for years."

I caught Michael studying my reaction to the surroundings. He was sizing me up, I feel, trying to see if I was insane or just normal with an exaggerated reputation, which I didn't realize I had. Many kids brought up the gold story, it was expected. Everyone dreams of discovering buried treasure and when one finds a person who actually did it they want to know how and why and who. I always left out the who part because no one believes a dead bandit told me where to find it.

"How did you infer that I was talking to Manuel? I could just be crazy." I said bringing Michael's total attention to me.

"I didn't just read the standard news story of you and the gold, I also read the medical journals they wrote about you when you had your accident. Sometimes a brain injury can induce certain qualities. Some can speak languages they never knew, others see things no one else can see, others were healers. But many seem to share a knack for speaking and seeing the dead, according to certain circles."

"I've never met anyone else like me. But I never looked."

"Maybe you should."

"I think I am too afraid to." I was being honest here. I had read the same articles as Michael. The cases that matched mine always had awkward side effects, but nothing substantiated. The one thing that seemed evident was they all died prematurely. Whatever gave the power to see and speak to ghosts was a death sentence. A slow-moving shadow over the brain that would eventually swallow it whole, snuffing out the life in the human. I put this out of my head as often as I could.

"You could charge for your services. I think most people believe in ghosts. Why not get something out of it?" Michael was not being glib. He folded his arms and nodded his head, going for his wallet. "Let's say, if I gave you fifty bucks to see if my aunt is still hanging around my house?"

He handed me the green bill. I held it in my hand, hoping this wasn't some adult's way of mocking me.

"I am not trying to hustle you, Henry. I am just a curious pebble on the edge of the shore with millions of other pebbles. Looking for something more."

"What do you want me to do, exactly?"

Michael had inherited his aunt's house after she passed ten years ago. It was a two-story Victorian with a wraparound patio, the place used to be a half-way house, a makeshift hospital during the Spanish Flu, so who knows how many other ghosts are hanging around this place. I stood on the porch, feeling uneasy. I immediately had the feeling of being watched and lo and behold I look up to the top bedroom window to see a ghostly womanly figure cocking her head at me.

Michael opened the door, allowing me in. I was shocked to see the enormous collection of vintage movie posters hanging throughout the house. Any movie of merit in the last sixty years were on display. Pristine against canvas behind thick glass, museum quality history in front of my eyes. I was lost in grandeur.

"Not bad, huh?" Michael smiled with such pride it took me by surprise. I never saw this man smile at the college.

"It's fantastic, how do you have so many?"

"Aunt Sherry owned a movie theater with her father back in the day. She kept most of the stuff the studio told her to destroy. She was a borderline archivist. Or borderline hoarder. But it's cool, so who am I to complain."

"So, what do you want me to do?" I asked to get to the point. I could see apprehension in Michael as I stood in the foyer. I scanned the entirety of the house, trying to see if Aunt Sherry would form. Nothing stirred.

"She died upstairs, in her bedroom. I want to know if you're for real. I asked her a question before she passed. If you repeat it, then I'll know." Michael stopped there, lost in his thoughts.

"Know what?"

"That she is okay. That she made it to the other side. That there is something out there to wonder about. I am an agnostic man looking for a silly answer."

"How did you find the medical records about me?"

"I read the journals out of curiosity. Most of the stories are debunked, but the one Dr. Murphy wrote about you when you were ten in the reports, nobody has come up with another diagnostic or theory. Plus, the story about the woman you saw in the MRI, what was it?"

"The Red Robin Broach Lady?"

"That's it. What a title, huh?"

"I would have called it, The Scariest Shit. She had an eternal choking face. That's how she died. When she crawled into the tube with me, I lost it. Afterward she was in my room as I recovered. Her face was normal. She apologized and that's when I started talking to ghosts. When I stopped being afraid of them."

"Anyone else ever come to you?" Michael asked hoping he wasn't the only one.

"You are the first." I said it distinctively. I wanted to see the shift in him, and I did.

"Let me show you the room."

Throughout the halls the movie posters continued. An occasional cardboard display stood along within the shelves of books and family pictures where I finally gazed upon Aunt Sherry. She was beautiful, engaging, alive through the Kodachrome. She could have fit in with the starlets on the canvases. Sherry and her husband stood in front of their cinema palace in the main photograph in the center of the hall. No other poster or picture stood around this one.

"My aunt and uncle loved each other very much. He died ten years into their marriage, I never knew him. He loved the movies, he loved spectacle, he loved my aunt. She used to tell me all their adventures, they traveled everywhere during the winter months when they closed the movie house." Michael seemed to be reporting a eulogy. His eyes were sad, his face tired. A part of him seemed to be against this whole situation, another side was more than curious. I could see the shifting thoughts rush through his mind as we got to the room.

"This the room?" I asked.

"Yes. Should I go in with you? Or do you do your thing better alone?"

"Alone. I can get the full attention of the ghost. If you walked in, she might shift, and I'll lose her."

"Okay. Sounds fair. I will be downstairs. If you need anything."

"Great. Thanks." I opened the door, walking into the lush bedroom which reminded me of the old fashioned decorative gaudy boudoirs of a high society creature long lost to the modern era. The bed at the end of the wall was large, with a canopy. I could imagine building a fort inside this massive edifice of comfort. A wheelchair stood in the corner in the darkest part of the room. Only two posters hung in this room: *The Ten Commandments* starring Chuck Heston and *Once Upon A Time In The West* starring Charles Bronson.

"Those were the two films that book end my love." Aunt Sherry phased in and out in the corner opposite the wheelchair. "I felt I had to explain the placement."

"Two great movies."

"Two of the best movies ever made, yes." Sherry moved into the light of the sun coming in from the single window. Her youth was present as the shifting subsided, allowing her to keep her entire body still for many more seconds than normal. "I saw you at the window. But I felt that was years ago. Time is odd when you are dead."

"Your nephew sent me to speak to you. He wanted to see if you were here or not." I told her the truth out right; she didn't seem to be interested.

"I was so old when I died. I was mad at God for that. So many years without Marvin. That was my husband's name. I met him in 1956 and lost him 1968. These two posters are a reminder of my time with him. How I wish that's where I could be now."

"Do you ever see a door?"

"Oh yes. But I don't deserve to open it." Sherry pointed to the invisible door. She walked to me and floated around me, reaching out to see if she could touch my head. Nothing occurred.

"He misses you very much, your nephew." I said routinely. I didn't know what I was supposed to ascertain in this meeting.

"He is and was a good boy. But I poisoned his soul with my pain. I hated seeing his torment with every gasp of air I spat out with a touch of blood. I knew I was dying but it was such a long time of pain, that I forgot everything I was blessed with."

"Why do you stay? I think the door opens the world you once had with Marvin." I felt bad for Sherry all at once. This was a truly remorseful spirit the like of which I had never encountered before.

"My sins are mine. Yet, Michael shares the most mortal of my sins. And because of that I have no hope of being reunited with Marvin. Or even be allowed to see the edge of the steps of heaven. My choices affected another one's soul. Its cursed Michael's soul."

"You asked him to kill you?" I realized what she was afraid to say.

"And he did. So gently, so lovingly. Yet he still cries at my wheelchair. I watch him beg for forgiveness to an empty room. I can't tell him to let it go. I can't tell him I don't blame him."

"I can tell him everything. I can tell him the truth. But, for me to do that, I need you to step through your door. I want to see you smile. I want to see if what I believe it to be is true."

"The door to the other side? You think it's for heaven?"

"What I know of the door is that everyone I have seen open it, saw what they wanted to have in life but lost in death."

"Are you telling me the truth?"

"I don't lie to the dead."

Aunt Sherry walked to her invisible door; I stood behind her hoping that I could finally see something. Yet nothing yielded. Sherry turned her head, laughing, crying. She made an about face to see my eyes.

"The door is what you say it is. Tell Michael, I want him to sell this place. Tell him I want him to live like I did with Marvin. Tell him, I never liked Kubrick." Sherry laughed with that last bit, leaping to the door, disappearing before my eyes.

I was left alone in the empty room. All the energy that existed in it was gone. I opened the door and headed downstairs to find Michael nervously sitting at the table, a bottle of whiskey opened half gone.

"And?"

"She doesn't want you to keep her sin. Let her go, Michael. She's gone to Marvin now. That much I saw."

Michael broke down. Tears flowed as if he had never spilt them before. "She was in so much pain. She didn't deserve a death like that. Inhumane way for a fucking saint. She raised me when my mother dumped me here. She had no husband, just a movie theater that would go up and down like a yo-yo in business. She took me to the box office every day and let me take tickets. My mother wanted nothing to do with me. She abandoned me and Sherry took me in. I owe her my life, but instead this shit happened." Michael slumped into a soft large antique chair, nothing stirred off it, this place was cleaner than most museums.

"You loved her, a lot." I tried to offer a soft response to him, allowing him to think instead of blubber.

"Love isn't equal to what she did for me. Saving me like she did, with nothing to gain from it. I failed her."

"She asked you to do it. She needs you to let her go now. She wants you to sell the house. She wants you to find yourself a Marvin of your own."

Michael smiled at that last line. "My own Marvin? Those are hard to find today, Henry. I hope you don't hate me for what I had to do. For making you be party to my mistakes."

"I can't judge anyone. I have heard more than a few confessions from the dead. Usually they don't concern the living, so this is new to me. But I don't look at you any differently. You will though. Now that I know everything, you'll stay away from me. Most people wander away from me after a while. When you rub against the dead, they leave a trace on you. I can feel it sometimes. It's like a throbbing in my head, but it's quick. Once I step away from them when they go to their doors, I lose that throb."

"Doors?" Michael wiped his eyes; he began to sense relief. I could tell he had only been half listening to me. I think he was still lost in the guilt of his deed. Now, with his sudden forgiveness, the weigh on his soul was lifted. I was just a footnote for him to refer to if anyone ever asked what it was like to speak with Henry Clermont.

"Yeah, doors. Every ghost I talk to sees them and I just tell them to open it. They see heaven, I guess."

"Any ghost ever see hell?" Michael poured himself another drink.

"I have seen something similar. I just don't know what it was."

"You should swing by my deathbed down the road, give me a heads up if I really am in the clear?" Michael knocked the whiskey down like a professional.

"She also said she never liked Kubrick."

Michael laughed. "I knew it."

After the revelations delivered, I was sent off back home. I didn't go home right away, I just drove. Watching the world unfold before me, allowing me a glimpse at the reality of other people. No such reality existed for me. I just seem to float in it, coming across the most desperate people. They always seem to find me too. No matter where I would go, there was some person looking for closure. Michael gave me fifty bucks for my trouble this time. In the future I decided it was fiscally feasible to ask for two hundred. Nice round number if someone needs closure. The next time I saw Michael, he was putting the posters away from the classroom. The school board had no means of paying for a superfluous class like History of Cinema. Michael sold his aunt's house, securing him enough finances to move out of this joke of a city. I never did hear from him again or get an invite to his death bed.

When the time came to prepare for a transfer, my parents wanted to talk to me in the kitchen. My sister Casey was twelve years old, showing signs of a prodigy. I think they saw that as a sign to nurture a new breed and allow the other to pasture. They had a check on the table with ten thousand dollars written on it. I knew this was a buyout.

"Your mother and I feel that it's best for you to maybe find your own path. Move to Los Angeles, like you always wanted to. You're twenty-one, I think that's time enough to want to be out on your own." My father was stoic in his banishment. He displayed a hint of regret, so did mother. I could see they were not comfortable with this but when I saw them look at Casey, I saw their discomfort dissipate. She was their reason for parenting now. I was the mistake they wanted to hide. Too many people were talking about what I could do, most of them didn't believe it but they still gossiped.

"I can still come for holidays, right?" I asked wondering if they could say no.

When they took a moment to answer I was shocked. This was a simple "yes" or "no" answer, yet they hesitated. That's when I realized they wanted me truly out of their lives.

"I keep hearing about your walks, Henry. You talk to air. You spend hours acting a fool when no one is around. But out here, there is always someone around. They like to talk too. And if we are going to be taking Casey into these high-end schools, we can't have the baggage you might bring into it. That's the issue, here. Casey has a bright future, and you might impede it. I know it's not your fault.

And we don't blame you. We just can't afford to risk the what if factors." My mother was more to the point.

"I get it. I want Casey to have a future too. I get it." I said holding back my tears. I just focused on the check amount. Ten thousand was a nice goodbye note.

"Holidays, we might be able to do something. Let's just plan it by ear."

That night I spent with Casey, watching our dogged copy of Ghostbusters on VHS. We laughed at the same moments getting lost in the hour fifty minutes runtime. Casey buried her head in a pillow next to me. It had been a long time since I spent this much time with a living creature. With Casey she just had a brother and that was all she needed. My comfort in that moment had to last. I was leaving my home, yet I felt it had stopped being mine years before. When my grandmother came to me and not my father, I feel that it hurt him. When the gold coins were taken away from us it hurt him publicly. And now with the gossip of the town speaking their low murmurs about me, the embarrassment started to return. We had moved before because of me; I think they didn't want to do that again. Best to give me a wad of cash and send me out into the world. I left the next day on the first bus to Los Angeles. Maybe there I could succeed. Maybe there I could find meaning.

5

Los Angeles, the Mob, Horses and R.C. 1997

My first job was the first call back. I was looking at the ads in the paper and circled the many low experience jobs needing a sucker like me. The racetrack was going through their busy season, and I was lucky to snag a job in their one eatery offered in the whole establishment. It was called The Epicurious Equestrian, many who made the track their home could barely pronounce it. I, on the other hand, could not only pronounce it, but I added a flourish to it that tickled the hiring manager. She was a portly woman named Ruby, red hair in a bun, giant boobs being strung together by an old broken bra, the tight gladiator blouse she showed off gleamed in the sunlight along with her brow beady with sweat. Her capri pants were tight too, leaving little to the imagination of her front organs. Still, there was something about her, as if she had the goods years ago and knew it. This current form she existed in rippled with a sexuality that only confirmed her Nymphomania from a former life, long lost to time but recalled with smiles and satisfaction.

"When can you start, honey?" Ruby had a pad of paper out, no computer in sight. This system was still ruled as it was in the 70's.

"Whenever you need me." I said not realizing she was desperate.

"How about today?"

"Don't I need training?"

"On the job is the best way to go. Throw you into the fire and watch you dance. I think it's the best thing for you." Ruby kept her eyes on mine, they were nice and calming green.

"Okay, let's go."

Right away I was in the fry room, dipping the fries, chicken breasts, beef patties, egg rolls, tacos, tater tots, cheese, brownie chunks, and anything else dipped in their secret batter. After the first batch goes into the oil, I had to rush to the hot dogs spinning on their rollers, checking which ones were ready to be made into their carb beds. I had thirty-five people in line at 12:04, ten minutes before the third race. Most wanted hot dogs, due to the speedy delivery. However, being my first day, I had turned the roller to the highest temperature not realizing that the dog in the center was not being cooked thoroughly. Most noticed right away as they tore into the bun with three teeth visible in their heads. I had never heard so much profanity pointed at me at once. Ruby turned down the heating element and smiled. She knew it was my first day.

"Don't let those idiots get to you, dear. But next time, don't be fucking stupid." Ruby showed off her perfect teeth with that smile of hers, blouse untucked, showing off

her small rolls of flab. She walked with such bravado, that you didn't see her physical imperfections. You saw the sexuality she exhibited. As a twenty-two-year-old working for minimum wage, she wasn't looking too bad.

The weeks went by without too many hitches. I learned quickly, I failed, I listened, and as the time went on, I began to see Ruby as my first real adult friend outside the ghosts I saw roaming the track. I was hesitant to take lunch away from the dive restaurant because being near Ruby, was alive and fresh, the antithesis of what plagued me since I was ten. So, when I did discover a ghost discovering me, I often tried to ignore them. I didn't want to show off any sign of insanity.

"I said, do you think this is heaven or hell?" The ghost asked with the ever-shifting clothes but maintained a small fedora hat. "I realize you probably don't want to make a scene, so I will just accept a nod for perhaps this is heaven. Or a shake of the head for this is perhaps hell."

"Neither this is just living." I whispered to the middle-aged Irish man.

He smiled and laughed heartily, "knew you were paying attention to me. Wow. That's a first time for me. In a long time… what year is it?"

"1997."

"Shit. I've been in that column for twenty years now. Well, the bones of me. Are you sure 1997? I keep seeing 2000 on the board there." He cocked his head, checking the winner board. "Oh, wait, it's 1997. Looks like Buttercup and Tuesday Red won the long shot."

The racing form was on the table, I pursued the names on the form and neither of those were on it. Race five had already started so most of the races had been played out and the winners were being shown on the newly installed plasma screens.

"What was the day on the board?" I asked.

"If I remember correctly, it was Tuesday, October 12, third race and sixth race."

"That's two weeks from now."

He gave me a deceptive gaze, he then smiled.

"You know what this could mean for you?"

"It could mean early retirement. If what you saw is accurate."

"I know the races winning boards. I know the horses. I know the jockeys. I know how horses shit. I could've been half horse in all honesty, at least that's what the Wops used to tell me when I won them money."

I was excited but then remembered Frank and Hershal. I remembered the Feds and the helicopters. I buried my head in my hands, realizing the lottery I may have just won. Excitement filled me, suppressing the guilt and shame that could arise chasing ghosts for financial gain. Though in all honesty, maybe this was God's apology to me? I leaned into the sky around me, silently speaking to the Almighty, seeking a course to take. Hardly a reaction erupted from the abyss, so I took that as a sign to get some money.

"I'm not saying that I want you to report on the winning boards. But I just need to hear what you saw on the winning board two weeks from now? Out of curiosity. I mean, hell, we could be wrong in our observation." I spoke low, not letting anyone see my lips move. As I got older, I got better at this skill.

"Yes, I understand. We don't want to broadcast a winning ticket just yet. I could be dyslexic. I remember two long shots, Buttercup in the third race. Tuesday Red in the sixth race."

"Tuesday, the twelfth?" I wrote down the ethereal report.

"True that." He smiled, feeling good to finally find another racing buddy.

"We shall see if that works." I thought he would've walked on after I said that, but he lingered. The grey hat on his head reminded me more and more of a caricature than a person. As if he was a living cartoon character at my disposal. I didn't care for the feeling. I didn't want to look down on a dead spirit with such incredulity. Especially if this guy could win money. I stared him down momentarily, watching him react to the modern world moving around him. He wore a smile akin to a child waking from a nap. All he knew began to flutter to the surface, allowing him to access memories he probably lost before meeting me.

"So, you were murdered?" I asked pointing at the concrete column keeping the C Section erect.

"Yeah. When you work with the mob most of your life it doesn't end well for you. I used to run numbers for Joey Turkey, that was a nick name and Eddie Spumoni, that was his real one. And if you questioned it, he would pistol whip you. I think he had issues with his weight and being named after ice cream didn't help."

I wrote the names down to check them out later. Maybe they still ran this place. I had to be careful wading through new territory. But my excitement for what could potentially be a windfall of financial gain overtook the bull shit of sensibility.

"My name is Henry."

"My name is Archie. But most everyone called me RC." He extended his hand as he would in life, only now I couldn't shake it in return. The pantomime alone would create too many uncomfortable stares and I just started working here.

"Oh, I get it. I'm dead, no one can see me. And you don't want to be shaking air." RC laughed then spun around checking the boards. "This is going to be a nice way to buy some acreage in heaven. And for you to buy some commercial property downtown."

Back home, in my studio apartment, I began to see the lacking appeal of being me. Where am I going to go? The first job I get out of college is barely able to pay rent, let alone, purchase food. I have answers to questions most have been asking for thousands of years and here I am standing on a carpet that may or not be stained in blood. I didn't notice that when I was looking at this place. No amount of Dawn liquid soap is going to take that shit out. Being alone in this place forced me to face what path I had to take being an adult. I had the ability to take advantage of things no one else could be able to do. So, why was I feeling this nag in the back of my head? My soul was in a state of entropy, frozen with guilt I didn't accept because I couldn't believe in it. Why should I be guilty taking advantage of a situation delivered unto me by powers I have no control over. I think God would be fine with me getting some sort of Universal Basic Income while I could. It wasn't stealing if it was my cash being put on the line.

I went to a drawer in my room my grandfather, the last one

standing, my mother's father, left me a stack of five single one hundred-dollar bills. He was always sending me money when he could. My grandfather was never too talkative but knew money took care of a lot of hanging threads between people. It was simple, to the point of love. Money to him was crucial to living. Without it there was no chance of coming through it alive. People tend to spit at the idea of money, yet when they hurl their indignation to it, if they discover a wad of hundreds in their suit jacket, they'll throw it at the air to illustrate how it means nothing to them. Though, no one ever sees them lurch down in horror, picking up those dollars as if they would never see them again. Cash is not a monster. It's just another ghost.

The first six weeks of the betting happened simply. I would lay my bets down on the first morning break. Head back to the Equestrian and do my shift. Then head to a terminal on the way out and cash in the tickets. Thankfully, this was the first automatic cash machines inserted into the track. It cut down on the need to hire people. The future had arrived, and I was going to leach the shit out of it. I bet small at first, learning about the system. RC kept me in the know of track and horses. Just in case anyone ever asked I could respond with some sense of prior knowledge. Not like it would matter. I forgot most of what he told me. To say this was a scam was erroneous, this was the surest thing a thing could be. It was a license not to steal, but to invest in.

Ruby noticed the occasional glimpses at the racing track. She would always slap it out of my hand and then spank my butt. Literally, she spanked my butt. I could have sued if I didn't mind the attention.

"You better not to get too acquainted with that piece of paper. I don't want to see another lovely boy lose himself to this shit." Ruby was showing off her new bra today, purple with some embroidery on the giant cup. She wouldn't show it totally to me but did show off the straps. She would show it off to Matty, the dishwasher, multiple times because they were screwing every lunch break.

"I was curious. I wasn't betting." I said meekly.

"Right. Just because someone in the lunch line that you see three times a day, doesn't mean they're experts. It means the opposite. They're fucking losers.' She adjusted her bra again, showing off some areola. I was quick to look away out of respect.

"I understand. I get it. I see who eats here. I'm not taking any of their advice. Hell, if I did, the chicken sandwiches would have red onion in it."

"They asked for red onion. Jesus, ingrates. They are lucky they get the mayo in a pouch of plastic. Shit." Ruby returned to her normal peach skin tone as the red heated inflammation subsides. "I just don't want to lose you too soon, Henry. Guys like you, out here in this real world, sometime fall to it to easily. I don't want to see you hurt."

"You're the best boss I ever had, Ruby. I wouldn't want you to see me like that."

She smiled and spanked my butt again. "Now that's what I want to hear. Get to register 4, Marley called out again. You want to work a double?"

"Sure." I shrugged my shoulders not shocked to hear about Marley. She called out every two days due to some new infection she thought she had. Ruby couldn't fire here because she was connected to the managers in the Counting Office. The best job a dip shit like Marley could get was through nepotism at the Racetrack and that says a lot.

Laying the bets down was tricky. I had to manage to get away from my register, long enough to lay down the two long shot bets and two average winners just to throw anyone who was paying attention off. This was RC's rules.

"Always play it safe twice a day at the track. You bet the long shot, put down thirty percent more than you should on that. Then you take a sure thing and bet small with it to keep up appearances. It's like watching a novice from afar at Twenty-One table. At first, they bet small on everything, then they get a liking and comfort to the situation and that's when Pit Bosses bounce on the guy taking him for all he is worth. You, right here, though, have more than just a sure thing. It's the truth. It is the honest to God winner at the end of the race. So sayeth the board! And God be with the board in return. For as I, the dead, know, the perpetual nature of good things. God taketh them away."

"Who's going to be watching me put bets down? How would they know I won anything?" I was whispering typing in the bets.

"Trust the dead, kid. Someone always knows something is up when someone is winning. In anything."

"I don't want to work here forever, you know."

"I don't want to be spooking this place up forever either. I 've been seeing this door from time to time. It just stands there, all by itself. People seem to not notice it, yet they all walk around it. Weirdest damn thing I ever saw, next to the future that is."

"I wouldn't open it yet. Maybe it would spark a black hole. Suck the whole place into your dimension of the dead, kill all life. You never know about that metaphysical shit." I didn't want my cash cow to leave so soon. We had only been doing this for a month and the returns were growing large.

Collecting the winnings after the races was not as difficult. I would use my bathroom break to pick up the first five race and then when Ruby was getting serviced by the dishwasher round 4:45PM, his break, I would collect the last five races' winnings. Ruby's office door was conveniently located three feet from the sink. The massive dish washer would lower over the racks of plates and cups to mull the sound of humping emanating from three feet away. Nothing worked so well in the kitchen, so noise was a common occurrence.

Ruby and Matty could hold court for about ten minutes. With the occasional post-coitus cigarette, I had roughly 12 minutes to do what I needed to do without being seen. RC was always at the machine, waiting for me, always providing a second set of eyes.

"Maybe we should relax the amounts. This week we took advantage of four races a day. I say we switch it to two."

"That seems meek. Or should we bet bigger but only twice?" I suggested.

"Not a terrible idea. Maybe we should try it tomorrow? If I remember. I always seem to forget certain things."

"I call it ghost senility. All of you guys go through it. It's the timeline problem. You exist in all times, I gather. The future, the present and the past. All three of those timelines are running amongst you simultaneously. I have started to take notes and put them together. Maybe I can crack some mysteries of the universe on the side as well as invest in some solid opportunities."

"What are you going to look for next? A ghost realtor? Then you'll need a ghost lawyer and then ghost management."

"I can hire a living lawyer. And look up a realtor in the paper. I just need to know where the best place for growth is."

"Anywhere Disney builds a shithouse."

"Florida?"

"An actual shithouse." RC laughed. He was the first ghost since Frank that seemed to like spending time with me, even if time was a different thing to him.

"You ever get bored out here? I mean, as a ghost, do you feel boredom?" I had wanted to know this since I stumbled onto the time concept.

"I don't really think about it. I mean, there's moments where I see someone I used to know and it sends me in a flutter, like a seizure. The closer I am to them, knowing who they were, the more it triggers me to seize up. I shake, I really do. And in that moment, it's the only moment where I sense time ticking by as opposed to being just here. I don't know, it's weird."

"I saw that once. When I was a kid. A ghost connected with a man, and it killed him."

"No shit? I never tried that. Jesus. I don't think I would want to do that. I never had an ounce of murder in me even alive. I liked everyone. I just owed too much money to people with nary an iota of humor in them. That's the secret of life, I think. Find the humor in it."

"I won't put you in that situation. If this works out."

RC smiled, "you just jinxed us, Henry."

If this works out, kept me up that night. I couldn't sleep, I couldn't lose myself to useless television. I just stood in the middle of my shit show apartment replaying the possible failures. I didn't feel bad about it morally. Stealing from a racetrack that stole millions every day from crumb bums who read the racing forms religiously and clung to their old mantras told to them by the great gamblers of the past didn't seem like a sin. Using RC did though. His smile and wide-eyed nature of being himself kept me uncomfortable as I made him repeat the dates and their race outcomes. He never mentioned the door to me again. I felt bad about that too. It was as if his only shot at redemption in life was slipping away because he had to help a little shit like me win money to secure financial stability. What was wrong getting a job at an insurance company? They do all right. I was smart enough to do that. I just didn't like the idea of being behind a desk. Being trapped by any job scared me worse and worse as I got older. The dead didn't scare me, the living did. Watching them ride their buses, or broken cars down broken streets their taxes never went to. The living world was for suckers. And if I was blessed with this gift, I might as well use it to my full power. Even if it cost a sinner his road to Damascus.

Money rolled in as RC and I continued our arrangement. I would cash the winning ticket after my shift. Take the cash home, stuff it into a false coffee can and head back to the track. Even on my days off, I was there making bets. I was sure to be incognito, I even purchased a high-end fake mustaches and heavy padded suits to hide my slender frame. It was an adventure each time. I was beginning to enjoy myself especially after counting the daily winnings. After eight months, I was running out of cupboard space, I didn't have any room for actual food, I only had stuffed false coffee cans loaded with cash. I had to bury them at my parent's house. I made so much money I had created an extra savings account just to be on the safe side. Another three months rolled along, and the bank began to question me every time I waltzed in.

"Sir. Please fill out this form, it is to determine a certain parameter within our banking system." The blue haired clerk said this to me as I was dumping another thirteen hundred dollars in fifties into the account.

"Parameter for what?" I asked, keeping my eyes on the fifties as they roll through the nicotine-stained fingers of said clerk. Her skin was orange and peeling with black smudges. As if her body had been smothered putting out a house fire. I sometimes mistaken her for another member of the dead, just maintaining their daily routine as a bank clerk.

"It is to allow certain parties to ascertain that this money is not being created illegally. Or, if you would be involved in any nefarious activities to earn cash as opposed to a normal paycheck with deductions."

Oh, there it was. Deduction. A word I knew too well. I had been screwed by government over money earlier in life. You would think I would've learned my lesson. Cash wasn't gold, right? I figured cash would be alright to put into a bank without drawing attention.

"Wrong move, pal." RC spoke gazing at the boards, seeing the future winners.

"I thought it was a smart move." I was stunned.

"Banks monitor everybody's money now. Since Prohibition. If it's on paper, it's public. When it's public, the business partner you never asked for steps into the picture asking for their forty percent. And they, like the mob, find you. Why do you think I ended up in a concrete column?" RC shrugged his shoulders. "Sometimes, you need to realize you had the moment. How much money have you made on top of your earnings at honest work?"

"I think we are sitting on seventy thousand."

RC didn't shift at all for a brief ten seconds. It was amazing to finally see him as a whole entity. He was human. With no phase shifting, I could finally see his eyes and face. He was exhausted. As if he existed in a perpetual nervous sleep. A man who would close his eyes for a second, only to rush up out of bed to see the clock was forty minutes ahead of where it was last time.

"That's pretty good, huh?" RC began to rephase in and out of the multitude of outfits he wore in his living period. His clothes would grow shaggy in some spots, then would blossom forth a high-end suit, then retreat into a pair of cargo shorts and Hawaiian shirt. All at once, his demeanor changed as a gaggle of Mobsters rose from the bottom floor of the racetrack. The one in lead seemed familiar to me too.

"What is it?" I asked RC, trying to figure out who the shortest Italian was.

"It's Lonnie Sprinkles."

"Sprinkles?"

"Not his real name. He's obsessed with sprinkles; don't ask me why, I think it's a nostalgic kick for him."

"His best memories of life revolve around sprinkles?" I asked.

"Now that I think about it, I think he had his father killed in an ice cream parlor and there was a picture of the sprinkle jar covered in blood. Hence, Sprinkles."

"That's much worse. "

Lonnie Sprinkles did in fact have his father killed in an ice cream shop. Lonnie Sprinkles was the last known true mobster left on the west coast. He made the jump to Los Angeles back in the late eighties, developing the gambling structure out here for his bosses back east. He had worked extremely hard to maintain control of the gaming industry in the Southern California area enforcing the local governments to enact edicts to quash any Indian Casinos or slot machines from ever putting their mark in a two-hundred-mile radius around his territory. No one ever crossed him, but word on the street suggested a mega corporation was interested in buying the entire racetrack and surrounding parking lot to build a stadium for a National Football team yet to be determined. No one thought it possible to put up a stadium in this part of town, but weirder things do happen.

Lonnie turned the corner, never seeming to look towards me. So, when a pair of Friends from Jersey pulled me out of my lunch booth and into the abandoned office beneath the winner's board, I was surprised.

"Sit down, kid. Relax, Lonnie has some questions for you." The Friend from Jersey was decked out in a fine tailored suit. I was examining it, wondering if that was what I was missing in life, a fine tailored suit.

"Where did you get fitted for your suit?" I asked honestly wanting to know an answer when the gruff thick New York accent overtook the room.

"He got it in Providence. Same place I got mine." Lonnie Sprinkles sat in front of me. "You got older. What a strange world we live in. So many questions I had to ask you roughly twelve years ago. I've been going through that afternoon in my head, trying my damnedest to understand what happened. "

I realized at once who Lonnie Sprinkles was. The original Friend from Jersey who had me at gun point on the mountain with Hershal. "Holy shit. Small world." I said forcing a laugh out of Lonnie.

"Shit. Under statement of the year." He lit up a cigar and then handed me one out of his coat pocket. "Nicaragua tobacco is what used to be Cuban tobacco. All those farmers left when the Commies took over, shipped their abilities to another place with the same climate and proliferated. Much like me, I came over to California with my abilities and proliferated. Though the climate here is far superior."

"How long have you known about my winning?" I knew what this was about. RC was standing across from me, lost in Lonnie, like he had seen a ghost.

"You know I heard rumors about how you found that money on the mountain. This was after I had gotten out of prison. You set me up for ten months inside. But I don't blame you for that, you were just a kid. Hershal is who I blame. That cock sucker with his delusions of a Vegas outside of Vegas kept the bosses happy in their nostalgic haze, thinking back to when they ruled whatever they touched. Now, they spit in napkins and shit in wheelchairs with no more power. I keep them happy with money, we make so much here that your earnings don't concern me. What concerns me is your ability to be correct every time you make a bet. And two years working here, you seem to enjoy. Most people last six months to eight working that dive restaurant. You smile when you ask these rat puke fucks how they want their cheeseburgers."

"I like to make people happy. I am a math savant. I count the horse's hoofs. See if a grey horse is in the race. Grey horses always win, I have realized. I know the horses. I know the jockeys. I know how horses' shit. I could be half horse in all honesty." I realized immediately quoting RC was a mistake. Both RC and Lonnie Sprinkles stretched back, realization streaming through them.

"RC." Lonnie whispered. "Gentlemen, I won't be needing you. Henry and I need some alone time in the Emperor's Suite."

High Rollers from every walk of life knew about the Emperor's Suit, but none had ever been allowed inside. It was reserved for the Sheiks and oil barons and Japanese Whales, all of them carrying cash and gold just in case things got interesting. Lonnie poured himself Japanese whiskey from a decanter in the form of a Samurai, gold and diamonds adorn the sleeves of armor.

"Japanese whiskey. They got our number on that one. You know how much this one glass costs?" Lonnie was scanning the room. "Is RC in here with us?"

RC was in fact in the room, but he was too busy enjoying the atmosphere. He was admiring the art on the walls, the pictures of the racetrack's history. He found himself in one of the pictures.

"Holy shit, it's me and Lonnie! That's the night he shot me in the face."

"I shot him in the face, you know." Lonnie reluctantly spoke this fact.

"I heard. RC knew that was a possibility living the life he led." I said checking to see if RC was fine with that assertion. RC gave me an okay signal with his hand.

"I didn't want to. Orders are orders when you are a soldier. Now, I am a Captain. I don't have to do that none sense anymore. I hope he knows that I do apologize for the murder. I figured if I dumped him in a concrete column, he would appreciate it."

"I did!" RC shouted, smiling at the pictures leading all the way down to the bathroom. There were many with himself in it.

"How did you figure I could talk to ghosts?" I asked point blank.

"Like I said, it took me a long time to figure out what happened that day. Hershal fell down a shaft a healthy man but was pulled out carrying a two-pound brain tumor in his frontal lobe. That takes effort." Lonnie opened a ledger from under the black marble table at his knees. The windows lowered their automatic shades, blocking the sun from entering the room. RC was beaming with pride, realizing he had made the grade to be featured in these photos in the Emperor's Suite.

"I didn't do that." I said, retreating into the suede couch. My entire body was engulfed in its comfort, I had never experienced a couch like this.

"You'll fall asleep in that couch if you let yourself go. But right now, you and I must be talking. So, get off the fucking couch and sit on the stool."

I quickly hopped onto the stool.

"As I was saying, a two-pound brain tumor formed in his head on the way down a fifty-foot shaft. I'm no doctor, but that is damn near impossible. Then I remembered Hershal saying something, a single name. Grant."

I was taken aback hearing that name. I had almost forgotten it myself.

"I see you remember." Lonnie said, snapping through the ledger with his fingers.

"Yeah. I recall."

"I researched that name, discovering the Grant Gang and what they did up in them hills. Stealing government gold, then smelting it down to make it their own. Smart. Gold is gold. Same thing today too. But this world and time, gold is cash. Even if it is coming out of a machine. You have placed one hundred and thirteen bets in the last seven months. You have amassed a total of 87,000 dollars. Cash."

"Yeah. I should have been more sensible."

"Hershal tried to take 32 million dollars of gold off you and now I will be taking a fraction of that. But, again, I have questions. What did you do to Hershal? My recollection was myself with my gun out, then suddenly Hershal screamed, you screamed, then I blacked out. Then I woke up, Hershal in the hole. FBI in the sky. Can you fill in the bits I missed?"

"Grant attacked Hershal. Somehow, he was able to attack him.

Grant went for his skull, as if by instinct. I felt the same pain he did, in that moment. As if the ghost was using me to enter the physical world."

"A conduit? He needed a charge off you. Interesting."

"I wouldn't do that again. It hurt too much. And there was something else." I stopped myself, not wanting to bring the Devil Dogs back into my head. I had never thought of them since that day. Now, faced with that memory, they didn't want to retreat. I almost thought I saw one move across the racetrack. Giant testicles being dragged across the mud with oversized backward hunches and thick arms carrying its weight. The human face on the deformity seemed to smile as it got closer to the steps leading up to the Emperor's Suite. I dismissed it as a figment of my imagination.

RC noticed my dismay, "you okay, kid?"

"I didn't ask for him to get killed. I didn't want that."

"I know. You were a ten-year-old kid. Put into a ridiculous situation by grown men trying to scam you. Now, you're a grown man trying to get away with a scam using a ridiculous situation." Lonnie crossed his legs, lighting up a cigar. "You can smoke in the Emperor's Suite. Yet in a year we won't get to smoke in the parking lot. New laws are coming our way in this state. Lots of changes are coming and I am sick of them. I grew up in the world of smoking jackets and space suits. Now, there is just health and organics. I want out of this life."

"How much do I have to give you?" I realized this was going to come up eventually, I figured get it out of the way.

"You can keep five." Lonnie blew smoke out and toked another round.

"Five?" I was shocked.

"You're lucky you get to breath still." Lonnie had a way of going lovely to psychotic in milliseconds. I guess all murderers are like that. "But that is the first payment. You will work for me. I'll let you keep five percent. The rest goes to me until the allotment I want is collected in full."

RC shook his head, laughing, "he's got you now. Here comes the next favor. I am sure you and me will be working with each other till Jesus comes back."

"I want you to use RC to make me another million dollars in cash. One million and then you can do whatever it is you want to do. But you won't be able to do it here. I cannot have any connection between me you or RC. No one would believe it any way. But I don't take additional chances in any business arrangement."

"That means he's going to kill you after its all over." RC was afraid, he looked at me and then tried to move his hand into Lonnie's head. Nothing was connecting. He just phased in and out falling through the couch and Lonnie landing on the other side. "It didn't work."

"I will do it. But what are my guarantees that you will in fact let me walk away."

"I saw what you could do with a ghost. I expect you would try to do it to me if it came down to it." Lonnie smiled. "Knowing RC, he might have already tried it."

"Astute of you." I swallowed back my fear.

"I know you don't trust me. I wouldn't either. But, like I said, I want out of this life. I want to leave the country. I have a way out. I don't want to put you in jeopardy. If the bosses knew about you, they'd take you for themselves."

"Would they believe you if you did tell them?"

"When it comes to money, they don't give a shit."

RC was pacing more than I was at the coffee cart. He kept looking at the future boards, shaking his head. "This is my fault. I should never have bothered you. Should've just stayed in the folds of time and space, enjoying the spectacle. But no, I had to be needy. Stupid."

"It's not your fault, RC. I deserve this. I should've sent you off to the door as soon as I saw you."

RC wrinkled his nose at the mention of the door. "So, that's what it is."

"Well, what the hell else is it?"

"I thought it would be more of a vortex with fluttering angels, or devils, depending on where you were off to. I don't know. A normal door? I see those all over the place. I see one right behind you, now."

"Maybe you should just go on through it. I don't want you to be a slave to a man named Sprinkles again." I was being nonchalant not realizing he was in fact a real murderer. In all honesty, with this power of sight comes a relaxation of death. None of that bothered me anymore. In fact, I never thought about the future, well, my future. I sensed it would pan out and I would die eventually somewhere. Just not in the present and not by a guy name Sprinkles.

"In the meantime, let's give Sprinkles his winnings." RC went to the winning board and began to read out the long shots. "Hopefully we can do it in six months and not another two years."

When I got home the door was ajar and the goon squad was working overtime cleaning out my coffee cans. All the cash I accumulated evaporated before my eyes. I just sat on the small love seat to turn on the television. It was a lesson in futility. Then Lonnie Sparkles himself sat across from me on my little love seat.

"You understand how this works now?"

"I got it. It's the same lesson as before. I make money, someone will find a way to take it."

"Just wait until you find a wife. Bitches want it all."

"I'm not making that mistake." This I was so sure of being twenty-three.

"You say that now. But trust me. Someone always finds a way into your heart. Women are like that Amazon dick fish. Swims up the urethra, fucks up your bladder and shit. Women." Lonnie scanned the room and smiled. "You have good taste. I like the flow of this place."

"Are you going to hire me to remodel your house?"

"Something to look in to… RC isn't here is he?"

"No. He can't go beyond the track, it's his home. I think he prefers that."

"Interesting. All this newfound knowledge. Anyone else would be rocked by the awe of it, you seem so indifferent. Why is that?"

"I used to be afraid of it. Now it's just a pain in the ass. Doesn't help me in any way. In fact, it only gets me in trouble."

Lonnie giggled to himself, he nodded his head, "you will discover that most things get us in trouble. We need to learn how to maneuver. In doing that, we can adapt and adjust better. Most people don't. RC was one of those people. Why I had to shoot him. I don't want you scared of me. This is personal. RC was business. Assignment."

"You told me that."

"Yes, but I needed to explain. RC was not just a gambler; he was an informant. Tried to put us all out of business. Bosses don't like rats. I don't either, but I liked RC. For me to rise in the ranks I had to put four bullets into his head. You don't say no to that order. I never liked killing people. It's a sin God is a little tougher on than most."I shocked him when I asked, "are you okay?"

Lonnie opened one of the fake coffee cans. "Neat trick. You got a lot of time ahead of you, kid. Some of us don't. I want you to know, me taking this money is not personal. It is just a maneuver. I just hope this move was perfectly timed." Lonnie tossed me the coffee can. "You could get about twenty bucks a piece for these. I know some people who may buy them. Bring them to the counter. Stack them up. Give you a little bonus."

"Thanks." I did mean that as I had no idea what to do with these things. Lonnie pulled out a wad of hundred-dollar bills tossed them to me.

"Your five percent I said you could have. I would put it in the bank." He laughed to himself throwing me a wink out of the door.

I put the cans on the counter like Lonnie told me to. Within two hours they all sold out. I was ahead two hundred bucks. Ruby reminded me of the truth of the world once again, this being her counter, she was entitled to twenty percent. I gladly handed her the bills as she always stuffed extra cash into her bra, allowing me a glimpse at her ample dirty pillow. I would always shoot my eyes away, but she would smile knowing what I was seeing.

"There's going to be some changes coming our way, my buddy." Ruby said settling on a stool across from the Coke machine. "Don't be too scared when yellow tape is strewn across the office doors and the racetrack closes for a week or two."

"Feds?" It was the first thing to come to mind.

"Absolutely, the Feds are moving in. I saw you got introduced to Lonnie. He is bad news. Even if he's trying to be human. Don't think he is your friend. He's a murderer. He killed an old friend of mine, RC." Ruby swallowed back emotion, as a sudden rush of men in black suits ran into view from all angles strewing out the yellow tape.

"All right, men, get the office situated now, break through to the count room, now. Allow no exits!" The voice of the FBI agent ran through the concrete walls reminding me of another time. A time of chopper blades and a hard, strong American voice breaking through the Earth itself. I was in the presence of the same exact FBI from the mine. This guy must never sleep.

"Hey!" I shouted pointing at the agent.

"Hey, kid! Looks like another day, another bust. You're a lucky charm!" He smiled at me, pulling out a military shot gun, cocking it, he blasted the door frame down into the count room. "Let's get these sons of bitches!" He led the charge into the count room.

"You know Agent Thompson?"

"Let me tell you a story, Ruby."

I told Ruby about my little run in with the mafia back when I was ten. The gold, the mine, Hershal, and his connection to Lonnie Sprinkles. I didn't mention the ghost part or the quadrupedal testicle monsters with teeth.

I was informed that after a three-year sting operation, led by Ruby, Agent Thompson finally nabbed the one criminal on his list he had been pursuing since 1986. That day on the mine, after Hershal was eaten alive, after they took my gold coins. If only they had arrived three weeks earlier, I would have been ahead eighty-five thousand dollars.

"You should write a book, kid." Ruby smiled, pouring herself a soda, "come on, let me buy you lunch."

Lonnie Sprinkles had already skipped town by the time the FBI arrived. After he took my cash, he boarded a flight back to Jersey where he absconded with his kids and wife. Within six months they caught him in Paraguay. Not any of his family was present. At the end of the year, I received a letter from him with Riker Island heading. I didn't know they had stationary.

DEAR HENRY,

Thanks for your coffee beans. My family planted them with such care that I believe they will be able to create their own blend. They don't need me to help them anymore. My beans were too coarse and bitter. My recipes were disastrous choices mandated by too many cooks in the kitchen. Too many ideas and orders. Too many bad choices made to get ahead in the market. This spoils beans and people. Clean beans and good people will prevail from the kitchen's staff. You'd probably been happier if this experiment with our mutual friend, RC, worked out for you. Just because you lost a big step doesn't mean it was for nothing. My kids are safe. They will be situated too by the coffee investment. I think your ability to maneuver will strengthen your resolve. You're like the farmers who left Cuba, remember? Take the talents you have and proliferate somewhere else. You will not be visited by any one I know. The kitchen staff is no longer working. I will never see the lights of the city again or the Emperor's Suite. But light a candle for me and RC anytime you find yourself in a church. Men like me don't last long in cages. Maybe we will meet up again, me on the other side this time.

Lonnie.

RC seemed to tear up as I read the letter to him. I had put in my two weeks' notice with Ruby. She promised to write me up a killer professional letter. But this one was what I needed.

"Lonnie wasn't so bad. I always liked him." RC said beginning to read the winner board.

"He murdered you."

"I'll forget about that in a few minutes; besides, you want the last three races of the day? For old times' sake?" RC smiled, pointing to the board.

"RC, you don't have to read out the winners for me anymore." I felt a pang of regret, but I had made the decision as soon as I read the letter.

"But we are a team, with Lonnie out of the way, we could really make a run for it."

"You ever see that door again? The one that pops out to you every now and then?"

"Sure, but what does that have to do with winning some money?"

"I want you to have your peace. I want you to go home. You can go home now, RC. You don't have to help me anymore."

RC smiled brightly, "I made it to the Emperor's Suite after all. And I got to see it. I never thought I was that special."

"You were. And you are. Thank you for helping me, RC. I will miss you."

RC opened the door and cracked a giggle that rippled through the universe.

Within a millisecond he was gone.

The loneliness hits when they step through the door. I always feel it. A wave of horror, pain, lust, love, power, awe then laughter. I believed it was all their hang ups in life phasing out of themselves before they're able to step into their new world. Every time I felt it, the wave grew stronger. I began to think maybe it's a warning. The forbidden knowledge must be paid for somehow. Adam and Eve were thrown out of Paradise just for eating an apple.

I might be fucked.

6
Aimless Walks 1999

Without a stable job but enough money saved up from the extra wins I took advantage of when Lonnie ran off, I began to take my long walks along the neighborhood sidewalks. I would take my three-to-four-mile jaunts to think and contemplate what to do next, in the words of Sprinkles, how to maneuver into a next phase. People always have chapters to their lives, which one was I in now? Everyone has the poor part of their growth, the part of the story where you tell people how much you earned last year, and they look at you with such sympathy and remorse, responding: *How do you live?* Usually, I answer with a shrugged shoulder, more like a spasm form one side of my body: *I just do.* Which ends the conversation at any party if I am at one.

Walking was the only way for me to really relax. Breath in the cold fall air of Los Angeles, realizing why was I here? I was interested in acting, but I didn't have the money for a coach or seminar. I wanted to do theater, but you had to buy yourself a spot through working for the company if they were even interested to begin with. Maybe I could write a screenplay. I had seen enough movies to understand the structures, to plug in the formula. Shit, just look at what was green lit, monkeys with typewriters were doing the work now.

Out of the lull of my mindless walking, I came upon a girl sitting on a wraparound porch of a massive compound of a house. Windows all sealed shut, black curtains blocked any view in or out of the home. Security lights snaked along the brick wall encompassing the property line, garbage cans were out in the street to be picked up by the trucks this morning. Two black doors bolted shut allowed access to the side of the domicile where the garbage cans came from. Pristine rose bushes lined the fence, it was as if they were designed to take your eye off the house itself. The red against the white blocked any roaming eye. I found it odd for so much paranoia in a neighborhood this quiet. That's when she first spoke out to me, her smile still hits me hard reminiscing.

"Yeah, it's a bit of a mystery as to why so much security. You are the first person to notice anything, then again, you are the first person I have ever been able to speak to. Which is odd because I am dead."

"Funny, I have that effect on people."

"Dead people, I assume? I am not the first?"

"Far from it."

"I died in that room up there. I was kidnapped, drugged, and I don't want to remember the rest. I wasn't murdered if that's what you're thinking. I had severe diabetes. I went into shock and that was that. I knew one day it would get me but not like this."

"Is he here now?"

"No. He works a regular job. But I need help in saving the other girls. Three of them. Locked up in there. Why I sit out here every day, looking for a way to break this place open. And you just walked around the corner... Maybe God is real?"

"I still don't know that answer, but I assume so, what I have seen, I can only assume."

"You don't sound convincing. Then again, here I am, with no light vortex sucking me into heaven. I just seem to wake up every morning seeing the same metal shutters sealed with mortar. A fan above my head allowing air flow. A steel fan with rust caking along the edges of the blades from the very few days of rain we get here." She lost herself speaking to me, her phasing continued like the other ghosts, but her face was frozen in such a torment that I wanted to curse God for putting an innocent beautiful girl in this place. "Sorry, I like being descriptive. I think I wanted to be a writer in college."

"That vortex doesn't have to matter. I'm going to help you."

I spent over an hour on that porch speaking to air if you were to walk around the bend. Luckily, no one came. This place was an empty nightmare. No one living saw what existed here. Her name was Laura, she was a UCLA student excited and scared to leave home. A full ride in scholarships she earned working her ass off all to be taken away one night in 1980.

"I was at the movies that night. First date with this guy I had in my class. Bill Miller. *Empire Strikes Back* opening night. He won tickets and took me. I was super excited. He wanted to take me to his car and drive me back to the dorms, I smiled and said I wanted to walk. I was afraid he was going to kiss me. I liked him, but I wasn't sure if I wanted to date him."

"I gathered. You wouldn't have known anything different. It wasn't your fault."

"No, but I still get pissed about it. This cock sucker picked me up along Westwood. Didn't see him coming too. He just grabbed me, put the either over my mouth and I woke up in that god damned room. Didn't last long. Odd thing to watch yourself be buried in the middle of a fruit yard. The back is loaded with orange and apple trees. He sells them on the side at a farmer's market. Best ones in the state he says."

"How long is he gone for?"

"Don't know. Time is different for me. Some days I know it has been just one day, others I don't know if it's been six weeks or six years. I just don't know anything anymore."

"How would I be able to get into the house?"

"The storm doors in the back are always opened. He uses those more than any others. Front door is made of metal, always locked. Front windows are all sealed shut. He parks on the side, leaves early comes home late. When the weekend hits, that's when he has his time for the girls."

"Tomorrow is Friday." I felt sick. How the hell was I supposed to do this?

"And the sun is almost down today. You must get here tomorrow."

"I will."

"If anything changes, I will be here on the porch. I will tell you if its safe."

I began to leave but she stopped me.

"Could you stay a while longer? It's been a long time since anyone has even looked at me let alone spoke to me. And I don't want to go back in there."

"How many girls again?"

"Three. One is new. She's not going to make it if this goes on."

"It'll end tomorrow."

I couldn't stop thinking about her. Shopping for a claw hammer and a crowbar I kept going back to the small moments where she smiled. I was falling for Laura. Of all the ghosts I encountered this was the first one that truly was a victim of evil. It was the first time I ever questioned the concept of God. How could someone this innocent, beautiful, full of life and ready for a future of achievement be snuffed out so unceremoniously. Laura was a used tissue paper tossed aside by the universe. It infuriated me so much that a store clerk worried I was going to be violent with the claw hammer. I cast those thoughts aside as soon as I focused on Laura's face. It calmed me down. It made me focus on what I needed to do.

I paced in my apartment, going through every possible scenario.

What if he came early and I was in the middle of a hallway, trapped between chain link fences and locks designed to snare an escaping girl or a rescuer. What if he was armed with a gun? What if he had dogs roaming the interior of the house? So many booby traps deaths went through my head. I saw myself die thirty different ways with thirty different implements. Axes, bullets, fire, knifes, the girls themselves. I was sweating profusely, about ready to puke. Again, all I had to do was focus on Laura and every scenario ended with success. This was my chance to be a hero. Who could turn that chance down?

The kidnapper walked from the front door, checking the locks, to the side of the house where his truck was parked. The electric gate opened, displaying my first look at this monster. It was what anyone chasing a monster would expect, he was normal. Just another man living in the world of the blind. I waited for twenty minutes, thinking he was going to come back for a forgotten wallet, but the truck didn't make a return trip.

"Fuck it." I said out loud to myself. Then Laura appeared on the porch, she didn't see me beyond the fence. I wondered what she did see. I was going to make it a point to ask her as I crossed the street. Once I walked through the little gate and stepped onto the cement Laura smiled and rushed to me.

"You were real." She said almost lost. "I thought I dreamed you. When did you come to me?'

"Yesterday. It's only been hours, really."

"Damn, time is odd. It feels like it was months ago. Why is that?"

"When you're dead, I think, time is a constant flux. It's moving in every direction to you at the same time. To me, I exist in the present, you existed in the past but also the present which means the future is moving too. Can I ask, what do you see when you look past the fence?"

Laura at first didn't know how to answer the question. She

squinted, gazing out to the landscapes beyond me. "I see desert, then cabins, then an ocean, then city scape. But it happens all at the same time. Why I always came out to the porch. I liked to see the shifting. It comforted me. It helped me forget my life. When I think about my life, my parents, my brothers, I just cry. I couldn't do that all day. But, as I began to understand what had happen to me, I just became angrier. And now I have you to save not only me, but three others."

"Point me to the storm doors."

I broke the lock with the crowbar, easily. The doors lifted with nary a squeak. Concrete stairs lead down into the darkness, Laura stayed behind me.

"There's a string connected to an alarm at the second to last step. Step over it when you reach it. "

I looked down and saw the fishing string connected to a rudimentary electrical box. It must have sent out a silent alarm to him just in case someone managed to get this far. "Now what?"

"There's a staircase heading into the house to the right. Again, there's a string connected to another alarm on the first step. Then right before the door, another one."

Again, I stepped over the first string, then the second. I had my hand to the doorknob leading into the house when I saw the CCTV camera glowing red with recording life. I was being videotaped.

"I see a camera looking right at me, Laura. Does he have a computer system linked to it?"

"No, the camera is for the house. I see him checking out the cameras in the living room every night, double checking for anything out of the ordinary. It won't matter if you get the girls out today."

"Okay." I opened the door, not realizing that the mistake I made not breaking the CCTV program.

First room was the kitchen, a state-of-the-art high-end kitchen. It was like he was a chef. Clean, knifes lined the magnetic strips along the island, copper pots hung delicately, food processors and an orange juicer aligned the tops of the counters. Everything was in its place with such a precision that it scared me. This was a house of a sane mind, not anything rotting or smelling. In fact, the house smelt of fresh roses emanating from the row of vases filled with roses freshly cut. There were three vases filled with roses.

"Three vases, for the three girls. He gives them a fresh one every week." Laura came to the last vase; a single orchid grew out of it. "This is for me. It's been here since the day I died. No roses, just this orchid. See the purple? Almost looks black." Laura phase shifted to the stairs, pointed at the third step. "Another wire to step over. Sorry."

"Thanks." I started to head up stairs, carefully raising my leg over the string. If Laura weren't here, there would be no way in hell I would've seen any of these. "He's paranoia knows no bounds. Does he cut these when he's home?"

"No, he just steps over them. He knows every angle, every corner. This is his domain. Anyone in it is his too."

"Not for much longer." I said it with such bravado I impressed myself. Laura was lost in her shifting, she appeared at the top of the stairs.

"The first door is here."

Walking up the staircase I saw family photos framed on the wall. Up close, I saw a home with a real loving family inside this house removed by twenty years. This guy must have inherited the house. Kept it pristine and neat for himself and his locked-up guests. The last picture was him and three girls. Each one lost, the camera captured their fear more than love. They were each different, each with a separate hair color, body type, eye color. One was trim and lean, cut with muscle. She could have easily beaten any man up let alone be held hostage to one. The other had blonde hair, demure, she wore a lowcut blouse showing off her cup size. She was rounder, softer than the first one. Her eyes dismissed her supine position, yet she took the picture. The last girl was exactly like Laura. Her eyes were nothing like the others, her eyes were empty, as if she were struggling to accept this new world. This must have been the new girl.

Laura had her hand on the door, as if she could communicate through it. She smiled wanly. "This is Trina. She reads a lot. She's been here four years, I think. Time is hard to figure out, I hope I am not misjudging the years."

"Trina? My name is Henry, I am here to get you out."

"Henry?! Where's Tony? I can't be outside without Tony."

"That's his name." Laura said with disdain.

"Did Tony send you? Are you one of his friends?"

"No, I don't even know the guy. I just came here to get you out." There was a long pause.

"Tell her, Teresa and Jazz want out too." Laura said.

"Teresa and Jazz are going to leave too. All of us."

"Open the door, then." Trina said defeated.

I opened the door to find the first girl from the picture. In the corner was workout equipment, a bookcase filled with paperbacks, a small tv mounted on the wall with an old Nintendo system attached, a row of games lined up against the wall. She had one window in the corner looking out to the street. It was sealed with black coating; a white curtain covered it. Protein bars, water bottles and carrots were stacked in a short cupboard with no doors, a minifridge next to it.

"How did you know?" Trina asked with tears in her eyes looking up at me from her bean bag chair. A small mattress hugged the wall with two large pillows and clean sheets.

"Not important, look, when you get out, stay behind me. Tony has trip wires all over the house. Let me guide you through them. We are all leaving together." I offered my hand to Trina. Her grip was incredibly strong.

"Grab those protein bars." Trina pointed to the stacks of bars fresh from their boxes. "I have grown fond of them."

Trina and I were hugging the walls slowly heading up in this domestic prison. Laura would phase in and out as we inched up each stair. Laura shifted back in front of us, she blocked one of the doors with her body as I went to open it.

"There's a shot gun pointed at you. There is a side door from the other bedroom that he uses to get around. The computer is in there with the cameras. He never opens this door."

"Then we must remove the shotgun. If the cops get here, they might not know it's booby trapped." I spoke to Laura forgetting about Trina.

Trina backed away from me, squinting at the white door I spoke to. "How do you know there's a shot gun in there?"

"Oh, I just assumed so. Look, I am going to be strange leading you girls around for the next few minutes, so, take my little interludes with a grain of salt. You have to trust me."

Trina bit into her protein bar, "just get us out of here, I see nothing."

"Where's Teresa?" I asked Laura, suddenly she phases shifted, landing next to a curved staircase leading to the next floor.

"Up here. This one has no tricks, not enough room. Narrow stairs. You'll have to break the door down, she's a deep sleeper."

I finally got to use the hammer. One smack, the door buckled, with another swing I was able to knock out the entire top section. I saw Teresa slowly rising from her cot in the corner. She had enormous pillows all around her. They smelt sweet. Candles lined the walls, all of them lit, providing the aroma. There was a picture of a woman in yellow against the wall. Framed in gold. A small table in the corner had art supplies, markers, pencils, paints, anything an artist would want. A small fridge also included in her ten by fifteen room.

"Who are you?" Teresa asked lackadaisically, rubbing her eyes.

"My name is Henry; I'm getting you out."

"Okay, fine." She got up, unlocked the demolished door, then collected her art supplies placing them in a leather bag. She leaned against the wall next to Trina.

"Where's Jazz?" I asked Laura.

"Who's he talking to?" Teresa asked yawning.

"Don't ask." Trina said looking over her shoulder.

"Probably Laura. She's the only one to die here." I spun around, catching Teresa smiling. "Is it? Oh, shit!"

"How did you know?"

"He talks about her. He feels bad about it. Always blaming himself for not knowing she was sick. Makes sense that she would still be here. I would be."

"Why?"

"Make sure he paid for it."

"We got to get to Jazz, come on."

"The girls need to get out first. Jazz is a prize. Too many traps around her. Too many obstacles." Laura phase shifted, arriving behind Trina pointing down to the staircase out to the front door. "Follow me, Henry, lead the girls out."

"Change of plans, you guys get to get out first. But you must follow me and listen."

Laura led us past the trip wires again, Trina and Teresa followed closely. Teresa was beginning to break out of her doldrums. Hope was rising in her. When I busted opened the front door, she ran out screaming and crying. Trina simply walked out stretching, laughing heading east as if she knew where she was heading. I stood at the door watching them head off in two separate directions. Laura was at the top of the stairs, her face lost. Almost as if she didn't know what was happening. As if this was another dreamscape stare from the front porch seeing every timeline rush into an explosion of ethereal dust.

"We need to get Jazz out of here." Laura woke from her spell, she appeared directly in front of me, I was so close to her I thought I could smell her. I wanted to kiss her, I wanted to hold her. All the strength she had was tossed out of this world years before. All that exists now is this ethereal shadow of what would have been an amazing living creature.

"Show me." Was all I could muster.

Jazz was held in the attic. Laura took me through an array of fishing line booby traps, shot gun embankments, false floors with dead drops. Jazz was the treasure in this collection. I was wearing thin, avoiding the number of traps, I couldn't imagine this man having to deal with this every time he wanted to see her.

"This is ridiculous, how the fuck does this guy get around his own home?"

"He is trained and disciplined to live like this. He feels more evolved, an apex predator unlike any in existence. His hubris is his weakness."

"I am just a regular omnivore... How am I going to lead her out?"

"You'll have to take her through the window. There is a slight slope to the house on her side. You can lead her down the side of the house, perfectly safe, but there will be an eight-foot drop on the other end. Eight feet is nothing if you're desperate. Plus, she hasn't been here long. But I fear she isn't built for this. Tony has been trying to break her in, but it's not taking. We need to get her out now."

"Okay." I never felt fear in these moments. I don't know why. When I looked in Laura's eyes, I was lost to them. She was a ghost but felt more alive than anyone I ever knew. I hadn't known that feeling since Samantha, and what was that worth?

Laura phased completely around, the sudden jolt forced me back, her face filled with fear. "He's here."

"We got to get her out now!" I shouted, keeping my excitement from forcing me to move without caution. "Just tell me what to step over or under and I'll get her out."

"Not much more to go, lift your left leg over that rug, now, bend over and pull the rug."

I did so, revealing a small dead drop, fourteen inches deep to a series of jagged blades sticking out of a cement block. A homemade foot killer. If anyone let their foot fall through the rug, you were not walking out of here.

"Take one of the blades out of there, or the whole block of cement if you can. We can use it against Tony if he comes too close."

"I don't know if I can do that." I didn't want to kill or maim anyone on this day. I didn't have that hatred in me even if this man was a monster.

"Maybe I can help you." Laura rushed into my being, I felt her inside of me, using me to lift the block of cement from the dead drop. I didn't realize I was so strong, as I lifted the cement block with ease. The blades sticking out were secure albeit one. That blade fell out as soon as I flipped it forward. "We will throw this at him if worse comes to worse." Laura and my voice echoed each other. It was a brutal, wild vocal, almost subhuman. She rushed out of me, as I stood holding the block of cement. Suddenly I vomited, feeling the loss of her presence inside of me. For a moment I saw her memoires. Laura and I shared all we were in a matter of nanoseconds. I had tears sting my eyes, feeling her loss of family, her years of existing as a specter in a house of evil. I was ready to kill Tony.

"We haven't much time. He's unlocking the front door. Jazz is in this room."

I took the hammer from my belt and bashed the door in. It took a few moments; this door was reinforced. This was his prize horse in the stable and not any one was just going to bash down a simple wooden door to get it. I was able to get a chunk of the door broken through, I could see inside the room. A large window stood against the side of the sloped roof. I could see the tile of the roof through the clean glass.

My attack on the door was becoming more and more futile. The reinforced bottom and top forbid me from breaking through.

"He's through the door. He's coming up the stairs." Laura said, shifting back and forth. "Just tell her what to do. She can do it."

Jazz stuck her head out, I saw her scared, defeated being as she backed against the window that led to her salvation, she couldn't speak, let alone scream. Her essence was almost drained completely from her.

"Jazz, I am here to save you, don't be afraid. I just need you to take this hammer and bash the window out. You can head out down the slope of the roof, there's an eight-foot drop. You can do it. I can't lead you out, but you can do this on your own."

Tony made his appearance at the bottom of the narrow stair well.

"What the fuck is this?" He asked calmly. "Who are you, friend?'

"I'm just a nobody." Was all I could muster as Jazz shattered the window with one swing of the hammer.

"No, Jazzy! Not my Jazzy!" Tony rushed up the stairs, he leaped over the first false step with a dead drop, he made it halfway up before I threw the cement block at him. Due to the weight of the block, it tittered in the air, the blades tilted up as gravity took over. Tony was able to catch the block, but the weight was too much, he rolled backwards down the stairs, his hand fell into the first dead drop. I heard him scream as blades from that trap ruptured his hand and forearm.

Jazz began her descent down the side of the roof. Her feet were nimble hugging the edge of the gutter. Her small frame allowed her balance and the proper weight limit to allow escape. If it were not for Tony attacking, I doubt I would be able to lead her off the roof, my weight would have been detrimental to the escape. It seemed to me that more eyes were on us then I realized. Maybe there was a God? Then again, Tony may kill me yet.

"You cunt." Tony shouted lifting his bleeding arm out of the hole. "Why are you taking my angels from me? I loved them so much." Tony started to sob madly. "You aren't allowed to take them from me!"

He stood up, blood dripping into a massive puddle below him. When lurching forward he almost collapsed entirely. I gazed at him from the stair above. He looked pathetic, small, worthless. Laura went into me again, I fell victim to her inner thoughts, I felt her anger rise, her pain channeled through every pore in my skin.

"Laura never wanted you, Tony! I never wanted you! I wanted a life! And you stole it from me! You are ending today. The girls are going home. And you can die knowing no one ever loved you." Laura's voice crept into mine with nary a vocal reverberation. Her voice was my voice long enough to scare Tony to madness. His expression twitched from sad to insanity. His eyes fluttered, he stumbled against the wall, heading back down the stairs.

Laura left my body and phase shifted to watch Tony fling himself against the door with the shotgun behind it. I managed to make it down to see Tony rolling his head along the door surface.

He looked up to me and smiled. "You always have to have a way out, my boy! Fuck you, Laura!" He raised his leg with all the strength left in him and kicked in the door. A blast from the shot gun behind the weak wood erupted through him with ease sending him through the window behind him. He fell thirty feet to the ground below. Laura and I shared the broken window witnessing his last movements as a human being. Tony crawled to the nearest fruit tree. His blood-soaked hands wrapped around the trunk, he pulled himself to the bark and kissed it then slumped over and died.

When his final breath left his mouth, the earth became dark again like the mine shaft when I was a child. I knew what was coming. I dreaded seeing them but this time I wouldn't look away. This time, I wanted to see them. What nightmares they were.

Laura and I gazed upon a trio of four legged monsters more akin to a giant, breathing phallus. The head had a human face with a prodigious maw. The arms pushed the girth of the testicles the legs maintained the balance at the front. A reversal of anatomy. From this distance I could clearly see the faces; a woman, her long hair perpetually swinging back and forth in her blasted engorged eyes, as if they were being pushed out from the inside of her skull. The second was a dark-skinned man, tattoos adorning every inch of flesh, even the thin membrane covering the massive testicles. Eyes the same as the woman, his hair was buzzed, tight, clean. The third was Hershal. I fell back when I saw him. Laura noticed my recognition and tried to comfort me with an extended hand, but it yielded before it could touch my head.

"You know him?"

"Once. The same trio came for him. Now I see why."

Hershal, now a Death Birther, smiled at me. It was more terrifying than the act they were about to perform. Tony, now awake, saw them up close. He screamed as they began to lick his body. A secretion formed, within moments, he was covered in a slime. It sizzled his flesh, it burnt the clothes and hair off his body completely. In seconds he was a shivering, pained, nude model, open for their enjoyment. Hershal opened his mouth wide, able to take the entirety of Tony's feet. Suddenly, Hershal propped up, member raised up as if becoming erect. Tony slowly slid into the pulsating shaft. The toes and legs began to press against the membrane of the sack. Bile threw up as Tony dropped inch by inch into Hershal's mouth until only his screaming face was visible though the shooting puss of a consummated damnation.

The earth opened beneath the fruit tree, only a hint of yellow could be seen against a vast black void. The Death Birthers were nimble as mountain goats, leaping to outcroppings leading down into the passage of Hell. Before he went back, Hershal looked up to me, smiling. With a slight nod of his monstrous head, he laughed, coughing up the remaining mucous from his throat and trotted down the passage as if he had been doing it for an eternity.

"What the fuck?" Laura said as she stood shocked.

"I guess that's what you call a death birth?"

"Makes sense when you call it that. But what the fuck?" Laura began to come out of the shock and smiled. With that gesture she saved my cracking psyche. "Let's get out of here."

Jazz made it down from the top of the house. The slope of the roof was more like a nine-foot drop, but she managed to land safely. She ran to the nearest phone, called the cops. Within twenty minutes sirens were wailing on their approach. Laura and I stood on the porch for those few remaining moments.

"Huh. Look at that." She said, smiling.

"What?" I asked.

"Time isn't moving anymore. I just see the neighborhood. And look who decides to come out of their caves to see the truth, finally." Laura was speaking about the neighbors, all of them standing on their front porches or white picket fences. All of them wondering what the sirens were about. "You see that door all of a sudden?"

"I never see it. Those aren't for me. It's for you. It means time for you to finally go home." I said with such a sadness I let tears fall.

"Why are you crying?"

"Because I love you. And you were never here. You existed in a time before me. And it hurts me so much."

"I lived and I died not on my time. You know, I don't think I was ever angry over it. I just stayed because I wanted to protect the girls who could have a shot at life. Their time wasn't up yet. I'm sure I was born to do that. If life doesn't allow you the chance to make a difference, maybe death can."

"I would kiss you. If I could feel you."

"I would've lovingly accepted it. But my time is now no longer mine." Laura phased shifted to the door. She turned to me, smiling. "One day, the living will embrace you like I did. One day, you'll have love. Though, in life, time is different. In life, it is one day after another, seconds into minutes into hours. So much can be enjoyed in those fleeting glimpses. Don't take them for granted." Laura opened her door leaving me on the porch, alone.

I stayed for the police so I could warn them of the traps within the house. I wanted them to move about safely. Trina, Teresa, and Jazz came with them to my surprise, they were wanting to personally thank me for what I did. They also brought the local news crews with them. When the girls rushed up the porch stairs to hold me the police gave me a round of applause. I felt so much vindication that I felt guilty crying over Laura. The dead were dead, the living needed help. The three girls pushed me to the forefront of the news crew cameras. Speaking of my heroic nature, my lack of fear in saving them and my coolness facing the monster, Tony.

"How did you know they were being held here?" One of the pampered newswomen asked.

"How did you break into the home?" Another asked.

"Do you know you're a hero?"

I smiled hearing that one. "I just did what anyone in that situation would do." I said into the camera.

"We got a body here!" One of the cops shouted, forcing all the news crews to rush over to the fence line, leaving me behind.

"You killed him?" Trina asked.

"No. He kicked in the shot gun door and blew himself away."

"Is he really dead?" Jazz asked next.

"I need to know he's dead." Teresa spoke out, leading the trio to the fence line. They stepped beyond the yellow tape, beyond the camera crews, the reporters, the ghouls standing on the sidewalk wanting to see death. The three girls parted them all like the Red Sea. They were entitled to see their captor lying in a pool of his own blood. No one saw what I saw. Only Laura. She was able to see the divine retribution. She was able to move on in triumphant. I didn't know what would happen to these three girls left alive to pick up the pieces of their missing world. Hopefully seeing Tony dead was the rope they needed to pull themselves out of the darkness. Teresa laughed and kissed me on the check.

"I'll be okay." Teresa let out tears, the other two followed suit.

I held them tight, their tears soaked through every inch of my shirt, it was a baptism bringing me into the fold of what my power could do. I could save both the living and the dead. This was not a curse but a blessing.

Three weeks later I was called in for questioning. I was told it was procedural. They had to put the X's and Y's together to complete the picture. I understood, so I was not at all scared walking into the police department. As soon as I stepped into the headquarters, I was given a three-minute cheer. I was red all over, forcing them to laugh. All of them whispered how I what I did was insanely brave, wonderful, justified, honorable. I got high from the adulation, when I sat down before the two detectives in the interrogation room, and they noticed.

"You smoke a joint, Henry?" Detective Harris was laughing to himself.

"You look high as shit." Detective Mullins was doing the same.

"Sorry, I just never thought I could be a hero."

"You did good, kid." Detective Mullins was big, burly, a typical hard ass with thirty years being in the thick of the shit of the street. You had the feeling he couldn't lie but could read a liar.

"We just need to ask you some follow up questions. It's like I said over the phone, all procedural. We just need to make our reports logical." Detective Harris was keeping something hidden. He wasn't as big as Mullins, he was demure, passive in character. They were bad cop, good cop on any other day. Today they were just concerned and more concerned.

"How did you know Tony McCall was harboring three girls in his house?" Detective Mullins sat across from me, lighting a smoke.

"I had walked the area few times. I saw a girl at a window one day, he pulled her away. I thought that was odd. Went back to see if I could see anything else, that's when one of the girls wrote out help on this white card. I saw it, went up to the window and I think it was Teresa, she was the one who was able to get to a window. I could see she was scared; she didn't say much, just repeated, *he has us prisoner. There's three of us. Find a way in, please.*" I had practiced this speech knowing I had to spill it eventually. I figured Teresa was the best girl to use because her door was never locked. Tony had beaten her down so badly that she had free reign in the house. She even backed that in her statement.

"The problem that we have with your story is when we watch the security footage from the house, we see none of the statements made by the girls or you make any sense. In fact, one could say they were lies. Not that you are in trouble. You are a hero, no one wants to take that away from you. But we need to know what exactly happened for our report." Detective Mullins spoke directly, putting the cigarette out.

"The video footage isn't going to be released to the public due to the context of it. You look like a crazy person talking to air." Detective Harris stuck a piece of gum in his mouth then offered some to me, which I took graciously.

"We know who you are, Henry. Detectives must do research and sometimes the time we put into it gain results quickly. The science papers about you and Dr. Murphy come to mind. The events with Peter Hershal are another. All documented and known if one knows where to look." Detective Mullins took a second, giving his partner a nod.

"Did you know who was buried under the apple tree in Tony's Garden?"

"I could only assume it was Laura." I didn't lie. I knew it wouldn't do any good.

"Only assume?" Detective Harris spit his gum out, not knowing what to do next.

"You were speaking to her in the video, weren't you?" Detective Mullins wasn't fazed by this statement. He accepted it full cloth. "Like I said, it didn't take long to discover your history with Dr. Murphy. He was adamant that you had developed a mental stigma which you said allowed you to see and speak to, lack of a better word, ghosts."

"Okay, I can't deal with this. I need a break. You want to finish this off. Go for it, you're retiring. Let me have what's left of my sanity for the next five years." Detective Harris left the room.

"Never ceases to amaze me when people find out about me. It's either your reaction or his. My parents had his. They just left me to my whims and some cash to start again. Why I live here. It's California, dreams come true here? Right?"

"Not really." Detective Mullins waved at the mirror, signaling the gathered group to exit the room. "Turn off the tapes too. We can't have this shit come out." A knock through the mirror was the retort.

"Thanks. I didn't want to be a media sensation, again." I said remembering my father making a fool of himself on local television leading to mockery on the national scene.

"We got a problem. We need to close the books on this case but can't do it if you were being led by a ghost. The ghost of Laura, who we exhumed from an eighteen-year-old grave. This can't make the papers or the news. It's too much."

"Now everyone out there is going to look at me like a freak." I said, spitting my gum out into a tissue.

"I won't let that happen. Most of the guys out there will always look at you as a hero. Tony McCall got what he deserved. The girls came clean with us two hours ago. Telling us what you were doing. Then we watched the security camera footage from the house. You should have erased the tapes."

"No kidding."

"You're not a freak. You're brave. I need you to sign off on this document. Detective Harris and I have written it out as you, detailing the events, and we matched it to the girl's statements. It keeps all the truth out of it. Maintains the story we as a department is willing to let out. This case won't be further investigated."

I signed the document, feeling such disgust over it. This dismissed Laura for her bravery. For her sacrifice in staying behind waiting for me to be the conduit for her honor.

"You now get a big check." He slid over a cashier check. It was for seventy-five thousand dollars. "Trina, Teresa, and Jazz had rewards put out for their safe return. You deserve it, Henry. Let that be comforting when we lie our asses off to the public outside."

Lie we did. The cameras of the news casts and the papers flashed across the steps of the police station as the sun went down behind us. Detective Mullins did all the talking as Detective Harris bit his tongue. He still couldn't accept the truth of what had happened. I was asked to raise my check up, making it a Lotto winning ticket story as opposed to a story about Laura. Not one question was asked about the lone dead body found on the property. Laura's body was taken back to her hometown in Indiana. Her parents were finally able to let her go. And then I received another check for her return. I had made almost one hundred thousand dollars being a hero, then the government took half of it.

The following days left me lonesome. I kept thinking about Laura's attempted kiss then her final shift exiting through her own door. The closest thing I had to a girlfriend had been dead eighteen years. I wanted to call my mom and dad. I wanted to hear their voices, and hopefully Casey too. Hopefully they didn't change their number, I dialed and waited, then realized what if they did pick up the phone. What was I going to say? They left me; I didn't leave them. I was still angry but as time subsided, I lost the heat the anger created. I just wanted to hear someone familiar. I just wanted my mom and dad to say good job. When the phone picked up Casey answered.

"Hello?"

"Casey?"

"Henry?! Hey! I just saw the news, holy shit, you're a hero." Casey's voice was shrill, puberty was hitting. Her feminine throatiness was becoming more and more pronounced. She was going to be a Lauren Bacall sound alike for sure.

"Thanks, Casey. I was just doing what I could."

"I'm going to tell everyone at school that you are my brother, the hero. Even going to do a special presentation. We had to pick a family member that we admire, and I picked you. Everyone always does their mom or dad, that's boring. You are way cooler."

Casey's excitement was legitimate. No sign of apprehension or fear. If my parents were on the line, that would be all I would hear. I was glad they didn't answer. I was glad Casey was able to have this time with me.

"If you ever needed me to show up for anything let me know. I will be there for you in a heartbeat." I was being honest and then when the long pause crept into the phone, I realized that I said too much.

"Mom and dad said that wouldn't be smart. You'll be a magnet of attention again and they just don't want to do that. They're still upset over the last time."

"Yeah, I figured that would be the case. It's fine, when you're older and have your own place, just think of the fun we could have then." I said this with so much hope it hurt. I wanted to be with my sister.

"I can't wait for that day. Could you call more often? I feel like we talk maybe twice a year and that's not working for me these days. I'm doing a play at school this month, we are doing Kiss Me Kate, I'm playing a cook. Not a big part, but I'm going to do an Irish accent. Way more fun for me that way." Casey's smile could be felt over the phone. I closed my eyes, remembering the last day I saw her. Casey was fourteen now, she was catching up to sixty. I was missing her growth. But it wasn't meant for me. My parents needed normalcy. I was the sacrificial lamb to allow it to return. I took it as a duty. Allowing my parents, the freedom they desperately wanted. I didn't ask for this power, and they didn't either. When my father asked me to leave them, to go on my own, I felt it was appropriate. I still didn't harbor any ill will. I just missed them that's all.

"You like being called a hero?" She asked laughing.

"It's nice. I must admit."

"Mom and dad are proud of you too, know that. I have to go, but if I called you at least twice a week, would you be able to answer?"

"Sure. Of course. I would always be a phone call away from you. Sounds like a plan."

"Then it's settled. I will talk to you later, Henry. Love you." She hung up quickly.

Silence returned to my world allowing me time to cry. Everything hit at once and all I could do was sob. I had a few seconds of blubbering before the phone rang again. I wiped my eyes, forcing myself to laugh as I answered:

"That was fast."

"Fast?" It was the voice of Detective Mullins. "Did I miss something?"

"Detective Mullins?"

"Yes."

"Sorry, I thought you were someone else. What do you need?"

"Can I buy you a hot dog?"

7

Cold Case: Charlie Hailey and a Vengeful Soul 2000

I had a two-chili dog with onions and garlic special accompanied by a forty-ounce cola and then added a large cheddar fry with bacon and then opted for a soft serve cone. I was depressed he was paying.

"How long have you been able to do this thing you do?" He was whispering as the world around us was shouting and enjoying their dogs. I began to cut into mine, taking the first bite with such a joy because I was seeing him linger waiting for me to respond.

"Since I was ten. You read the medical reports? It's all in there. But Dr. Murphy refused to believe it even when I made connections no one could with dead patients. Some men just can't accept different perspectives. I didn't care if he believed me or not. I was just wanting to get out of the hospital. I was tired of the probing, the tests, the questioning. It made my parents uneasy which led to them dumping me. When I get a chance to do something useful with this power, I use it full on. And if I can help someone else when no one else can, I tend to do that too. Pass me the ketchup."

"I have this cold case. Been working on it for, hell, twelve years. You may have heard of it, the Charlie Hailey murder?" Detective Mullins slid the ketchup over watching me eat. I motioned for him to eat too just in case he forgot.

"I don't know how I can help. I mean, when I do come into this stuff, it's not by choice. They just find me. If I had to focus or meet certain anomalies--" I didn't want to say the word "Ghost" out loud— "I don't know how the reaction would go."

"I understand. I do. I'm just trying to tie up loose ends at the end of a career. I've tried doing it the usual ways, but sometimes, one can't do that. You got to take a leap of faith to save yourself and that's where I am at right now. I don't know how else to approach these cases. I have exhausted every way." He finally took a bite of his plain hot dog. He tossed me his bag of chips then a photocopied police report. "You've served the dead before, now let's see if you can serve closure to the living."

I was afraid to open the police report knowing it was something terrible. I didn't want to help the detective at all. Something felt off to me. My instincts were blasting sirens of foreboding. I never listened to myself and now I was about to open the first page of the thick file. On the first page was a photograph of a small demur boy, thirteen years of age, found in a pile of leaves twenty-five yards behind the school he was abducted from. His eyes gave off a hidden darkness, something mystifying. As if he knew his own destiny and accepted it. I shook off that feeling to remember Laura. Her smile kept me happy these days even if they weren't real. Ghosts don't have physical form, yet when she entered me to speak out, I felt her deeper than any man ever could. Soul to soul breaking through time and space to forge a single vocal eruption of anger toward another living being. It felt incredible. I could feel my skin crawl with an ex-cited heat. I hadn't had sex, but this seemed to be the next best thing, maybe even better. Now, she was gone. Lost to me forever, she was just another victim. No more victims if I had any say in it. Maybe I could assume this as my true calling. Destiny is a hard thing to understand. As I gazed at this boy the foreboding seemed to melt away. Or maybe I was simply good at burying it. The child's name was Charlie Hailey and I decided at once I was the one to help him.

Detective Mullins picked me up from my apartment in the wee hours of the morning. I was groggery, felt the burden of this kid's past on me already. The file was not as detailed as I thought it would be. Maybe Mullins kept sections of it from me to see if I could fill in the blanks, to test my ability to see if this were all real. I wouldn't mind the exercise. I want to see if I can really do this. To solve a cold case like this might open avenues for me. I might be able to make a living doing this. I don't know how, or what court of law would allow a Soothsayer, or Medium like me get away with solving anything without any real evidence. I doubt this was going to work out for me or the court systems. I think this was all designed to appease a single man's conscience and maybe that was enough.

"Charlie Hailey was my first case as a detective. I was five years into the job, street beat, then some clerical nonsense to get a feel for the red tape aspect of police work. I was young, excited to take a case this big."

"Did you volunteer?"

"No, it was given to me because I was the fresh face on the crew. I had transferred from out of city to this job because it offered the detective position. Smaller town, I felt I could make an impact. Boy, was I wrong. This case was designed to be a cluster fuck. A lot of the guys knew it was an inside job, or a case that was protected from higher powers. They gave me the case because they knew I would fuck it up. And I did."

"In the file, I noticed it never mentioned a murder weapon. What was the cause of death in the autopsy report?"

"Massive head trauma, multiple stab wounds to the stomach and back, anal rupture, suggesting rape. Aggressive rape." Detective Mullins was quiet for a moment, he twitched, holding back a tear from forming in his eye. I knew now that I had to help solve this, mostly for him as opposed to Charlie Hailey.

"Was a knife ever found?"

"No, the wounds weren't a knife. It was a sharpened piece of metal. Construction steel rebar, most likely. But in the searches, we never found anything remotely like that. Hard to connect anything to the murder without the actual murder weapon."

"That's why you're taking me out there? See if I can find him? Charlie?"

"I am hoping that's the case. The report doesn't go into detail because most of the pages were confiscated by the State Police, they were thinking the technology and services they had allowance to would guarantee a faster conviction. But they never got one. This case smelled funny the day I got it. Now, you can help me verify what I already figured. Only this time, we can be proven positive by the victim himself."

"So, I take it, this case is never going to trial?"

"Fuck no. I bring you into the DA? I would be cuffed myself and put in the padded cell. And then lose my pension. No, this isn't on the books. This is beyond the laws of man now. I am going directly to God itself. That can be the judge here."

"I never saw any sigh of God yet, Detective Mullins." I was being honest with him.

"Doesn't matter. Charlie needs justice. I'm going to deliver it."

It took us four hours to drive to Bantam, the town where Charlie was murdered. Bantam was a small-big town, located in the center of California. Founded by an Industrialist, Wallace Bantam, it was a thriving factory town. Fruit packing plants, seed packing, potatoes bagging, with a railroad line straight from the factory floors to the main line laid out hundred years before. In 1929, Walter Bantam, the son of Wallace, decided to dive into the chocolate business. The town became world renowned once upon a time, they say, for their recipe for specific items. Hersey, Mars, other sugar merchants begged them to share their special approach to creating their brand of chocolate. No one ever knew the secrets of the Walter Bantam formula. Almost sixty years of chocolate factory fame coated this town in such a proud glow that it was featured twice in Time Magazine and Parade. Then Walter Bantam got sick, he couldn't maintain a control of the factory like he used to, so his children were left in charge, creating a massive wave of mistakes to put the company in financial ruin. The rumors swirled that Hershey would purchase the plant, but that fell apart after they dealt directly with the children of the owner. They were called the Horrid Four: Maggie, Marcus, Marshal, and Manfred the four children given the keys to Bantam's future. It took them ten months to sell out the old man's secrets. Twenty thousand jobs were lost. Bantam become a ghost town overnight. Most of the upper management men, who had been with the company since they were eighteen, were robbed of their pensions and retirement, they didn't have stock options because the company never went public. They were given bonuses instead during Christmas and Easter. When the old man died, that all ended. Many people committed suicide that Christmas. Real estate prices plummeted, forcing people to sell off their properties for forty percent less their worth. It seemed to all begin to end the day Charlie Hailey disappeared.

"Like a plague. Charlie was patient zero and it spread from there, ruining anyone within reach." Detective Mullin took a deep drink from his flask he was nursing for most of the drive. This was the first time I had seen him take a swig; he was an accomplished alcoholic.

"How long has it been since you were last there?"

"Ten years. I transferred after the case, couldn't face these people after it went to shit. I took the brunt of it. Took me a few years to recover. But I closed most of my cases after this botched one. Made a name for myself four hours south. Didn't have to worry about what these people thought anymore."

"But here we are." I added to push.

"Most of the people I failed are dead. Time took care of that."

Driving through the main drag you could see the cracks in the veneer. Most of the buildings were empty, modeled with those eighties square cubed glass bricks. Stacks upon stacks of gleaming cubes glistened as the sun began to lower itself. Every other store front was an updated thrift store, then you had your grocery store with no recognizable trademark name. Most were just titled, Liberty Market, Sam's, Toni's, Tony's, or Maybelle's. This being California, you also had your taco trucks and Mexican eateries comingled with disco Tecca stores and leather shops. A junkyard hugged the end of the street as if keeping the town cupped off from the rest of the world. If you turned left, you would hit the freeway out of there.

We turned right.

Three four-star hotels used to exist in this part of town, but now there was only the Hamlet Motel, a series of adobe style huts that should've been condemned in Yemen. Though the garden around the grounds added a charming English quality.

"I booked you Bungalow two, I am in one. I need a shower and a nap. What do you need?" Detective Mullins asked unloading his bags.

"I need a walk. See if anything moves our way."

"Be safe. There are some gang kids roaming around here."

"I'll be fine."

Walking the town proved to be fruitless. This was the first time I ever walked an old sad street without seeing a ghost. Any living human I passed was amazed to see me. Not many visitors stopped this way anymore. Even if the sign said they had the best tacos in three counties. In some alley ways old imprints of the chocolate factory peeked through the graffiti and missing dog posters. It was an art deco vision of the factory on a hill, the sun peeking through the smokestacks carrying confectionaries of all types inside its rays. Cubism figures lined the factory doors, all with bright smiling faces, squared off jaws and knees up high seeming to show off the unity of the march. It was a call to arms from this angle. A war with the bigger companies was in play, so they never had a chance.

"Hello, there, friend." An old voice rippled from the doorway inside the alley. I stepped back, startled. "Forgive me, I just was taken aback by someone actually looking at this old advertisement I painted." The voice belonged to an old feeble man, maybe late nineties or early eighties depending on his choice of afternoon delight. He lit up a giant cigar and sat on a rickety chair hanging from a hook embedded into the brick.

"You painted this?" I asked nodding approvingly. I did like it.

"Oh, that had to be sixty years ago. My youth I painted a lot. Then I drank. Then I got married. Then I drank more." He brought up a torch used to soften metal to light his stogie. "Then I just stook to tobacco. Figured, rather lose my gum tissue than liver. Then again, I never lost either one. So, a fluke of nature am I." He smiled. "You smoke? I may have another one."

A fluke of nature? You and me both, pal. "No thanks. I was just stopping through here."

"Reporter?" He asked after spitting.

"No."

"Writer?"

"No."

"Photographer?"

"No."

"I am going to keep guessing until you tell me."

"Investigator."

"Oh, my next choice. I figured it had to be one of five things especially if a man of your age is walking these streets." He smiled again, stretching his face skin back making him look younger still.

"Charlie Hailey, you were around for that?"

"Sadly, I lived here my whole life. I saw the town live and breathe then collapse and die. I could've left many a time, I just didn't want to give in. I still see the past in these streets. I see Miss Marby picking apples at the corner store, with her big breasts hanging out of her shirt, she couldn't help herself, the lovely. I see Marvin Houston lining the stack chairs along the street to guarantee prime position for the Fourth of July Parade. And then in the same glance I see the present. Leading me to believe in no future. And when I die, I take that all with me. And then I hope this place collapses on itself and falls into oblivion."

"Where's the factory?"

The old man didn't want to go, but he told me how to get there. It was a two-mile hike across the main downtown section, across the railroad depot into the derelict business district. Even the trains that hauled the chocolate out of town were broken and defeated along the tracks. Graffiti tags had long faded in the hot sun of an uncaring decade. Rusted metal twisted and churned against the still summer day, as if welcoming a living soul for once in a long time. Weeds wrapped around most of the freestanding metal structures, every window was broken, every door busted from marauders looking for treasures. File cabinets were stuck in the ground from the years of rainstorms slowing trying to suck them into the dirt. Any papers sticking from the drawers were crispy and dried. I went to touch one and it shattered like glass. I looked up gazing into the rows of windows three stories above me, trying to see if I could detect any movement but saw nothing. Usually if a ghost were roaming a place like this, I would have seen them already. Here, nothing but the wind sounded. I stepped over the first door I came to and started to head into the factory itself.

The ovens seemed Teutonic, ancient totems to gods long dead. I thought of Robert E. Howard in these steps, Conan sitting on a cold stone throne surrounded by ruins jetting out of the ground and ceiling. Nature's teeth collapsing over man, in this case it was the rusted metal of industrial ovens and mixers, giant pots lined the walls holding them up. Nature had ripped through most of them, black scars snaked across the once polished steel. This place seemed to be frozen in time, yet the elements had their way with it, destroying any hope of resurrection. I headed toward the staircase leading to the managerial offices above the factory floor, maybe something could be there.

Office boxes stacked along the stair well holding the many tax forms and records in case the auditor made an appearance. I opened one of the boxes finding a family of rats renting the spot. I covered it to keep them in their dark comfort. A series of timecards remained unharmed. So many names, so many stories that ended due to the whim of a few managerial decisions. Delicate balance for simple things that can destroy lives. Walking in the factory, I felt the sadness of it, a humid weight that stuck in your chest. Feeling the bursts of lament from every employee receiving their pink slips.

"You looking for Charlie?" A voice echoed from the broken doors leading to the conference room.

I turned around discovering a man, his phase shifting confirming his status of existence. "Yeah. How did you know?"

"You have the look. Besides, I've seen you before. Time is different for us."

"I know that bit. Thanks."

"My name is Harold Beaker. I used to be the Plant Manager. You?"

"Henry, I see ghosts."

"Interesting. I was wondering why you showed up. I'm beginning to put the pieces together now. Time is different for us." Harold repeated himself. "Charlie is going to be anxious to meet you. He knows what you'll be doing. He has told me a few times. And now that you are truly here, maybe you should leave."

"This wasn't my choice. I am trying to help a friend. I need to help Charlie now too. I might be the only person on Earth that can." I meant what I said believing in a destiny laid out before me. When Harold mentioned leaving, I balked.

"Choice? I believe in it now more than ever. I chose to hang myself in this factory. I thought it would change things. They didn't find me for three weeks. It took me death to realize no one cares in life." Harold shifted to the hallway, he kicked towards the boxes hoping something would stir but the phase shifting didn't allow contact. "Damn boxes, I wish the crews would've taken this out. Such an eyesore."

"I'm sure some one cared about you. Didn't you have a wife? Kids?"

"Nope. I waited too long. I thought if I didn't own a house, I couldn't have fill it up. I was dating Carla Mosier, but she was married. Her kids were awful. Now, it doesn't matter. She left right after the plant closed, the kids I have no idea."

"You said no one found you for three weeks?"

"Yes. I thought I would make an impression, maybe shock the people into attempting to bring the plant back to the community. I thought if I were the sacrificial lamb, I could garner a change in the attitude toward the plant. All for dick. The Horrid Four had already sold out the plant to copper miners. When Charlie went missing the factory was in the middle of the closure. In that entire time, I was hanging from the cross beam in the conference room. We used to hang decorations from it, the last Christmas here was wonderful. I like going back to those times, I get to see them, roaming around here. I thought I was going to be in Hell for what I did, but I think God understood my reasoning. My example was his Son for Christ

Sake, literally." He stifled a giggle as his uniform from his early years morphed into view. "I just feel bad about leaving my dad behind. I think that's my biggest sin. I was selfish and mad when I hung myself. I don't want him thinking I did this because of him. I want him to be happy. I wanted him to move on."

"You ever see a door?" I wanted Harold to move on. I think he deserved his door by now.

"I see about thirty, all leading to offices."

"This one is different." I was starting to move the boxes from the hallway, for Harold's sake.

"I'm not quite sure what you mean?" He noticed what I was doing and smiled. "I appreciate the gesture. You don't have all day for this bull shit."

"I don't mind. I can at least clear out your hallway."

"It was never mine." Harold's shifting continued as he flashed forward to the end of the hallway pointing to a stair well. "If you want to see Charlie, he's up there. Be careful. He's not a kid. He's too mad to be one of those."

I approached Harold looking at his feet with his finger pointing to the stairs. He seemed nervous and scared which was something a ghost had never been to me. I felt sorry for him, a man all his life spent in one place only to have it taken away for no reason other than bad management. A man's life lost to whims of ignorance is as old as time itself. I still never understood why a ghost had to stay in the place of their physical death. If the soul was forever, a piece of the universe itself, how was the basic structure of it stuck? Why couldn't it travel beyond the railroad tracks or the cement walls of the physical? Perhaps that was the point. The reasons ghosts have a sort of dementia to prevent them from interfering with the living world. Or to allow a punishment for their sins in life, being able to see and not touch or taste the ever-changing world around you must be misery.

Immediately I felt such a pressure on my chest and legs. I stumbled as I crossed the plain of the emergency stair well. Above me was ancient CCTV cameras, long dead. The board members had pictures along the hallway, still framed in oak. Dust and muck caked on them so thickly I couldn't make any of them out. I went to wipe one down when the heaviness returned, forcing me to go to my knee. It was like someone was putting a plastic bag over my head, then releasing me free of it, then ten seconds later the suffocation returned. I stood up out of frustration, throwing the picture off the wall.

"Stop it!" I shouted, sending a visible wave through the hallway leading to the last door facing me. I fell again out of fear this time. I had never seen that before. A ripple through reality, the waves of it crashed against the decrepit walls creating cracks suddenly.

A giggle echoed from the last room.

"Isn't that interesting? A sudden flood of energy? Visible? Able to penetrate your world of the living?" It was a young boy's voice but with none of the innocence one would expect. It felt like an impression. It felt fake.

"Charlie?" I asked knowing full well it was him.

"Ding, ding, ding! I have seen you before, too. I just could never hold on to your name." The voice moved to the back of the hallway.

"My name is Henry. Henry Claremont."

"Claremont! That's right. I remember now. But then again, I will forget just as quickly. Like Harold, down below, we tend to forget things."

"Show yourself. Tell me what happened?"

"Come on in, Henry. Come on in. I could use someone with your ability." The voice had returned to its original point. The door at the end of the hallway opened with nary a creek. "You were right to assume I was killed here."

"I figured it was the only place no one would check. Too many bad memories."

"It was closed three months before I was brought here. My parents worked here, my grandparents, my cousins. My friend's parents. Most had moved away, knowing they couldn't sit and wait for a miracle."

I walked to the door, discovering the conference room. Crown Molding stretched along the curved dome leading to the same mural from the town plaster in the center of the rotunda. Fluorescent light tubes were split, shattered along the ceiling. Cracks in the plaster were visible snaking along the entire mural suggesting the entire thing was about to collapse. A single long brown table stood in the center, it had to be fifteen feet long. Any chairs had long been sold off, the table itself was too big to manage, let alone sell off. It was left here to rot with the rest. A singe shattered window made up the rest of the room showing off the entire factory floor from this height. This was where the owner stood to watch his dream come reality. This is where someone brought a child to be murdered.

"Lovely view, right?" Charlie stood next to me, smiling. "I have grown used to it. In fact, it was what I was staring out at when they raped me."

"I'm sorry, Charlie." I turned to see something I had never seen before, a ghost fully formed without any phase shifting.

"Wacky, huh? No shifting, unlike Harold." He walked to the end of the table and jumped on it, standing three feet taller than me. "I like to look down on you like this, it allows me some piece of pride. Have you ever met a ghost with pride? Or anything remotely aggressive? Or are they all border line retards like Harold? Lost sense of time, self, and reason. A sad state if ever there was one." He leaped off the table, but floated slowly to the floor, giggling all the way down. "I never had a life. I was born, I was a child, I was killed. That was my existence. That was my destiny. Barely a speck in the wheel of time and space. So, I guess that means I am awarded this one form, this one outfit." He smiled at me with such an awkwardness that I knew he meant to unnerve me. It was working.

"You are truly different." Was all I could muster.

"You want to know a secret?" He whispered, leaning into me. I could feel so much heat emanating from his form. His hate had turned to a metaphysical wraith, looking for physical blood. "I know almost everything about you."

"How?"

"We have had this conversation before. And right now, you will tell me your story. You will be forthcoming with most of it, especially the time you saw Laura and saved those girls. Your ego is quite a thing, but then again, that is something to be proud of. Taking this gift of yours and utilizing it. I had gifts too. Now, I am just a spook. So, tell me your story. All of it."

After I finished, Charlie grinned, he was savoring the tale. I don't know why I just confessed my life to him. Maybe I am vain. If that is true, then I was more afraid than ever before. I shouldn't gloat or exult this power. I should be stronger than that, I should be wiser. I knew things no one else did, yet I carried it like a bargaining chip to get me into places no other human could enter.

"Did that bother you?' Charlie asked with his Cheshire Cat grin. His face almost seemed to disappear forcing his white teeth to shine ever so brighter.

"No. I just didn't expect to be so, honest."

"You're not a liar. Good on you. Besides, I would've known if you did. I had a feeling you weren't like most others." Charlie gazed down to the floor. "That's the murder weapon."

I went down to my knees, discovering a J hook rebar.

"Don't touch it, just look at it." Charlie was quick to speak as I reached out to pick it up. "You don't want to contaminant the evidence?"

"They beat you with this?"

"And much more."

"I am sorry."

"Don't be weak. You have the evidence the cops never found it because they didn't bother searching here. Ask your friend, Detective Mullins about that, drunk fuck."

I grabbed a wad of old newspaper that had blown into here years before, picked up the J hooked rebar, wrapped it and lifted it like it was a newborn child. It was so light, but hard, a diminutive woman could have lifted this and used it as a weapon.

"In the days of the factory, they used those to beat the chocolate pipes. Sometimes coagulation would occur, you had to beat the metal pipes a bit to get the flow going again. Simple, really. No one ever made the connection. They all thought it was a crowbar, or a heavy cane."

"With this, we could start a new trial. There's actual evidence." I began, but Charlie laughed it off.

"Evidence? The trial is over,* I need you to bring the guilty to me. Brother Manfred and sister Maggie. They did this to me. They still do this to others. It's time they pay for their crimes. It's time I get to be an avenging angel with a demon's bent."

When I made it back to the Hamlet Motel it was dark, I could barely make my way back if not for the streetlights of the broken town still glittering. In my backpack was the rebar, wrapped in cloth. I didn't know if I should show it to Detective Mullins or not. I should just leave. Leave him here to stew in his own past, allow me distance to have my present. He trusted me with this pain, and I couldn't leave him. I couldn't leave Charlie, angry and bitter in his ethereal form either. I was pinned in by an odd sense of honor. I don't know where it came from.

The old man from earlier was back out on his stoop, watching the slow passing of time.

"You find what you were looking for?" The old man asked pointing at my backpack, noticing the strain on the straps due to the J Rebar.

"I found something, I don't know if it's right or wrong. It certainly is something though."

"Be careful. Right and wrong don't really have a place out here. These dead old towns seem to be a vacuum for hopes and dreams. Perverse dreams can shatter too. And if this town has stood long enough to devour the ones who murdered all the good in this place, so be it. Then maybe I can finally fall asleep and go home."

"Home?"

"I always referred to the afterlife as home. At least it should be right? Look at it like this, see, there you are, dead. Lost and confused because it might have been before your time, well what you perceived as before your time, and you're sitting there, dead. All the world around you is the same. Yet, you can't touch shit, probably can't read because you need a brain for that. You are just standing there, oblivious to the fading world around you." He spat out a wad of tobacco and greasy spittle, akin to bacon fat flying out of a frying pan. "A door, maybe we see a door when we go. Allows us to just react. No thought. If one is faced with a door directly in front of you, of course you would just automatically open it."

"Unless you had second thoughts. If you were still able to." I couldn't let him know he was correct in his deduction.

"Most people I knew, all they had were second thoughts. Maybe they're waiting for me to show them the way."

"Probably. Out of curiosity, who would you open the first door for, if you could?"

The old man shivered as the cold wind began to whip through the streets, he covered up with a blanket under his rickety chair. "I would be first to open my son's door. His name was Harold Beaker."

Detective Mullins couldn't move gazing upon the murder weapon. It was his monolith delivered unto him to answer his life-long questions. It was his Savior awakening him from his stupor of drunkenness for the last twenty years.

"How did you find it?"

"Charlie."

"Jesus."

Detective Mullins brought out his dusting kit and began work on it. I saw the prints materialize out of nowhere, hopefully it would be enough.

"It's not enough." Detective Mullins must have been psychic.

"How?" I asked fearing this was not going to end simply.

"I can cross reference the DNA on this with any other unsolved cases in the country. I could put this guy away forever if he isn't already in the system. I just need to be sure this ends the son of a bitch."

"Sons and daughters." I replied.

"Charlie told you that too?" Detective Mullins knew exactly who I was referring to.

"He wants them for himself. He wants to kill them. I've never seen a ghost like this before. He knows he's an unsolved mystery. He knows about you and the present world around him. Usually they're lost, clinging to emotional connections with such a ferocity they refuse to see anything else. But Charlie, he's different. He can see the future and realize it. The others just shook it off. Charlie clings to it."

"How can he kill them?"

"Through me. Laura did it too."

"But I haven't checked this out yet. How could we bring them here if we don't know anything?" Detective Mullins was already packing his gear to head back to the city.

"It's them. But you want to know what else they did, so you can justify the execution Charlie wants."

"We both want that." Detective Mullins wrapped the rebar in the cloth and then secured it in an evidence bag. "Come with me, maybe if you see what else these cunts did, you'll let Charlie have his way."

I didn't know what to do at that moment. I didn't want to be a puppet for some victim even if I sympathized. It wasn't up to me to bring justice but maybe it was since I was the only avenue to take to allow it to be served. I knew there was a Hell, the Death Birthers were evidence of that. I wanted them to pay for their crimes. I wanted to see the Death Birther eat them whole and spit them out.

"I think Mitchell still works the late desk. We could use the local computer." Mullins collected everything like a seasoned collector dealing with prized pieces.

"I can go?" I was amazed I was being allowed inside the hard-boiled world of the homicide detective.

"You can't do anything, see anything or touch anything. But you can wait in the hallway. I am sure there's a nice couch somewhere. You could take a nap. I think they still put out donuts around 4 in the morning still."

"Good enough."

The Bantam police station was still at two in the morning. I would've thought the place would be filled with pimps, prostitutes, drug runners, dealers, murderers, and thieves. All I saw was Mitchell, the night man.

"Hey, Detective. How's it hanging?"

"Never low enough." Detective Mullins made Mitchell laugh out loud with that response. "I need to access fingerprinting and then check out DNA scrub kit send it in to the database."

"All doors are open to you, but your buddy here, I can't allow him access."

"Can he use that couch, Mitchell, is that still around?"

"Oh yeah, it's down the hall, last door on the right. Break room. I don't think there is anything in there you could screw up in the appeal process."

"How long does the DNA take to process?"

"Too long, but I have fingerprints on file in the database of everyone questioned in the case. Those two are in the system still. I remember how smug they were dipping their fingers in the ink. I knew then something was off about them, I just couldn't prove it and they knew it. That's the worst part of all of this. When everyone knows, yet you can't just point and say guilty. You must build a case, evidence and hours of testimony and recording eyewitness testimonies. Just to have a prosecutor twist the words on record to fit a narrative they created to save their client. When you're creative in court you can do anything." Mullins went for his pocket but forgot the bottle was still in the hotel room.

"I'm going to find that couch." I said yawning, allowing Mullins a moment to smile back at me as I walked away.

"Hey, Henry."

I turned to see him, glassy eyed and full of hope that reminded me of Laura before she opened her door to the unknown.

"Thank you. My life has more to it now."

"Nobody is less." Was all I could say in return.

The breakroom was more akin to a frat boy house than a police station. All the cool and fun contraband was sitting in tubs lined up on folding tables against the wall. A giant widescreen television, 45 inches max, its square squatted appearance was hiding two giant speakers on the bottom. A DVD player and VCR deck stood on a side table with coasters and pens situated in a local baseball team coffee mug. An assortment of action, horror and comedies lined the bookcase next to the giant wide screen block of a television. This was better than Blockbuster. I put in Evil Dead 2, leaned back in the armchair in the center of the other armchairs and watched Sam Raimi do his thing.

Detective Mullins woke me up, the channel had a quiet hiss of static and flicker reminding me of Poltergeist. The shadows played on Detectives Mullins' face making his grave look much more disturbing.

"You found them?"

"I found them. The prints matched. I am sending the rebar to be tested for DNA, but that will take months to process. But I think if this enters the national database we will get a few hits, maybe close more than just this case. And after what you have showed me, I don't need to wait for the results from the lab. I have a plan."

Detective Mullins had kept tabs on the Bantam brood for years. He always had a noise for guilty people and those four never escaped his gaze. Even if it had been a decade. They had broken up in the subsequent years, Marcus Bantam retreated to the Pacific Northwest residing in a self-sustaining doomsday prepped compound. Marshal Bantam had committed suicide three years prior, overdosed on sleeping pills in his swank apartment in Paris. Marshal, ever the art lover, wanted to be close to the Louvre. Maggie and Manfred seemed to stay together. They cohabitated the same address for years, never leaving each other's side for more than two days at a time. Most people in the town had the feeling they were lovers. The Bantam family kept their relationship close to the chest, no one outside of Maggie and Manfred truly knew the exact nature of their relationship. They had maintained a series of homes in Europe for the last eight years. Maggie and Manfred were the two main negotiators in the sellout of the factory. They kept the lion's share of the profits after revealing the secret ingredients for their chocolate marsh mellow nut cream, their mint n chip brownie bar, the Custard's Last Stand Chew, and the Indian Chief Fire Gum.

Manfred and Maggie had netted themselves over four million dollars along with selling off and splitting the properties owned by the family trust garnered them another three million after splitting it with the other siblings. Everyone on the Executive Board received benefits and pay outs as a result, any one below that received a voucher for the water park that opened six weeks later. That closed six months after that.

"I knew it was them. I knew it." Detective Mullins repeated to himself, shaking his head in disgust at himself.

"Instinct and evidence are two different things, right?" I said to cheer him up.

"Instinct should lead you to the evidence. I second guessed myself, never thought to look at the factory. We wanted it to be over. I think that was our biggest error. All of us law people want to close a case as soon as possible. Not for glory or the media, but for the family. To close the wound, to seal it. Let it heal. Any time you let a murder hang out in the open air for long stretches it affects everything and everyone. It corrodes, it breaks, it burns anyone in the wake of it. And if it you can't shut it out with solving it, then it festers. It lingers and kills you in the end too."

"Now you can close it. You can end it."

"Yeah. I think I have a plan to do it too."

The plan wasn't too complicated. Detective Mullins took Polaroid pictures of the weapon with the words: COME BACK TO THE FACTORY scrolled under it. Subtle, but effective. We were forced into the waiting game now, however. With this extra time, I figured I could at least try to save one person left behind in this dead town's story.

"Come again, son?" The old man who painted the mural, blew out a load of cigar smoke that could choke a donkey.

"I need your help at the factory." I wasn't willing to tell him much. I felt he would want closer nearing the twilight edge of his existence. But he just re-lit the cigar and sucked in another load.

"I don't see why I should go out there. I can barely walk on the cement, and it has no cracks."

"I think there's a way to save your son. Give him peace."

"What do you mean? He's dead, that's it. Peace comes from the Almighty and a secret handshake. I got nothing to do with it and neither do you." He was getting shifty; the old man shoulder crunch took effect.

"I saw him out there. I talked to him." I was desperate and to the quick.

"What are you saying? Make sense, now, God damn it."

"I can talk to the dead. It's why I was here to begin with. To solve the Charlie Hailey case, which I did. But that's not the point. Your son is there too, he needs you. He needs your allowance to move on." That all came out too fast. A lot to process for an octogenarian.

His eyes were blazing with thought, his eyes rolled around, his brain working overtime processing half of what I just spewed out. With a cough and a slap to the knee he spit and laughed. "You know the worst part of all this is I believe you. What does that say about my mental state? If my wife were alive, she would have me committed tomorrow. Shit, I just might do it to myself." He kept the grin on shaving years off his face.

"I've always been honest, to a fault. I don't know how to lie." I wasn't sure if that was a lie or not. I felt like I have been honest most my life. It's just exposing myself to people usually ends up with me finding out dark secrets and mortal sins hanging over other people's lives. It's very tiring when you think about it.

"Help me with the chair, kid. Am I going to be able to see him?"

I put away his lounge chair. "Most likely not, but I think there might be a way to cheat." We began to walk toward the edge of town where the broken factory stood.

"My whole life with my son can be seen through this walk." The old man had a spark in his step, so much so that he almost knocked me over twice. "That's the ice cream parlor I used to take him after baseball. He was a hell of a hitter, even at thirteen. I always thought, dream of dreams, he would go pro. He went to the minors for a time. The factory had a team, he led them to a championship run three years in a row. One day on the floor fell off the conveyor busted his knee. Life happens." The old man paused his grin disappeared for a moment I think the fear of the unknown began to take effect. "You think this cheat may work? That I could see him?"

"I don't know. There's a way for you to talk to him, for him to see you, but it would have to be through me. I don't know how it works, but it has happened to me before. The ghost can use me momentarily. I'll be putting it to the test today." I realized this was what Charlie was going to use me for. To murder those who murdered him. A vessel of retribution I wasn't so sure I wanted to be. I understood it but I wanted no part of it. I was praying for a way out, maybe I could discover a way to push out Charlie using Harold as practice.

"If this was any other day, I would have told you to fuck off. But for some reason, this is all happening on the same day my Harold killed himself. That's the scary part."

Maneuvering through the factory I noticed the stairs leading up to the corporate level. I felt the phantom tugs of Charlie Hailey gripping my chest. It was oddly still for now. I was expecting him to laugh or gloat or demand the heads of his killers. There was nothing. Maybe he couldn't exert himself multiple times like that. Hate takes a toll, but right now I was more worried about what love of a father would feel like under these circumstances. When Hershal was attacked at the mine, it was out of self-defense. A reaction without any emotion, a static response to a moment. Charlie wouldn't be static the old man wouldn't be static. Two yearning beings needing closure may kill me yet.

"Harold?" I shouted down the hallway, the boxes I moved were still in their places.

"See the hallway? It's way better now. Thanks for that." Harold didn't seem to notice his father sitting in one of the rolling chairs nestled in a corner.

"Is he here?"

Harold turned around, phase shifting to his youth wearing the baseball uniform. "Dad?"

The old man stirred, as if a chill went through him. "Did you see him yet?"

"He's here."

Harold phase shifted back to his adult self in his factory overalls. He knelt beside the decrypted figure that used to be his father. He was lost in the image. "Has it been this long? I never thought it would be so long."

"I can feel something. I could swear, I can feel sadness." The old man was crying now.

"Harold, you can go through me. You can talk to him." I prepared myself for the intrusion.

"I don't know if I can." Harold whispered.

"You can do it. I will allow it. Please, Harold. Give yourself the permission for forgiveness."

Harold lifted his head, his being turned into a type of gaseous form engulfing me whole. Within a millisecond I saw his entire life. Every moment of importance, every Christmas, Halloween, baseball game, lover, accomplishment, failures. They all rushed through me like an unending stream. I couldn't breathe or move. I was buried by the waters of memory. I opened my eyes and saw it for the first time. I saw the door. It was standing next to the old man. It was as if the old man had the door with him the whole time, keeping it open, ready for his son to go home again.

"Harold? I see you, boy. I see you." The old man embraced me with the strength of a bear. It was as strong as Charlie's wave but softer, love was dripping from this energy.

"Dad. I'm sorry. I'm so sorry."

"No. You never failed me in anything."

"I knew I hurt you. It wasn't meant to be this way."

"That pain went away a long time ago, son. I love you always.

There is nothing else left. Hurt fades, my boy. Love is all we get to keep, really."

I could feel the tears soak into my sleeves as the old man bawled. I didn't let go. Harold didn't let go.

"You see it too, don't you?" Harold asked out loud to both of us. "The door? I see it and I know you both can too."

"Yes." The old man stepped away from the door, he pivoted with such fluid grace, it almost made us all laugh. "I would say your mother is getting ready for dinner."

"I can't leave you now, dad."

"Yes, you can. Because I am already there. I am at the front of that table with a knife and fork ready to eat that roast. Waiting for my son to come home."

The door opened and I saw what the old man said was there.

Then I fell to the floor, shaking, bleeding from every orifice.

I awoke at the Hamlet Hotel. Detective Mullins laughing, watching some true crime show. The Old Man was next to him chuckling along.

"He's up!" The Old Man smiled and hit my feet.

"I was worried there for a moment. But the doctor said you would be fine." Detective Mullins poured the old man a celebratory drink from his flask into a plastic cup.

"Doctor?"

"I used the phone at the factory, luckily the land lines were still plugged into the emergency services. You've been knocked out six hours."

"We were scared for a bit; the doctor gave you a look over and realized the wounds were superficial. Gave you a dose of something in your arm, called it a day."

"Any word from Maggie and Manfred?"

"Not yet... Did Charlie do this to you?" Detective Mullins asked legitimately concerned.

"No. This was something else."

"I will be off, now." The Old Man began to move before I grabbed his arm.

"Let me walk you out, please."

The Old Man smiled at me, "if you're up to it."

The moon was full giving us a clean night where I could see the empty town in a blue hue betraying the sad banal browns and glass cubes that seemed to swallow what little life this place had left.

"You would think the town woke up for a moment?" I pointed out the difference.

"It's having a death rattle. Anything worth keeping here is gone now. I can move on. Thanks to you." He laughed to himself.

"You know what scares me about all of this?"

"What?"

"If love could do this to me, what will hate do?"

"Everything happens for a reason. Let Charlie go."

"Charlie deserves better."

"Charlie is lost, based on what you told me. Sometimes justice can only go so far. Closure is the only real thing anyone can get out of a tragedy. Victims too. They say every house is a haunted one. So many lost to tragedies and injustice. Where would we be if they all just opened their own doors?"

"Nightmares would have nowhere to go. Maybe that's the point? We all need that terror to keep us on the path."

"Or maybe injustice forces us to be better. We need it to be there to remind us that we have a way to go. Then we could forgive, then we could move on without terror." He put his cigar in his mouth, taking a bite out of the end of it. "Then again, I am just an old man lucky enough to get closure. One in a million. No nightmares for me, now." The old man walked down the street to his perch next to his mural. He lit up a single cigar, took it in gently. He was blowing smoke rings for three minutes. I watched him from afar, he waved to me and retreated inside.

I didn't want to go back to the room, last thing I wanted was rest. I just wanted to scream. A deserved release out into the open but the sudden sigh of a familiar monster crept into my ear from the alley. I turned around to see one of the Death Birthers skulking along the cement, it's deformed elongated body digging into the cold concrete, a slime trail following. Another sound broke through the moan of this creature, a broken bottle crushed against moist puss filled pustules stretching across the shaft of the main body. Why were they here? Now? Are they coming for me finally? I just stood there, closing my eyes. Hoping they would finally take me. I didn't want this power anymore. I didn't want to make the choices of others or be used in making choices. I just wanted to be free. I just wanted to be alone.

"They will never hurt you whilst you breath air, Henry." A familiar voice replaced the guttural sighs. I opened my eyes to find Hershal sitting on the bus bench with a bag of caramel corn. "Hungry?" He offered up the bag.

"Hershal?'

"The very same."

"You died."

"Yeah."

"You used to be one of those."

"Yeah."

"What happened?"

"I paid my price. Eternity isn't quite what we think it is. Forgiveness is earned when you beg for it. And because we are human, we can learn."

"What am I supposed to do about Charlie?" I asked giving up hope. I couldn't let him use me to kill anyone, even if they deserved it.

"No one is allowed those choices, yet society has created panels and courts to determine what is best for the living. A corruptible system, a broken system, an old human concept of justice. Life is so precious, but the ones who steal it without pity are monsters in flesh. Outliers born of gluttony, greed, pride, envy, sloth, wrath, and lust. As you can see, the Death Birthers display those seven qualities with much gusto. Carrying that weight in a phallic shape too disgusting to gaze at. That is the truth of sin." Hershal pointed at the monsters huddled against the cold glass bricks. Their breath and slime left a visible residue against the clean glass. Lingering stares only seemed to concentrate their stench. A disgusting blend of stagnant piss, rotting flesh and burning hair. The very pungent aroma of death and rot.

"I didn't think anyone out there would be listening to me. I thought I was alone in this. Much like everything else." I was honest, but saying it felt hallow. I didn't want to sound ungrateful for life itself, as a man who can see and speak to the dead the appreciation of breathing and the physical world around me was so much more tantalizing. Though I was alone.

"You are never alone. No one is. The truth of the universe. If only they would listen to it. If you be still in life, you can almost feel the hum of the motor of the universe. Of life itself. A constant piston, an unending pulse that envelopes all in its wake. Very simple thing. Most block it with doubt, questions, anger, apathy, spite. Some don't care even if they do hear it. I was one of those people. For years I lusted for a life promised to me by a criminal. My grandfather poisoned me, but in turn, I allowed the poison to fill my heart. I know that now. I had to die to see." Marshal finished the bag, tossing it into the waste basket.

"What can I do to save him?"

"Charlie is more wrath now than child. Hate has turned him into heat which in turn burns anything it touches. Inside of him is a scared boy, still hoping for the innocence to return."

"They tortured him. Mutilated him."

"Yes. And you must find what existed before. Charlie must let them go if he is to continue. If not, he could become an abhorrent. A break in the machine, that could provide a dangerous repercussion to the rest. Synchronicity is purity." Hershal smiled, he investigated me deeply, I could see his form begin to shift, like the many ghosts from before.

"I'm sorry that happened to you. I didn't want it that way."

"It wasn't your fault, kid. It was mine. Maybe I can give you a visit again." Hershal smiled, evaporating without the need for a door. I went to the caramel popcorn bag in the trash can, feeling it. All of it was real, even the sticky residue of the caramel and the popcorn seeds that refused to pop. He was here, yet not here.

"More bullshit to think about." I felt that was the most appropriate response at the time.

Opening the hotel door, I discovered Maggie Bantam, sitting in the cheap chair of the corner table of the Hamlet Motel. All of her being reeked of malevolence. Fingers nails painted a hot pink, a barbed wire tattoo snaked around both hands leading to the top of her shoulders, tatted stables suggesting open wounds followed the barb wire line to an elaborate tattooed ripped open shoulder, exposing the anatomy beneath on both sides. A massive devil with mouth and tongue licking both nipples was visible through her sheer tank top, both nipples pierced, she opened her legs to me in a come-hither repose. Black leather pants creaked loudly as if someone was pulling the noose over a weak neck. Spread out on the chair, I was almost aroused, but I remembered what she did. How she laughed and put all her strength into bringing down the final blows to Charlie's small head.

"So, you found our toy?" She hissed.

"Maggie Bantam?"

"Obviously." She stood up revealing six feet of muscular stomach and legs. Tattooed ancient words rolled around her body as if she was a living Rosetta Stone. "You see the words? Spells of ancient tongues, some Latin, Aramaic, Hebrew, Hindi, any other old shit speaking of resurrection, death, chaos, blood. What else is there?"

"Innocence."

"Such a bull shit word. No one is that. Most of this world is ran by the perverts and slime Puritans rally against. All the powerful is littered with filth. The trick is to embrace it. Make it work for you. How do you think we get this far?"

"Where's Mullins?"

"My beau has him. He's safe. He doesn't bleed people until I get there."

"Your brother?"

"Watch your mouth. Brother and sisters have been fucking since time began. If you are lucky enough to find your soul mate at six, then I say fucking consummate. Have you ever been in love, little boy? Have you ever had someone hold you inside of them for moments that feel like hours? Then what the fuck you know about anything?" Maggie hand cuffed me, pulling on them forcing me to bend forward. Diving onto the back of my head she inhaled my scent. "Not one iota of sweat? Not a sign of fear? What secrets do you have in store for us tonight, then?"

"You have no idea." I looked up at her, my eyes scared her.

In retaliation, she slapped my face hard.

"We're wasting time."

One hundred thousand dollars' worth of machinery greeted me as we exited the hotel. A black Rolls Royce, vintage, so out of place in a dead town which was the point. Maggie and Manfred were back in town and anyone who would remember them shall gaze on with despair. Dark tinted windows held our reflection. On the roof of the motel was an old friend, the Death Birther, licking its mouth with such perversion it made me spit. A monster was lusting after another.

"Get in." Maggie opened the door for me, it almost felt like the prom date I never had.

I scooted as far away as I could from her, but this just made her stretch out her legs to pull me closer to her.

"Any other night, I think I could've let you have a go. You're cute with a little hint of something dark. It's a turn on."

"What would your brother say?"

"When is it my turn?" Maggie knocked on the black partition window. "Go to the factory."

Driving off, I noticed hordes of Death Birthers running alongside the car. All their faces toward me, they ran without needing to look forward. It made me sick to see so many of them. They wanted a feast. They wanted Maggie, Manfred, and Charlie. They wanted the child more than the killers. I could sense that. Hershal told me to find the child inside of the hate buried deep because if not, there was a feast to be held. I wasn't going to be the witness to it, I accepted the possibility of death as we arrived at the derelict factory.

"Jesus Christ, after all these years, it still looks like shit." Maggie spit on the ground, the cold was getting to her, a long fur coat was laid on her like a queen from the driver. Black fur, with red stripes, a custom job.

"Why are you like this?" I had to ask.

"It takes years. Long years, honey. But once you arrive at who you are supposed to be, with the person you are supposed to be with, everything is a blur of lies and needless remembrance. Living in the moment is what matters. Moments are all we get. Blaze it hard and to hell with the other world around you." She hooked her fingers into the chain of my cuffs, leading me to the conference room.

As we walked to the conference room, the palpitations began in my chest. I fell to the ground the waves of Charlie's heat were stronger than before. I screamed. Maggie could only stare in confusion.

"The fuck is wrong with you?"

"Stop it! STOP IT, CHARLIE!" I screamed, my chest burned through my lungs, embers were developing in the tissue, heat ripped through my nostrils, my eyes fluttered and twitched as I became a part time epileptic. Snot gushed out of my nose, then blood. Suddenly, it all stopped.

"What the fuck is going on?" Manfred screamed coming into the hallway, he was a masculine version of Maggie. His physique hidden behind a ten-thousand-dollar suit, but his eyes were wild, with a pension for raging violence, brute strength provided him the ability to break and maim with just his hands if allowed to. Manfred was a man not afraid to use his teeth in a fight or bite loose flesh if offered inches from his mouth.

"I don't know, he just fell down, I think he's having a stroke?" Maggie put her hand to my head, felt the heat, she jerked back. "He's on fire."

"Fine, one less thing to cut up. I didn't want to be here all night." Manfred stood over me, flipping me on my back with his foot. "You best die naturally, kid."

Charlie was lying next to me. His face reminded me of my sister for a moment. When she was young and sleeping on the couch above me one Christmas. I couldn't look away from her. In the briefest of moments, I saw what life was supposed be like. A safe place, a warm place, I heard the thrumming of carols and smelt ferns slowly drying out against the flickering Christmas lights. I heard mom put out the cookies for Santa and then her commanding us to go to bed. All of this attacked me at once. Then Charlie entered me, his void overtook the memory, drowning it out with bleak greys and black holes. I was standing up, not realizing it was Charlie moving my legs. My mind was lost in his shiftless nightmare. Then I remembered to find the light lost in this tortured soul.

"He seems fine, now." Manfred smiled.

Charlie's eyes took over, he smiled back, not me.

"You look like the cat catching the canary." Manfred stifled a giggle.

"You look like soft tissue. Easy to tear open with a vigorous mouth. My teeth need not be so sharp."

"Let's say hi to your friend." Manfred ignored the threat leading the way to Detective Mullins. His head was bleeding, his legs and arms tied to a large Captain's Chair built for their father sixty years ago.

Charlie was rolling in my head, all his past and present erupted inside my brain at the same time. I saw him born, I saw him brushing his teeth, I saw him sitting in front of the Christmas tree with its frosted white branches glistening. I saw his mother hold him after a nightmare, I saw his father working in the yard with Charlie lifting the rake up to collect leaves. Simple things that didn't mean much to anyone else but was the entirety of life for one soul. A child. I focused on these moments, I was pushing them into Charlie's anger and bitter dark void.

"He ain't talking much now." Maggie spoke rubbing down the blood from Detective Mullins' head.

"I just like to listen to dying people who believe they won." Charlie spoke through me. He was picking for a fight. He wanted one of them to throw the first blow, allowing him the excuse to let loose the fire of hate inside. Charlie was loving the view outside the giant broken window of the conference room, dozens of Death Birthers were crawling over the walls and ground floors, waiting for a glorious meal.

Let this go, Charlie! Look at what you're bringing out! I spoke out to him, trying to break through but the heat of his pain tore into me.

"So, you wanted to see if you could black mail us for a few hundred grand? So cheap. So vulgar." Manfred picked up the rebar, he licked it up and down. "Still a unique taste. If only the two of you understood what depravity can bring you."

You see what they are! I say let me out! Let me kill him now!

Charlie was screaming in my head. My hand, being forced towards the rebar left on the conference table. I felt the wet trail Manfred's tongue created, making me sick.

There must be another way! You can be free of them and of your hate if you let me have it! Give me the fire in you! We can both give it to him! He can have what you've been carrying! He can suffer a lifetime of pain in seconds! He can burn in your memory of what they did to you! I can deliver it!

The Death Birthers were swarming the conference room. Only Charlie and I could see the slime and puss trails sticking to the wood panels and ceiling. Maggie was almost surrounded by them, flicking their tongues at her.

"I think this guy had a stroke. He's just staring out at nothing." Maggie walked up to me slapping my face; I had no reaction to it. In my head, I was too busy battling Charlie's hate to feel reality.

Manfred saw me reaching for the rebar, a quick kick to the stomach dropped me to my knees. "What did you think you were going to do? Use that against us? You're so fucking lost. It'll be a mercy to just kill you now." Manfred was inches from my face, Charlie was pushing his hate to my hands.

I waited.

Making the power of Charlie's hate a cosmic quasar ready to launch.

NOW! USE IT! GIVE IT TO HIM NOW!

I slammed my head into Manfred's face, blood gushed out of his nose, I grabbed his head and held it to mine, transferring the hateful fire that burned in Charlie's soul into Manfred's brain.

"Manny!" Maggie shouted running to him, the amount of energy being released took hold of her, sending her flying across the room, crashing into the wood panels with such a force they shattered around her.

The death birthers were visibly disappointed. They sniffed at the living Maggie, lifting their noses up in rejection. Her unconscious state allowed her a single fleeting moment to see what was upon her. Maggie screamed in such horror, shaking as a seizure consumed her.

Manfred didn't move at all. His limp body was slumped against the wall, his eyes glazed over. His mind was in a cycle of unflinching recall. All the pain and torture visited upon Charlie was being delivered unto Manfred. Drool flowed from his opened mouth, snot from his nose. He was a vegetable in this moment until the day he died.

Maggie's spine shattered against the wall. Forever confined to a wheelchair, she would live out her days in a minimum-security prison, never able to sleep, whispering to herself about devil dogs wanting to eat her soul.

I woke up from the possession of Charlie, my equilibrium returned, I rushed to Detective Mullins, releasing his bonds.

"What the hell happened?" Mullins checked the pulse of Manfred, then rushed to Maggie. "They're alive."

"Of course. They need to live the rest of life in confinement. So, they may have a chance for grace." I said that with no thought. It was truth, a universal truth. Evil still had a chance to repent. Evil still had the ability to reach Grace. I didn't like it, but life is the journey to forgiveness. All of us have the chance to be saved. Even when all life turns their back on us.

"Charlie?" Detective Mullins was hoping to see him.

"He's gone. He took his door to heaven, where he belongs."

"I got to call this in. Get ready to be on television again."

"Maybe I can get a miniseries out of this?" I joked.

"I know a guy."

I shot Detective Mullins a raised eyebrow.

"When you're a detective in Los Angeles, you got a producer in your rolodex." Detective Mullins laughed, "but I don't know how much they'll swallow."

"We did it, didn't we? We saved him."

"You did that."

"You didn't let him go, Detective. You kept on fighting for him. And now Charlie is free. You're the hero. You should get the mini-series." I smiled weakly.

"No one will believe this anyway, kid. But I don't give a shit."

Mullins was right, we were on television again. Hundreds of camera crews were swarming the town of Bantam just like they did when Charlie was found murdered. Detective Mullins was on point, delivering the reveal of the true murderers, the new evidence founded and the reopening of the case for a new trial. I was on the news again, nationally.

My sister called that night.

"You did it again!" She shrieked into the phone displaying energy I didn't have anymore.

"I try."

"Even mom and dad are getting calls from the local news stations. They just finished a newspaper article. Now, I am being interviewed tomorrow by the Morning Zoo Crew, they're funny."

"Great. Hopefully I can come home for Christmas this year." I was jaded. Burnt out from Charlie being inside of me. The hate was still stoked, the heat he gave me was still throbbing. All my tendons felt stretched by horses, my stomach ached with dagger hits. But the worst part was the horrid loneliness Charlie lived in after death. All these emotions clung to me as if they needed me. A symbiote for pure hate and malice.

"You don't sound good."

"I am not." It was the truth.

"I am coming out there."

"What?"

"I need a break. I can take two weeks off for summer, I don't have anything on my calendar. Mom and dad will be fine with it."

Detective Mullins threw the newspaper at me, we owned the front page. I opened it to see the last page, a corner section with one square announcement.

HAROLD BEAKER SENIOR

Beloved Local Artist, died in his sleep peacefully aged 94. He is preceded in death by his wife EVA and his son, HAROLD BEAKER JR. No Service will be held. Any Donations will be accepted in lieu of flowers.

Barely a paragraph summarized a man's existence. How many even receive that? Now I felt worse. I could only go back to my sister's idea. "I think I need you to do that for me. I need something alive in my life."

8

TRUE HOLLYWOOD STORIES WITH THE DEAD 2001

Detective Mullins was a well-known detective in the heart of the movie industry, so he had several producer numbers in his rolodex. They would ask for ideas, time to allow their actors to train with real police and detectives on the job. Detective Mullins would always appeal to their whims because who didn't want to earn some extra money as a consultant and who would say no to see their names in the credits of a movie or television show. After the time in Bantam the rolodex doubled in size as the producers came out of every orifice of Hollywood's cavernous boutiques and agencies. Most were asking about me, the wild card in the deck of the whole story that somehow saved three women in a homemade prison not two years before and then to suddenly reappear capturing two vile criminals ten years after the cold case had been abandoned. I was becoming a hot IT property, and I didn't even know about it until about three weeks later.

Casey had come down and was staying with me, we had started the night like we left off four years before, watching a movie. Only this time it was a DVD and the sequel Ghostbusters 2 played before us. So many angry fans seemed to always attack this second attempt for more money, but I always felt it was a fantastic sequel illustrating truth for heroes. Years can go by and what was accomplished can be forgotten, leaving the ones who came to save the day to face the wrath of those they saved. It is easier to forget. I have felt forgotten so many times in my life, it was habit.

Casey's laugh brought me out of the sudden depression. It was the first time I had had family in my own apartment. I had afforded myself a two bedroom with the reward money and what was left of my racetrack winnings. If I had maintained the role of restaurant worker, I would have to have roommates, a concept I had not wanted to entertain. I wanted my freedom. I needed quiet moments when all I could hear in dark alleys where screams of help. I had done enough walking down the road of the shepherd. I wanted something for me. I needed my time in the living world.

That's when the phone rang.

"Hello, Henry?" A cold, throaty voice spoke, smoke audibly blown through two nostrils.

"This is Henry." I responded as my sister paused the movie.

"My name is Peter Roy I am a producer. Look, I spoke to Detective Mullins, he's one of my old friends. He told me you would be cool if I could talk to you about a gig."

"A gig?"

"A job. One that you seem to be born for." I could hear his smile over the receiver. "I can be more specific when we meet."

"Sounds good. Can I bring my business partner?"

This took Peter Roy off guard. I knew this may scare him off the bat, but I didn't care. Casey was here, the first time any living human had done that for me.

"Sure. I am open to anyone in your corner. Love it. Meet me at the Chateau Mormont, I have a bungalow there."

"Beautiful, we will be there. What time?"

"Noon, which means closer to one in the afternoon. You will learn time is different in Hollywood." He laughed.

"I have dealt with time differentials a plenty, Mr. Roy. I can handle Hollywood time."

He hung up and I was left smiling. "I think we might get famous."

"We?" Casey was lost.

"I think you might be smarter than ninety percent of every producer in this town."

"I'm only sixteen."

"I don't think that matters."

One thirty-two Peter Roy opened the doors to his bungalow. Casey and I were dressed in black to represent an artistic aesthetic he might not have thought we had. He was in a coffee-stained white button up that cost more than most used cars and a pair of work out shorts with sandals.

"You must be the great, Henry Claremont! And his business partner?"

"Casey." She extended her hand; he kissed it gently and then fist pumped me.

"Casey! Fantastic! I just woke up, so I am having a late breakfast, do you want salmon and bagels? Pancakes? Eggs?" He led us through the mess of a bungalow. Scripts were stacked against the couch, three on the floor ripped to shreds. An ashtray filled with broken cigarettes and cigar ends. A giant bong on the coffee table.

"That's not mine. I was pitching ideas with some Canadian comics." Peter pointed at the bong.

"Whatever works." Casey responded, stifling a giggle. She then noticed the panties of the floor.

"Those aren't mine either." Peter picked them up with his toes then tossed them into the equally destroyed bedroom. "So, I wanted to share an idea I had and one that Detective Mullins turned me on to, if you don't mind?"

"I am here, I will listen." I said coming to the breakfast spread on a long high-end table only seen through the pages of Architectures Digest. "Can we partake?" I pointed to the still streaming hot food.

"Of course, please. That's what it's there for." He sat and lit up a cigarette. "So, Henry, Casey, there is a new sensation about to break through to cable and network television. It had been bubbling for a while, documentarian style crime shows, real world scenarios with actors recreating the carnage of crime and machinations of the desperate. I want to cash in on this developing property."

"You want to tell my story about Charlie?"

"No. I want to tell the story of you."

Casey and I both looked at each other as we poured syrup on pancakes.

"Holy shit, there's no milk! How can you guys eat pancakes without milk?" Peter hit the phone hard, as soon as a voice came through, he spat out: "fucking milk in bungalow three! In like twenty seconds, please!" Peter looked at us and raised an eyebrow. "Whole? Or Nonfat?"

Casey immediately responded "Whole."

"Whole, god damn it." Peter hung up the phone. "You! What you can do. You see and speak to the dead?"

"Simply put, yes." Casey responded for me, playing her part naturally.

"And according to Detective Mullins, a man I trust, he vouches for it. He has seen what you can do up close and confirms what others have stated in other interviews."

"Other interviews?" I asked.

"The girls you saved at the horror house. The other detectives on the scene, your former physician, Dr. Murphy, he has since republished the articles about your time under his care. They are a buzzed with the potential of a series."

"They?" Casey and I both asked at the same time.

"*They* are always and forever. *They* are the idol makers and the ones who choose the statues in the pantheon of fame." Peter Roy lit up another cigarette and downed the last of his espresso. "Reality television is on the horizon. True stories, real people, not actors on the screen, representing the unsung blue-collar people and simpletons trying to eke out a piece of gold for their own rainbows. Real people. People with insane potential to illuminate a fantastical world within the reality of normal life. But not shot in 35! Shot on digital cameras, real motion in real time. No more twenty-four frame a second lies, now we have 30 frames per second of digital honesty. You can't hide from digital honesty. You can only embrace it and thus the audience will embrace you."

"You want me to act?"

"Fuck no. Acting is a sham! Reality television will reveal that in time. What we see is the truth of what you can do. With a few caveats."

"What kind of caveats?" Casey gave pause to Peter Roy; she opened the door to the milk man and took the whole milk in a silver pitcher. "Thank you." She poured me a glass and then herself. "You mean lie?"

"Lying is a second language to us in this town. But for you, it will be honesty. I don't lie to people willing to make us all rich. Caveats meaning, if a place isn't haunted, we say it has a presence. If it is haunted, we say it has a manifestation then call the Priests and Shamans to put on a Sweeps Week Event. Eventually, if we can pull off a first season, these haunted locations will not only open themselves up to us for free but might even pay to have us feature their little haunted burgs on nationally syndicated television. So much potential, and all I need is a man like you." Peter Roy held up the treatment for the show.

"The Ghost Walker?" I didn't like the title.

"We had a wonderful firm come up with that title through a three-week research program in which they assessed thirteen hundred responses from key demos in the Mid-West. You know, fly over people, they often flock to shows of this nature and would be our bread and butter."

"I thought you said this was going to be a first of its kind show?" Casey was point blank blunt. "How do you know anyone would flock to this show?"

"I like you. Look, this will work if you work with us. Let's do a pilot, then we can go from there. And if this works like I think it will... Me and us, will be buying Malibu property by next Christmas." Peter Roy was all smiles. "But for us to move on this, to be a head of the game and surly guarantee success I need an answer now. Are you up to this? Are you up for success?"

"This might be the biggest decision of my life. A choice that could forever alter my destiny, a path to ruin or untold riches. I need a minute." I swallowed down one last pancake square. "I'll do it."

The pilot revolved around three separate locations, a mansion in Bel Air twenty minutes away from the Chateau. A bed and breakfast in Riverside California, then a hotel in downtown Los Angeles. I noticed the pattern in the pilot. Peter Roy informed me that it was better this way, cheaper. All we had to do to travel was take a van. Casey was too expensive to take. The van could fit the entire crew and me. Peter Roy wasn't going to go, he had to stay at the home office bungalow.

A lean, Roman nosed man with gelled blond hair pointed in an almost aerodynamic shape akin to a hood ornament from the 50's sat in the back counting the tapes for the recording. Derek Whipple was his name, had been working with Peter Roy shooting behind the scenes documentaries for the last two years.

Next to him was the sound man, Adam Nunn, a former Mid-West resident who had just graduated from a one-year technical film school. He was marking the audio tapes.

Mark Ronson was the onsite producer, the direct connection to Peter Roy whenever Peter Roy couldn't be there, a middle-aged man, long burnt out by the Hollywood system, lit up a cigarette, going through a sheet of paper which he called the script.

"Okay, Henry, check this out." Mark handed over the sheet of paper, two paragraphs printed out with side notes written in red ink, detailing different emotional perspectives to utilize. "This first set is for the intro; we will record that in front of the building. Then we follow you inside, you shake hands with the owners, they'll detail the history, we will splice in some photos and old recordings we have in the old stock footage file. Then we will cut back to you exploring the halls, which Derek will shoot as we prep for the on-camera bits."

"Okay, so I just read this whole thing? I don't think I can re-member it." I said beginning to feel the tension of being a television ghost seeker.

"Just wing it. It will be a baptism by fire. I think you can pull it off. You got a good look to you. Sweet, innocent, a little naïve, that is going to give you a layer of likability. If you are too suave, too intelligent, you'll come off as an asshole. Even if you aren't one."

I looked to Derek, nodding his head.

"I don't want to be an asshole." I muttered.

"Don't worry, that's what I am here for. I can bring out that Midwest charm you possess."

"I was born in Nevada."

"Fantastic."

I began to read the paragraph to get an idea on what to say.

The building was an old hotel, western style illustrating its con-nection to Wyatt Earp who had maybe stayed here six months as he was prepping his Los Angeles estate working in the movies during that glorious time of early film. The paper had a bullet list of poten-tial ghosts lurking in the shadows, most of which I couldn't find. I doubt anybody interesting died in this place.

Adam put the mic on me situating my box against my belt at my back. He held up the boom mic to gage the sound quality through his headphones. He gave a quick nod to Mark and Derek as I stood right smack center of the hotel arched entrance.

"Okay, Henry, just be sure to state the hotel's name, location, and add a hint of mystery when speaking of the possible spooks lurking about." Mark was standing behind Derek holding a small monitor, headphones on. He then pointed to me, "action."

"Here we are at the entrance of the Cattle Way Hotel, a throwback to the wild west days of early California. They say Wyatt Earp roamed these halls during his early Hollywood days, as he waited for the completion of his estate in the hills. The locals say this hotel caters to every walk of life, even the dead. Guests have been known to check in early only to check out when the sun went down. Could this place be haunted? Find out with me, Henry Claremont, the Ghost Seeker."

"Cut!" Mark lowered the monitor, a smile on his face that infused me with all the confidence in the world. "I loved it. Let's do one more for safety."

We did three more takes for safety then began the tour of the hotel. I could tell within three minutes that there was not one ghost lingering in these halls. I felt bad about it too. Marsha Teal was the owner, she was a very attractive middle-aged woman, hoping that this episode could resurrect any hopes of income for the coming season.

"You're not seeing anything are you?" Marshal whispered to me.

"Not really. I am sorry."

"Do you think you could make it up?"

"Make it up? You mean, lie?" I was taken aback by that. I had never lied about my ability. I never used it to lie. All my exploits were proven to be true, but now, here I am sitting in front of a small crew shooting a reality television show that may or may not be picked up by some company.

"It isn't lying, it's television." Marsha raised her shoulders up as she accepted her loose interpretation of lying. She took out an envelope, a wad of hundreds sat inside. A bribe for the ghost seeker. "And since it's television with a possible audience reach of one to two million viewers in basic cable circumstances or the possible audience of dozens of millions of viewers if a national network picked you up. I could be looking at bookings lasting through the next decade. Especially during Halloween." She slid the envelope in my pant pocket. She made sure Mark didn't see this.

"Thank you?" was the only response I had.

She nodded leaving me. Now what was I supposed to do? Having a wad of cash thrusted into my pants left me feeling dirty yet I was obliged to accommodate. I had to give her what she paid for. I wanted her to succeed.

"Did she make a pass on you?" Mark asked, revealing a tinge of jealousy.

"No, she gave me money to guarantee a ghost sighting."

"Oh. Okay. Let's give her a helping hand then." Mark went to Derek and Adam whispering in their ears. They nodded and set up a new angle on the lights above. "I am going to flicker the lights on and off rapidly, react to it as if you just got a goose nip from the invisible man. Or woman." Mark directed me.

"Okay. I can do that. Just signal when the camera is on me."

"You got it, love." Mark was really putting on the Hollywood smarm.

The whole bit went off without a hitch. We did three takes of it, just to be sure. I even pushed myself against a chair scooting it against the tile floor making a screech almost popping Adam's ear, but it worked. With all the edits it looked like the real thing. Reality television is a lie, but so is television so are movies. I received a SAG card in the mail two weeks later. I'm still paying the dues.

On the edge of the property was the real haunted place though. The old hospital erected in 1912, which housed over two thousand patients at the height of the Spanish Flu Pandemic of 1918. It was a monster of a building, solid brick, foundation deep, most of the windows boarded up since the 70's when the state pulled funding for it.

"We need to get into that place." I told Mark as we shared the Arby's meal rushed over by Adam. Three bags filled with cheddar beef sandwiches, fries, and ketchup packets. Zero napkins.

"No one goes in there. It's condemned. The hotel is what we focus on. They can't give tours to busted out edifices." Marc was pounding down his beef sandwich looking for napkins then discovering something much worse. "Did we get curly fries?"

"I got the regular, curly was two bucks up charge." Adam reported checking his sound equipment.

"We get a six-episode order, we will be able to afford steak fries." Marc smiled dreaming of the future lunches yet to be written off. "And fucking napkins."

"Whoa." Adam pushed his headphones off his head violently.

"What happened?" I asked.

"I got real bad feedback from that building. Like a scream." Adam stood up facing the ancient hospital.

"It's probably the guy in the first window, second floor." I spoke.

Mark, Adam, and Derek stopped eating all at once.

"What?" Derek was the first to question it.

"He's been waiving for like ten minutes. Why I asked we should go shoot in there. I think he was getting excited."

"Anybody in the other window?" Mark asked chewing down his fries.

"Well, I would say there might be about thirty. They're all looking at us now." I was calm in explaining what I saw because this was nothing. After the incident with Charlie, nothing truly scared me anymore. If this was ten years ago, maybe it would've been different. Now, I was needing to head inside this place to let these roaming spirits have a way out. There were doors needing to be opened.

Marsha lifted a plethora of metal keys attached to large ring, like she was opening the catacombs under a medieval castle. It took her twenty minutes to find the keys as the handy man was the only one with access to them and this was lunch break time in California, which meant you had to wait. Derek had loaded the camera with new tape, Adam had his boom pole raised and volume adjusted just in case another blast of sound occurred. Mark kept to the rear his eyes scanning the remaining exposed windows trying to see something.

"We always thought this building was haunted but couldn't figure out how to cash in on it."

"Make it a maze?" Derek said playing with the zoom on the camera.

"I wish. Half the building is riddled with mold. If we had kids running around here and they got sick, forget it, lawsuit city."

"If it were a historical building, isn't it protected by the state?" I asked trying to find my way to the stairs leading up to the second floor.

"Reason this place was so cheap was due to this monstrosity next to the property. State never responded to the inquiries we sent. I think they want nothing to do with it. Too much work." Marsha walked close to me; I could tell she was itching toward fear.

"Honestly, even if you could open this place up, no one would see the ghosts. Mark has been straining his eyes for the last twenty minutes trying to believe. I don't think we are supposed to see all the secrets of the universe, yet."

"Then why do you get to?" Marsha asked as we made our way up to the second floor. Derek had the camera wide on the two of us as we head into the darkness of the hospital room floor.

"Because I hit my head hard when I was ten."

Rows of rooms without doors seemed to stretch for miles into the void of black the boarded-up windows allowed. Wood floors seeping in the waters from the rains of the past, the dead smell of mold punctuated the air adding the necessary dread this place had already been advertising. I was reminded of the chocolate factory in Bantam. I think it was the sadness of the place that was affecting me, I could feel the suffering emanating from the brick and mortar, all those years of suffering.

"Two thousand people came through these doors in 1919. Most didn't make it." Marsha informed us as we made our way down the hall to the cafeteria. She kept close to me as if I was a protective agent. She was nervous, but I didn't understand why. Nothing in these halls were like Charlie, these souls were just lost.

"I haven't seen anyone yet. Don't be nervous, Marsha." I whispered to her trying to avoid being picked up by the microphone, but Adam gave me an OK with his fingers as he kept the shot gun mic angled on us. I also forgot about the mics on our persons. The sound quality was of the highest degree. "What else do you know about this place?"

"Not much else, nothing nefarious happened. This place was just a holding ground for the sick and dying. I couldn't imagine bringing a family member here, taking them to their bed upstairs, mouths covered, afraid to touch anything or anyone. Leaving them to die here alone. On average, the patient made three days tops. I remember one of the last old timers who worked here speak about the blood."

"Blood?" Mark asked back, hiding his smile from the camera. He knew this would be gold for the show.

"When the coughing fits hit hard, most of the patients would vomit blood. A lot of them choked to death, and from what I was told, the blood would pool on the wood floor and glisten due to the infection. It was shimmering pools of blood, and in the summer months, the reflection was oddly beautiful. The old timer said it was a reminder that life is a moving painting, and God was the artist. You couldn't question his strokes, his color choices, or his technique.

You could only sit and stare, hoping your blood wouldn't mingle with theirs tomorrow." Marsha wiped her eyes.

I finally saw the man from the window. The excited man rushed over to me speaking, "I must say, I thought you were going to get here earlier, Henry."

"I wasn't here yet. You were seeing the future, most likely."

"Yes, good point. I figured, the one person who could explain the doors was the one person who could see us." His phase shifting was the quickest I had ever seen. Perhaps it was due to his excitement? I had never seen an excited ghost before. Learn something new every day, so they say.

"How many are left here?" I asked.

"Twenty-five. I was elected to speak on behalf of the group, I served during Wilson's War, so they figured I had leadership skills. Which is funny, because I survived that only to die of the Spanish Flu two years later. At least I travelled while I was alive. I must be thankful for that much, little Susie died when she was six, but she isn't here. You are Henry Claremont, right?"

"Yes, that is me." I was speaking to air.

Derek continued to roll tape.

Adam recorded my audio never catching this excited veteran's voice.

Mark could only give out orders, "get a reverse on this, Derek."

Derek maneuvered around Marsha, angling himself at the front of the staircase. Adjusting the zoom, he was able to get a two shot of myself and Marsha. What he didn't see was the confused veteran of Wilson's War.

"What the hell is going on?" He asked gazing into the lens of the camera. "Is that a camera? I took a photograph in Germany, but it was much bigger than that. In fact, this looks delicate as all hell."

"Can you repeat what you said, Henry?" Mark asked as Derek gave a thumbs up for the recording.

"I can wing it, I guess."

"I can rewind the audio, give me a second." Adam went to the log, marking the pause.

"What the hell is this?" The veteran asked.

"Don't worry, you said twenty-five others?" I was trying my low voice Minerva taught me years ago, it wasn't the best.

"Are you talking to me?" Marsha whispered.

"Why you guys whispering?" Adam asked, "I got your lines."

Adam fed me the original line to match the previous angle. Mark was sure it would cut together well enough. The Veteran's arms folded watching us work. I felt bad, making him wait longer. But then again time didn't really exist on his playing field.

"Show me where the doors are." I point blanked asked the Veteran.

He smiled, shaking his head. "You can tell us what those are! I knew it! Yes, yes. Follow me, they just seemed to appear the night we all realized we had passed on."

"We're on the move, guys." I followed the Veteran who had already trotted down the hallway to the next level above us. "I am being taking to the top floor. It's where the doors will be."

"Cut, cut!" Mark threw his hands up, slowing Adam and Derek who were keeping good pace with Marsha and me. "No running in this building, we don't have the insurance for this!"

"We'll just sign the NDA, Mark." Derek said. "I was getting some good action shots with this hallway. We got a nice light cascade with the sun going down. Real Golden Hour light happening."

"Fine." Mark pulled out a series of stapled packets from his backpack. "Marsha, I need your signature too."

All the momentum ceased, The Veteran stood in the frame of the third-floor stair, rolling his eyes.

"And don't forget to date that line. Initials here too." Mark was thorough. "Marsha, do you have a copy machine? I will need to make three copies for the production company. And we need to wrap up before six, I don't have the authority to issue over time."

"I just need to get to that room. And then we can be done." I told Mark, then going back to the Veteran at the stairs. "Sorry, modern day paperwork stuff."

"If you go up there, we go up there. I want to get this on camera, whatever this is." Mark said securing the paperwork to a brown manilla envelope. "Okay, we are good. Let's shoot this!" Mark patted Derek on the head building up the momentum that had just dissipated.

"Are we all coming up?" The Veteran asked tepidly.

"I apologize." I spoke to the Veteran, however Mark thought I was speaking to him—

"You're okay. It's just I must keep the I's dotted and shit." Mark shrugged his shoulders.

"I don't think he was talking to you." Derek said, pushing the camera in Mark's face.

"Come on guys, let's see what good we can do here." I said heading up to the Veteran. So many stairs I have walked up with ghosts leading me on. I was truthful in what I said, maybe it was a selfish need to save the forgotten. I wasn't thinking about the television show at this moment. My indifference to it shocked me. This was my gift, my curse, my existence all of which led me to this moment. Though, this time, I wasn't alone. I had a small crew that seemed to be believing what I was seeing.

The scope of the Spanish Flu never affected me; I had read about it in school saw a few documentaries on it but that has no real consequence. We look on the past like an old sitcom rerun. The context lost on why certain jokes were funny, certain references relevant, certain vernacular appreciated. Time is lost to the ones in the present, all of us are just trying to understand the now, never realizing we are just stepping through the dust of both future and past. Cyclical pattern lost to anyone even those paying attention. Now, I was faced seeing twenty-six people lined up along their long-lost brass hospital beds, looking back at me with lost eyes and worried faces. They were so afraid. So many years languishing in a void lost to all they knew. Seeing a world so removed from them though hospital windows.

"We knew you were coming. We needed to know if the doors are where we are supposed to go?" The Veteran spoke, embracing each ghost, all phase shifting as I walk amongst them. "It's an odd thing, we feel like it's been days, but by the looks of your crew it has been much longer than that, has it been so long?"

"It's been a long time. Though you don't have to worry about that anymore. Each one of you have a door, each is designed only for you. I cannot see them. It is not up to the living to open them. All I can do is give you the solace you were looking for, no need to be afraid anymore. Just open the door and step through."

"The simplest things are hard, are they not?" The Veteran smiled, as he put his hand around an invisible knob.

"Life teaches us that. Death teaches us to let go." I saw joy erupt on the many faces, in tandem with The Veteran pantomiming their door opening. In this moment, a large electrical field popped off around us. All our hair stood up; we giggled like children as this euphoric joy raptured us.

"What just happened?" Adam stifled a laugh.

"Look at my arm." Mark lifted his surprisingly hairy arm follicles erratic with electricity. "I've never felt that before. Not like that."

"Did they move on, Henry?" Marsha asked, her smile wide, her hair teased in such a way I couldn't help but laugh at her, moving my hands around the supernatural perm.

"They're all gone. Where they needed to go." Was all I could say. I always wondered if hell was on the other side of some of those doors. I had seen the Death Birthers, the Demon Dogs, or whatever other moniker you could give to those nightmarish beings brought on by the smell of dead sinners. The doors were meant for the worthy even if they had no idea there were up to that title. Maybe there were those who felt unworthy of heaven. I had seen that firsthand before. Ghosts unwilling to let go and try the knob to see what lies behind their magical doors.

"Now that is going to make a real nice commercial break." Mark had kept his smile. "We need to get a testimonial from Marsha, then let's do one of both of you guys, so this whole moment gets a little more depth. Allow the viewer to understand this wasn't planned. This will be a ratings winner if we edit this right."

After the testimonials, I went walking around the back perimeter of the property. Forest lined the rising hills stretching on above us, a quiet valley made still with the sun setting. It was getting colder, I turned to see Marsha walking up to me, a cow skin blanket wrapped around herself.

"It gets cold out here. I thought you would like to have something hot to drink. Making coffee in the kitchen it you want some?" Marsha had kept that smile on since the explosion of energy. "I can't get over it. That feeling that went through me. You saw it all happen, didn't you?"

"I never see them leave. They see doors, I tell them to step through. When they do, an energy is released. But this time, there were so many doors, I didn't think it would've been so effective on all of you. Yet, here we are, still shaking." I noticed her beauty as the waning sun painted her face in such soft light. Her blue eyes sparkled, her red hair shone, the cow skin blanket hung off her shoulders, allowing a clear view of the curves of her breasts. Marsha was something worth wanting.

"There really is something out there? I mean, all of this isn't the only thing we have. I can now be completely calm in knowing there is another life after this. Talk about a profound Tuesday."

"Just imagine what Wednesday might bring." I saw her make the move towards me. Her lips hit mine as I bent in, allowing the kiss to take place.

"You guys have rooms tonight. I think I can give you the Presidential Suite. That's what I call my room." Marsha kissed me again. She was sweet. A hint of cream and coffee on her tongue clued me in on how much they spent on high end coffee beans.

"I didn't want Mark to be jealous."

"He didn't make me feel this way today. And I don't expect you to be here Thursday."

"We got three more segments to shoot." I said going back to her needy lips. We were both wrapped in the cow skin blanket, its heaviness wore on me, then Marsha adjusted it, enwrapping the two of us. The heat was instant, the moment intense with sexuality, dense with want. Each kiss was longer than the previous. Making love was something I never thought the dead would grant me. Or maybe this was television celebrity beginning to take hold. Either way, I allowed it because moments are all we get. And when a woman kisses you as the sun sets, you best hope she's still next to you when it comes back up. I didn't even see her at breakfast.

Three weeks had gone by as we traversed the eighty-mile radius Southern California had to offer due to budgetary concerns. Mark was elated at the footage we were getting, that he immediately forgot about Marsha. Peter Roy was constantly sending us emails with mostly visuals, no words. Adam informed me that Peter was a man unable to use words when he was happy. When he was mad, he can scream profanities to make your ear bleed, but when he found things to be going well, he could only muster images of birds singing on a branch, or pigs in shit.

As we traversed across the state, I was worried about Casey. I left her alone in my apartment for three weeks, I remember my first three weeks in Los Angeles, I developed cabin fever because I didn't want to go outside. The only thing to push me out of the door was the fact I only had a VCR and DVD dual player and a square television set without cable hook up. I couldn't afford cable, so I took a gamble stepping outside into the world to find an antenna for my box television. The last antenna was purchased at the last Kmart along the Miracle Mile. The only way I found it was to blindly drive around the city. No map, no GPS, only my sense of direction which was meager at best.

Casey was much smarter than me, though. She had mapped out most of Westwood, pining her desired locations to an index card drawn out to actual scale. Granted, she was a prodigy, but this was ridiculous. I had to check on her.

"Where you at now?" Casey asked, someone else was in the background.

"We just wrapped over at, hell, I forget. But who is with you?"

"Mom and dad are here. They're helping me get settled.

"Settled? In my apartment?"

"It was my idea. I thought maybe they could bury the hatchet."

"I don't know if I can yet. They're not in my room, are they?"

"That's where they've been sleeping. Where else, silly? Don't worry I washed the bed." Casey had her smile up and bright, I could hear it over the phone.

"Oh my god, I didn't even think about that." I was now stricken for the need to return as swiftly as I could.

"Don't worry, everything is fine, they like your place."

There was a pause.

"What is it?" I was afraid to ask.

Casey relented, "I bought a suit of armor. I put it in the foyer."

"A suit of armor?"

"It really ties the room together. Plus, you are about to be a reality television fixture according to Roy. He has been watching the footage putting together a rough cut of the pilot. He says Travel Channel is desperate for it."

"There's a Travel Channel?"

"Apparently. Is there a way you could get mom and dad out of there before I come back?" Casey wasn't stupid, she knew what my parents did to me. Sending me off to start over. All of it still hurt me. I couldn't just let it go because Casey was there. I didn't want to look at them. I wanted it to be on my time, not theirs.

"I can do that. I will make something up." Casey sounded defeated but her bubbly persona popped back on like a light bulb. "I also got a coat of arms crest. It's above the bathroom door."

"Are you making my apartment a castle?" I was trying to imagine what that would be like. Stone bricks covering the drywall, tapestries of royal history atoning the walls leading to the sliding glass door to the balcony with my patio chair and table stood. Or did she replace that with a fourteenth century bench and throne chair? I cannot leave Casey alone in my apartment for too long.

When I arrived at my place, I scanned the streets checking for my parent's car. Even though I hadn't seen what they drove in eight years. I knew their taste, so I thought I could pinpoint their newest vehicle. Nothing looked out of place. Everything was pure Southern California street meaning most of the license plates were out of state signifying the army of actors and writers trying to make the big break. I stumbled into it. I could honestly say I was a television personality, but it was too early to boast. We only had the six episodes in the can, and we hadn't heard back from the Travel Channel. Peter Roy figured having six complete episodes would be the way to go. A mid-season replacement on the standby for any channel in need of a new show. Time and money are the major factors in Hollywood.

"Did it go well?" Casey asked, textbooks from college stacked on the coffee table. I could barely feel my feet at this point.

"I think we got something here. But I need to sleep for three weeks, so don't wake me up." I finally put the college books together, "what is this?"

"I'm going to UCLA. You didn't know that?"

"I do now."

"Mom and dad thought living here would be good for us. And it's free."

"Free for them. But you can stay if you want. Tomorrow is what day?"

"Saturday."

"Let's go shopping for your room tomorrow. I will sleep on this couch." I fell into the soft cushions and before Casey could move to send me off, I was out. In sleepy voice I ordered her, "go to my sleep zone, fall to bed."

My parents had realized that Casey was in fact a prodigy. She had always been ahead in the game of life since she was three years old. When she graduated high school at sixteen, I believed it. Though because she was now seventeen heading into the halls of an Ivy League school she wasn't allowed to participate in the dorms. Living with me provided a buffer. I was happy to be it. No boys in this place anytime.

As I poured coffee from the pot I finally came upon the knight in my foyer. It was black armor, immaculately shined, the rivets were a dead giveaway that this was made in modern era. However, the visor stuck out, instead of the black it was silver. The mouth of the helmet was black, holes punctured for breathing, eye slits so narrow no true knight could fight in this thing.

"The silver is the only original part on it." Casey spoke from the toaster popping down waffles. "He told me he had found the visor in the middle of Ireland, rusted, torn up, battle weary. Used in war or practice. Either way, cool."

"Did you buy this so I wouldn't bring up why mom and dad

came here?" I was upfront. I still had some issue with them telling me to leave.

"I think it's a nice piece, that's all. Mom and dad don't know how to say sorry. And you know that." Casey said pouring the syrup on top of the buttered waffles.

"They didn't have a problem telling me to leave."

"We need to buy bacon. Waffles alone serves no purpose." Casey took the last bite then washed down the plate in the sink. "One of these days it might be worth the effort to focus on the living people in your life. They're not ghosts yet."

The show began to take over my life. Six episodes in and I began to develop a muscle. Mark called it the beginning of metamorphosis from nobody into a television star. We were working out of offices in some back wood studio by Randy's Donuts. Television production was a very strange animal. We would spend ten hours bull shitting and then work for about three hours with snacks in between from the kitchen then eat lunch. We never got donuts though. The offices were connected to a recording booth situated in the middle of a large former airplane-hanger redesigned to aid lower budgeted productions needing postproduction amenities. I was using the booth to do voice over for the episodes. A screen faced me, forcing me to watch myself react to ghosts we never saw. Only the one night at Marsha's place did we find any real ones. In the neighboring building was the editing office, it was a cold room attached to a small common area with couches and a big screen television. Mark's office was connected to the kitchen and common area so he could keep an eye on us, Adam, Derek and myself as we went over the notes we thought would make for quality television. Morgan Damsky was our editor, a balding man with beard, always had shorts on. Mark dealt with him exclusively.

"You're on the cusp of something here, Henry. Peter is getting boners over the footage. And so is the Travel Channel. They might buy another ten episodes make this a twenty-episode season, the first time for anybody to get that deal." Mark was like a kid. "Well, a basic cable channel, but they all grow. More and more digital cable and dish subscribers every day. We will have the ability to launch into twenty million homes."

"More like ten." Derek muttered.

"That's second quarter numbers, they'll be ten million more by the time the show drops." Mark dropped the smile but as soon as he looked at me it returned.

"Great. When do we get paid?" Adam muttered that question.

"Yeah, when do we get paid?" I still hadn't received a check.

"You guys got to talk to payroll." Mark about faced exiting the office.

"Don't worry, we will get paid. Then we renegotiate." Derek spoke up. He had been working with Mark and Peter for years, he knew the game better than most. He never got stiffed but he never made enough to retire either.

"We need to hire assistants." Adam was going through the tapes, numbering them into his laptop. "If I write out another time code, I am going to lose my shit."

Mark came back into the office with a bucket of Red Vines, "don't even think about asking for that. You're lucky we got a kitchen and a toilet that doesn't smell like your apartment."

"Twenty million viewers will pay for assistants." Adam said.

"Twenty-five, maybe." Mark threw Adam a Red Vine. "Meanwhile, here's a lifeline."

"Maybe to diabetes." Adam handed me the Red Vine, I loved them.

"We need dried mangos. We had that on the last shoot, damn good." Derek was popping open a bag of chips then a soda can. "This shit is going to give us all cancer and diabetes."

"Shit, I'll bring a vegetable tray tomorrow." Mark made a note in his Blackberry.

"And bottled water. Why do we have so much soda?" Adam had brought his own water since day one.

"I need to hire fat guys again. They may be lethargic, but they don't bitch." Mark smiled at us.

"What?" I asked.

"This is fun. We are in the beginning of something special. You work long enough in this business you get a sense of what works and what doesn't. Success isn't marked by cash in your wallet, but how much fun you have earning it."

"What happens if you stop having fun?" I asked.

"Then it's time to get out. I have seen the best walk away because they get lost to the bull shit. I have seen the best wither away because they stayed too long." Mark was suddenly nostalgic, lost to the years of this job. Hollywood can take years off you if you don't pay attention.

"I would like a wallet full of cash. I can have more fun that way." Derek said digging into the Red Vines.

"Don't touch all of them, damn it." Mark said as his Black Berry came to life with the chimes of an incoming call. "It's Peter." He jumped out of the common area closing the door to his office.

"Even if they get a deal, we ain't going to see any pay bumps. Maybe next season. But don't get too excited, we will be getting our minimum for the next six months." Derek knew what he was talking about. "You'll have more power too, Henry. Keep that in mind if Peter tries anything. This show is you not him."

"I'm still learning. I trust Peter, I guess." I was naïve and Derek picked up on it.

"Learn faster. And always remember the little people. I would like to be gainfully employed for a few years."

"Me too." Adam spoke up, his tapes lined up ready to go on the glass coffee table. "I'm going to hand these over to Damsky. If you order anything, get me a salad. With shrimp, we can afford that now."

"We don't have assistants. We can only do take out." Mark reported coming back into the common area. His smile was bright. "We are twenty episodes in, baby. Next season guaranteed, and yes, we will be getting assistants."

I was excited, Derek just exhaled loudly and laid back down on the couch.

As we wrapped the last episode of the first season, I thought I would feel something more. It was a Tuesday night, no more important than any other Tuesday night. This was the only Tuesday night where I wrapped an episode of a television show, my television show. My parents were wondering when it would air, they spoke mainly though Casey, the launch date was going to be May 23 9:00 PM Eastern. It was six weeks from airing. In the six weeks leading up to the premiere, we had to go through an array of legal papers, signing off on every type of legal parameter one could imagine. Peter told me it was part of the grueling process of producing, why he got paid so much up front.

"The bull shit paperwork of the lawyers keeps this business afloat. Without it we would be suing each other every which way but loose. Agents don't do a god damn thing. The lawyers keep us honest here. I should have been one of them. But I have too much creativity in me. I have too much love of craft in me. The empty television is a canvas. I fill it with the moving images of something important." Peter signed and initialed fourteen pages in thirty seconds, I was amazed watching him move down the pages.

"Are you even reading those?" I asked.

"No point. It's all legal speak. And besides, if they came to my house demanding one of my children, I'd be upset at first, but a deal is a deal." He winked at me.

"Well, if you say so." I didn't even bother to read the pages either. I signed all the places marked, then initialed three more pages.

Casey had the bucket of popcorn ready as my mom and dad sat on my new furniture in my new house. Casey was adamant about them being here for the premiere. No one brought up the past, we were just there to enjoy the present. They were having fun with it; I couldn't stand it. Watching it for real this time, not behind a microphone on a sound stage or in postproduction was grueling. Peter felt the opening needed some creditability so the news footage of when I discovered the kidnapped girls, and the aftermath of the Charlie Hailey case was used to bolster my ability. To cue the audience into my power. Moreover, was the sudden recall of being in the news when I was ten years old, with my father gushing about finding the long-lost treasure of the Nevada Gang. I remember the scorn he had for me when it was taken away. It wasn't my fault, he wanted the cameras, I had no say. Now, all these years later, I see him laughing and grinning like a child. I couldn't tell if he was proud or if he was enjoying his son looking like a fool. I felt like a fool watching myself react to nothing. Post sound provided additional cues needed to signify something hitting the walls off camera, a howl, a shriek, an inaudible voice mumbling something about the afterlife. The last segment was the real event we all experienced. Marsha was on camera next to me, Adam popped into frame for a moment as the rush of energy hit us. Those few seconds of reality television were the only real moments of ghosts ever truly captured on video, and it was followed by a commercial for restless leg syndrome.

"I think you guys are on to something here." Mom sad dipping her pop corn into the tiny bowl of mustard. That was her thing, mustard, and popcorn.

"Half of that was fake, right?" Dad asked opening another can of beer.

"Yeah. Well, the last part was real. Everything else, made up." I said solemnly.

"It's television, Henry. It's not supposed to be real." Mom said sensing something amiss in me.

"I know. It's for the best. Keep the public guessing. If there's anyone watching that is." I was sure the show would flop. I hated the concept of it. The camera was so static, yet boring. Nothing was interesting in the entire hour. Even the music sucked. My cinematic sensibility was hurt. I was making filth. I felt dirty. I felt used.

"Biggest audience for a pilot on the Travel Channel in history." Peter was ecstatic.

"History? It's been available on cable for six months." I rolled my eyes.

"History making!" Peter reiterated, "look, let's not get too excited. Week two will be the real test. I will call you later, I am working on a documentary about GG Allen right now, not in the best mind to discuss anything. Love ya, Ghost Seeker!" Peter hung up.

It was a relentless hit. Every week the numbers went up. Every week more and more people were discovering the Ghost Seeker. Tourist numbers went up too, all the locations used in the show shot up forty to fifty percent. Marsha's place was breaking records that entire year. I felt good about that. By episode fifteen, Travel Channel ordered not just a second season but a third. We were off and running with bigger vans, better cameras, sound equipment, a salad bar, and assistants. I travelled all over the country as Casey kept the home fires burning going to college. I was afraid she would be the brunt of the jokes and scolding from classmates, on the contrary, she was more popular than me.

"You have no idea how many girls want your number." Casey would tell me as I travelled.

"They're all over eighteen, right?" I had to know.

"You are a sick man. Just know you are becoming a Tiger Beat pin up boy to these chicks."

"How do you know about Tiger Beat?"

"I had a well-rounded education. Where are you this week?"

"Philadelphia. Some one thought they saw Ben Franklin here. It's not him."

"So, there is a ghost there?"

"Some stableboy. I got him to his door."

"Well at least you're still able to help those who need it."

"Yeah, but it was off camera. I don't want to bring the others into it. It gets awkward."

"Isn't that the point of the show?"

"I have seen two genuine ghosts this whole season. I feel like a fraud."

"It's a reality tv show, you're making most of these episodes up as you go. You are a fraud." Casey didn't mince words; she was honest to a fault.

"Just keep those numbers around. I need to a break when I get back."

9

HAUNTED FAME 2003

With the second season premiere, Casey, mom, and dad maintained the tradition of watching it at my place. Mom and dad would fly in, stay for a weekend, fly back. It was more for Casey than me. My abandonment issues persisted, yet I could never tell them to their face how I was feeling. They would laugh and smile at me as the show played, seemingly proud of me. I just didn't understand how they could just let the past go so easily with me clinging to it as if was the only thing keeping me afloat in this reality television ocean. I didn't want to call it hate, but it percolated every moment my parents lingered. All I could do was hide my pain, give a fake smile to them allowing them the ability to let go of any of their guilt, if they even had it. If I could be a liar on the show, I could be a liar in real life.

When the second season ended, I went insane. Dating three girls at a time, hitting up the Los Angeles hot spots as if they were owned by myself. I was lost to the murk of stardom. I soaked it up because I felt I deserved it. I wanted to enjoy it, so I did. I have no regrets, I don't live in these moments when I daydream, because that kind of bliss came later. As of this moment I was the three-week boyfriend. By the time the third season was shooting the powers that be swooped in to save me from myself.

"We want you to date other celebrities. Or up and comers if you permit me?" Peter sat me down in the new production offices. "The studio wants you to date Sherry Maitland, she just got a new sitcom on CBS, her agent is a friend of mine, I am also the producer on her new show, so I can allow you and Sherry to meet up and be seen around town. In fact, here are two tickets for the premier of Matt Damon's new joint." Peter handed me an envelope with two glossy black tickets for the Cinerama Dome. I hadn't been there yet, so I was excited.

"Is she nice?" I asked.

"She can talk."

Sherry Maitland was a gorgeous raven-haired former teen star from Disney. The last two years of her career had been cratering, especially with her cocaine addiction that she had battling since she was fourteen. Hollywood had finally scooped me into its clutches as I was sitting opposite Sherry wearing a low-cut gown, making any man want to go down on their knees to beg for her attention.

"So, is that whole ghost thing real?" Sherry adjusted her boobs making sure they were amply visible.

"Yeah. Just the show emboldens it. I don't see ghosts every-where we go. That's just for the show."

"You're too honest. Better not have some pap overhear you say that. Your show would be done then we will be done. I need you for at least a season. You understand?"

"I think so." I was confused.

"I think you're a cute guy, really. Maybe we could have some fun out of this. But remember, out there, we are happy. In here, we are just playing our parts. How the girls looking?" Sherry posed us-ing that fake teen smile she mastered at Disney.

"Girls?"

"My tits. You are too cute." Sherry gave a genuine smile which was better than her promotional one. "Okay, here we go."

The limo stopped, the doors flew open, the lights of dozens of cameras popped to life around us. We made the front page of three grocery store rag magazines. Peter was ecstatic. The show went up five points that week, Sherry's show was number one in that times-lot. The fake chemistry between us worked, the studio was happy, Peter was happy, Sherry was happy, I was miserable.

"We have to take pictures on the set?" I couldn't believe the new orders from the network which I wasn't even a part of.

Marc shrugged his shoulder, "its one-day work. You're getting paid for it. Look, I know this is weird. I get it. You are in the thick of the machine now. But it won't last, believe me."

"How long does it last?" I asked.

"Depends. Right now, you are on fire. The show is a hit. You are on the cover of magazines with a hot television star, for the moment. It takes a bad month of ratings to make all the differences in the world. Always remember that." Marc was open to me here, the real person behind the producer. These were moment few humans ever get to see. "Oh, they got you a suite at The Standard on Sunset. You guys can hang out there this week for sweeps. Go out every night. Get the free room service. Enjoy the free parking. One day that will all fade away and you will be left with the ghosts of perks. And those you can't send through a celestial door."

"I am thankful, really." I was trying to sound happy but that was a lie.

"It's okay, my friend. Like I said, one day this will all be over. You will have great memories if you allow it. If you fight it, no one will appreciate you, because you are not appreciating the experi-ence. One can only be an asshole when they are on top. Everyone has their way down. And when that happens, all of us people work-ing alongside them, will bring out their knives to stab them on the way down. I don't think you are capable of that, but I have been wrong before." Marc handed me the envelope with the key cards to The Standard and the itinerary for our week.

"If I make a movie, they'll cease this shit." She smiled at me as I gazed down below through the windows of The Standard Hotel suit. "We are just marketing material right now. I get it, but do you? I don't want you to be hurt by anything that may happen down the road." Sheryl was being authentic. Say what you will about actors, they can be people too, sometimes.

"I get it. I didn't expect to be married or anything like that. I'm a tv star, I guess. So, I got to play their game."

"Reality tv star. Big difference, my friend." She came to me and kissed me.

"Is this all just a total lie?" I asked feeling her heart skip a beat as she pulled away from me.

"Yes. But, like I said, we can still have some fun. And we have had it." She gave me a coy smile reserved for me, as she never used this one outside in public.

"Does that make us whores?" I was being honest. This whole situation was beginning to ware me down.

"So what? Lots of people have dead end relationships that go on for years. At least we have employers telling us when to stop. All part of the job, really. You are different though, which is why I really liked you out of all the guys they put me with. Shit next year, maybe I'll be with a girl."

"Now that would be interesting." I gave her the coy smile back.

"Pig." Sherry laughed, putting her coat on, "let's get this dinner over with. Then we are watching some free pay per view."

Sherry's show didn't go down in ratings. It was a rocket ship heading for Alpha Centauri. By the time we were wrapping season two, Sherry was prepping for a summer movie, meaning I was on the chopping block. I spent six months with her. We went to Hawaii, the paps got pictures of her topless on the yacht the studio rented. A calculated moment, of course. Most of the Hollywood scene was calculated. A dream factory working overtime spewing toxic images of what relationships should look like. I couldn't complain though, in the real world not many girls would look my way, but because I was the Ghost Seeker on tv, they seemed to have a change of heart. Sherry explained to me how it was, we had some conversations when the two of us just sat in the hotel suits waiting to go outside for cameras to take our pictures to plug our shows. She was the only real honest person I knew. Had to give her credit for it.

When the time came, it was over. Sherry had her movie and I had season three premiere to worry about. Our ratings maintained their dominance, as I sat on the couch with Casey and mom and dad over to watch it this time in my new house. A five-bedroom enclosed property not far off from Fuller. It had an old Hollywood vibe to it, reminding me of Chaplin or Keaton. It was built in the 20's, so I figured why not buy it. I moved Casey into a nice town house in Westwood, keep her close to the campus.

"Sherry is out of the picture?" Casey asked as mom itched closer to hear my response.

"It was never a real relationship, guys. It's Hollywood." I couldn't sit still watching the new opening of the show. This time, Derek, Adam, and Marc were featured in equal time with me, pretending to see phantoms. I liked the fact due to contractual obligations, the crew got more screen time, maybe they could share the burden. As the show began the trepidation in me rose again. Mom and dad both in the house again for the annual premiere. I had to do something this time, I had to ask them for semblance of truth.

"Do you guys ever remember that day in the kitchen?" I asked noticing the pathos exit the room, the uncomfortable shifting took its place.

"It was a different time then, son. It was a difficult choice to make, but it worked out. Why do you want to bring it up?" Dad asked.

"I don't know. It just hurt. And I am glad you did it for Casey's sake, but it still hurt. I didn't want to go. I didn't want to be here." I didn't cry, I was too tired to tear up.

"Sometimes family handles shit badly. Your grandma used to say, hate me today, love me tomorrow. That's what it was. A hard choice we had to make. But it turned out great, look around you. All you have is due to your gift." Mother spoke of my gift as if she understood it.

"What gift? To see ghosts? To talk to them? If it wasn't for certain events, certain moments of me falling into something, I would be in a half-way house, suffering with nothing to show. I would just be a freak. Now I am just a part time celebrity. When that is all done, I am still the freak. Are you going to let me back in the house for Christmas dinner when the show is off the air? Are you going to speak of me with your friends when kids come up? Or are you going to just talk about Casey? The good one. The normal one."

"Are you feeling better now?" Casey asked holding mom's hand as she started to tear up.

"I can't watch this shit tonight. Hate me today, love me tomorrow." I spat it out stepping out into the street walking to the corner bar.

10

"**G**host seeker?" She smiled, putting me in a hard position to hate her. Hint of red in her hair, which always perked up male interest for some reason. She would tell me years later it was dyed on purpose, she made more tips as a red hair, a tactic she learned six months working in the bar arena.

"Don't tell anyone, please." I covered my face.

"You live around here? I never see you here." Bartender skills were high in this one, she kept the small talk going as the other ogling regulars kept their come-ons to themselves as she focused on me.

"Just bought a place down the street. Mom and dad are over for the season premiere, kind of a tradition now. Third season and all."

"Looks like you had enough of tradition if you're sitting at my bar."

"Long story."

"Let me tend to the regulars, then I am all yours. Give me a second. Sundays are slow and I got time for a long story." She went to the regulars taking their orders, listening to their chattering. All smiles, all a show. She kept returning a gaze to me, her blue eyes seemed to just see me as she maneuvered around the denizens. I felt like a ghost, no one seemed to notice me, but she did. Within twenty minutes she had made a dozen drinks, paid out three custom-ers, cleaned out five glasses, and washed her hands.

"Okay. Tell me your long story."

I gave her the broad strokes of my life story. I didn't mention Samantha, I didn't give too much away when I helped Laura. I didn't go into detail about Charlie Hailey. But I let everything out about my life with my parents. About what they did. How they told me to leave. It felt good to let it out. A stranger made me feel so much closure.

"I need to forgive them, don't I?" I asked her.

"Family is a funny thing. You're always running away from it, but one day, enough time passes, and you are left with memories and tombstones. You missed out on the days you should've been there. All because you were off being an adult. Living for your own time, never realizing you missed theirs. Then all you can do is make up a phony past, where you were always there to begin with. You lie because it's all you can do. At least you're not a liar."

"I lie on the show all the time. A big bull shit nothing." I let the honesty flow though me.

"I don't think your bosses would like to hear that." She smiled that authentic smile again.

I was about to ask about her life, but my father sat next to me at the bar. He looked up at the television and pointed.

"They did a two-episode opener this year." My father said taking a drink from my beer.

"I didn't mean to ruin mom's time."

"She's okay. Casey is taking care of her. She knows how to do that stuff. I don't." My father checked out the bar. "You come here often? It's nice."

"First time I have ever been here."

"Good thing it's down the street. I was half thinking I would find you in an abandoned house talking to air."

"I used to do that back home. You heard all about it."

"True. And I should've told them to fuck off. I should've said, at least my son is interesting. But I didn't. I didn't know what to do. How to handle that. No one could. What you have managed to do with all this burden on you is amazing." My father was being careful not to be overheard by anyone in the bar. Emotional revelation was not his strong suit.

"I still don't know what I'm doing. I needed you and mom to tell me it would be okay. You guys just sent me to the hospital. You ignored me thinking I could grow out of this. I wish I did."

"Whatever happens now, we are with you. Casey brought us back to you. I knew you were angry with us. I didn't blame you for that. All I can do is, nothing. What's done is done. You can hate me for yesterday. Love me tomorrow." Father paraphrased the family creed.

"I love you always. Mom too. Shit." I hugged him. For the first time in years, I felt whole again. I felt healed.

"Come back to the house. Let's get a pizza or something." My father stood up from the stool leading me back to the outside.

"You better come back in here, since you're so close." The bartender said as I put down a fifty for the beer.

"What's your name?"

"Liz. Simple. I am here every Saturday and Sunday. Five to close. I'll keep that stool open for you."

"Do me a favor, change that channel." I pointed to my mug holding a finger to my temple, looking distressed by a sudden ghost scream which was recorded in postproduction. "And I will see you Saturday."

So, my weekly ritual began. Every Saturday and Sunday I would spend three hours hanging out with Liz, only three because once eight hit the bar filled up and I let her work. In the lame five to seven thirty slot for a bartender, it allowed us time to talk. Liz was your atypical Los Angeles story, from the Midwest, artistic, put her toe in acting, writing, standup comedy, all the things people come out here to try and fail at. Liz considered herself a complex failure because she had literally tried every aspect of the industry in her twenties only to discover it wasn't her mind executives were after, it was her toned ass and perfect breasts. Not to mention she was beautiful to boot. A perfect combination for assault in this town.

"I was good too." Liz never looked away from me when she spoke to me. Her eyes were locked in on me as if I were the only guy in the bar. To be honest, I was the third guy in the bar, the other two were over sixty and drank so they could die faster. They were all former union members, guys who worked on television shows since the sixties, twice divorced with several addiction problems. They managed to kick most of them with beer and cigarettes being their only vice left. Liz was good to them, they tipped handsomely and had amazing stories about how fucked up Hollywood was. Nothing really had changed according to the old timers. They just knew how to hide it better now.

"When do you head out for the fourth season?" Liz asked as she closed a tab.

"Two weeks. We are travelling the globe now. Scotland castles, Irish castles, English castles and then a Spainish castle." I was excited to travel but not excited about pretending to see foreign ghosts. And if I did see genuine ghosts, if they spoke the local language of their era, I was screwed.

"What happens if the ghosts speak another language." Liz seemed to read my mind.

"Then I am screwed. I am not a translator. I barely speak English."

"I took some French, a little Latin, figured it would be fun."

"In college?"

"Yeah, well, it was Oxford. The real Oxford." Liz raised her eyebrows in a self-celebratory exultation. "I don't mean to brag, but I got a post graduate scholarship to go there for about two years. Acting. It was easier than mathematics."

"Wow. I barely got my Associates Degree. Math course demanded a test for placement. I had to go through three separate classes to pass the one I needed. It was a pain in the ass."

"You're a television star, you don't need shit now." Liz winked, pouring a shot for herself, and slamming it.

"Reality television, not the same thing. I wish it would get cancelled." I was being honest; with Liz it was easy.

"Ride the ride while you can, my friend." Liz mentioned "friend" killing my self-esteem. "Save your money, enjoy the adulation, it comes to so little few from the outside."

"The outside?"

"The normies. Average people who aren't related or married or born into this business of show. Every year it gets worse, so whenever a normie breaks in, the other normies cheer and project themselves onto whoever broke in the back window."

"I just answered a phone call."

"You saved three girl's lives and solved two cold case files. That deserves a phone call." Liz bit her lip, revealing she knew more than I thought she knew.

"You actually watch the show?"

"It's easy, you're a character. A real to life one too. Hard to find those. And to have you sitting at my bar. Well, I must admit, made my year."

I checked my watch discovering my time was up as the doors opened throwing in the Improv theater crowd coming in from the Herald Night. It was about to be filled with comedians and characters trying to be seen and heard. I put down two-hundred-dollar bills. My tab was never over fifty bucks.

"This isn't a charity." Liz put the bills away.

"I don't believe in charity. I pay for a good time." I realized that sounded off. "Not what I wanted that to sound like."

"I get it. You're a sweetie." Liz laughed.

"When I get back, dinner? On a weekday?" I was throwing it out there because I knew if she said no, I didn't have to see her for three months.

"Aren't you supposed to be gone six months?"

"Three. Is that too soon?"

"That's a long time."

"Makes it better. I now have something to look forward to when I get back." That line hit her right between the eyes. I could tell she was genuinely interested in me; it wasn't a show, she wasn't acting.

"You know that old saying, *everyone wants to either fight or fuck the bartender,* I often believe it."

"Well, first off, I need to know you more before I attempt either. Second, who would dare fight you? You have stage combat experience."

"You better hurry your ass back in three months." Liz bit her lip again, signaling true equal interest.

"I'll be counting down the days."

Liz wrote down her number on a napkin, "hey, Ghost Seeker, you might need this."

"This could be dangerous, I am not a guy to sit on a number, shit, I might call you on my way home."

"It'll go to voicemail, I'm at work."

The old world was certainly that, old. We had a schedule to hit up five castles, five hotels, five pubs, five estates, all supposedly haunted. Not one ghost showed up. We had to use all our creative skills to manage any content. Marc was referring to Hammer Horror films to maintain a motif. We went full blown Gothic horror romance on an episode as there were no ghosts to build off on. I was proud of that episode as we were forced to sit down and hash out a back story for this broken-down edifice. Half the castles didn't even have a ghost story associated with it. They were real estate hold overs from long lost Lords and Ladies who had fled to America in the teens and 20's. Adam and Derek were my same guys, but we had additional foreign crew members to meet the union standards as we were guests. They were less enthusiastic and hard to read. Marc offered them booze and cigarettes and that seemed to pick at their inner American. We had them pitching ideas for hotel two three weeks into the shoot. Peter was ecstatic, he informed us when he was younger in England, it took him far more to get the crews to align with the projects and he was English.

I was on week three two days in when I broke down to call Liz. I didn't realize the time difference, so we played phone tag for about three weeks. Casey was around this time which allowed me my venting partner.

"This is bull shit. It's like every supposed haunted castle has been exorcised." I was flustered and bunt out. We had to write the episodes as we shot them now, and I felt less convinced of my acting ability as time went on. Even though we always found the performance in editing.

"We're just late to the party that's all. Consider it a good thing. These spirits were sent up who knows how long ago. They found peace." Casey was dipping her potato fries into the Dutch mayonnaise for the last three days. I couldn't watch it. "What?" Casey knew what I was flummoxed on. "You're lucky I didn't fall in love with their deep-fried gravy balls."

"Am I being stupid?" I usually asked this because my sister was technically a genius.

"Yes." Casey took a healthy glob of mayonnaise down. "It's six at night in Los Angeles. Call that Liz."

"How did you know the time?"

"My job is to think of things you are unable to." She threw the cup with the remaining globs of fat into the garbage. "I need to walk a mile or three, to burn this shit off. So, I'll be back in the morning with some of that bad ass pastry and coffee from the café. Love you." Casey left me to the phone; I dialed as quickly as I could.

"Hello?" Liz's voice came on muffled, the reception was weak, but it was strong enough for now.

"It's me, Henry. I'm in Holland right now. Well, Utrecht. They got a flying saucer crashed into a building out here. It's like a Fry's."

"Sounds amazing. You going to see some flying Dutchmen? Literally?" She laughed at her own joke, but it worked on me.

"You're talented, you should be on the stage."

"I get enough guys hitting on me and trying to grope, need not more. At least these pricks tip more."

"I don't want to keep you too long. Your phone bill will eat up them tips."

"You can pay it, sugar daddy." She laughed forcing me to follow.

"Absolutely. My privilege."

"Just be careful out there. You're such sweet boy in the bigger world."

"Bigger world is a lot emptier I am discovering."

"Not seeing any spirits?"

"Not a single pustule of ectoplasm, nary a pirate, nor a beheaded duke. Just stone with slight mold in some spots."

"That's scary enough. Don't worry, Ghost Seeker, you'll find some left over spirit roaming some bleak cold tower. Or you make it up. Not the first time. And besides, isn't it a good thing the dead moved on over there?"

"My sister said the same thing."

"Genius too, right?" I could imagine her beautiful smile over the phone as the sound of her parking the car interrupted my vision.

"I need to let you go here, pulling a double tonight. I need to buy something special when you get back."

"You're way more than enough." I wished she was in this room.

"Yeah, but spending money is more fun. Talk to you later, Ghost Seeker."

She always ended with Ghost Seeker which always scared me. It was a throw away remark, like a joke. Something for someone to say when they weren't as interested as you thought. I felt like a fifteen-year-old boy again facing down Samantha. I was hurt then but dealt with it as best I could. This time I didn't see anyone better than me in her future. Or was that just arrogance? Confidence is a hard thing to develop when you have so many failures under your belt. I didn't count the set-up dates my management team created and didn't count the "ghost groupies" back in season one and two. I wanted more and I felt more with Liz. I couldn't explain it. I also felt time was slipping away. As if the world was beginning to slow down around me, forcing me to lean back. It was a tinge of fear running through me at first, then I didn't fully understand it was a warning. Time is funny when you deal with ghosts. It catches up to us all in the end.

"E.V.P." Marc held up a tape with Adam smiling proudly.

"Who?" I asked as Casey lit up understanding the trick.

"Electronic Voice Phenomenon." Casey broke it down. "It's a way to record a spirit on tape. Audio wise. You don't even have to respond to it. We can play it off like it was discovered after we asked questions to air."

"More lies?" I shook my head.

"It's not lies, it's bull shit." Marc was precise.

"Don't take it to heart, Henry, it's just a show." Adam was right.

"People watch not thinking it's real, they watch to want it to be real. This just adds to the mystery. Besides, we are looking at an additional one million viewers this next season as the channel has been picked up into cable services too." Marc handed me a Cuban cigar. "Peter told me to give this to you. We are looking at a very lucrative season five."

"How is it you always know what to say to me?" I asked truly wanting to know.

"Because I am the light. Now let's record some nonsensical ramblings that may or may not be dead people." Marc clapped his hands, and we were off shooting into the courtyard of a castle with nary a dead floater in sight.

Electronic Voice Phenomenon blew up in Season Four. We were the first show to pull that off. Any of the episode's problems were solved with a little E.V.P. segment. It allowed us to amplify the terror, securing scores of viewers. That year we went up three points securing a five million viewer rating on cable and satellite television. Another round of raises was granted, Adam and Derek were made producers as was Casey. I was proud of that more than anything else. These guys were the real pull, I was just the window dressing.

Liz was waiting for me at the house when we got back, I had called her the night before, but she was working. Seeing her smiling with her back to her Nissan was the best vision I had all season. Casey suppressed her excitement for me as she rolled her luggage up the driveway.

"You got my directions?" Casey laughed as I realized I never told Liz where I lived.

"Are you stalking me?" I asked standing eye to eye with her. Liz was almost to my height, maybe an inch or two shorter, but it was close. It was easy to get lost in those eyes.

"Well, I haven't gotten that much out of this yet, so I figured a little bit of stalking was in the cards. See, when a girl does it, it's cute." Liz winked.

"Sure. There better not be a rabbit in a pot boiling on the stove."

"No, I don't have a key."

"Let's dump our shit, and let's go to Cheesecake Factory. I want to tell you all about the trip." I ran up the driveway, digging into my pockets for keys.

"I like the fact you said dump our shit and then Cheesecake Factory in the opposite order of events." Casey already had her keys out.

"You are my sister." I kissed her forehead and threw my suitcase in the foyer. "Okay, let's get diabetes together."

Six months had gone by and mostly I remember laughing. Casey had met a decent guy in Los Angeles, Liz, and I both were in shock. His name was Steven Knight, a wannabe actor-writer from Northern California. He never took interest in the reality show as he was for the pure cinema or paycheck he could earn on his own. He never wanted a connection, he just wrote and had Casey read his stuff. She was adamant that it was good. So, I believed her. Mom and dad had relocated to the neighborhood as I was able to buy three properties next to each other developing our own compound of sorts. We were slowly healing the wounds. The scars were left but I wasn't looking away from them as much as I used to. Time heals and once more I was sensing its slow turn on the clock. How I wish I could stop it from moving all together. This time was heaven, and I didn't know it. No ghosts, just love. And love is ever so fleeting.

Things were starting to change as the technology improved. The internet was providing more content that was easily consumable, it was free, it was quick, it was democratic. Average people were buying cameras and equipment allowing them to crack the surface of mass communications. Ghost hunting was becoming easier for average people. So many videos of derelict factories, shuttered high schools, hospitals and abandoned homes allowed the verisimilitude of hauntings to become cost effective. A show like ours, going into a sixth season was falling into the bean counter sights of corporate cable. Peter Roy had to call a meeting.

"We want to bring in a new team to assist you this year. They're a fun group of guys armed with their own equipment and material. You will be more of a guide for them into the unknow. They will provide footage and sound that will guarantee more eyeballs on the screen." Peter poured us bourbon this time round. No breakfast, no assistant running off for a glass of milk.

"So, you are trying to tell us we're on the endangered list?" Casey had become a hardened producer. She was not easily dismissed.

"Not at all. In fact, I am here to provide you with insurance. A new contract that will allow you to maintain a position with the show for the next five seasons."

"What about Derek and Adam?" I asked. "And Marc?"

"All will be fine. I have Adam on another project. He wanted a break. Adam is still your sound guy for one more season. Casey can be included in this deal, but you would have to split the money between yourselves."

"I can live with that." I said glad Casey had an income still coming to her.

"What about the show? Isn't the whole point of the Ghost Seeker is to actually have a ghost seeker?" Casey was reading the contract opened to us on the desk.

"YouTube is creating a problem. The future is here and it's going to get worse for any corporate show, reality or scripted. At least to me this looks like the case. The conglomerate behind the cable channel isn't quite grasping this yet." Peter opened his laptop to display the channel of the Ghost Finders. He pointed to the views in the corner of the screen. They had close to three million hits.

"That's impressive." I admitted.

"Why I called you guys up. This video is their latest, it has been up for three days. They have an active fan base. With you prompting their launch into the television arena we will gain another few million viewers." Peter drank his bourbon down.

"You look worried for such good news." Casey noted.

"Yes, well, I am not a fool. If we don't give them a way in our way, they will make their own and double their money. In this way we can guide them and get an additional pay out. As opposed to letting them get a bigger contract with someone else who sees the future like me. Thankfully right now that number is small."

"You want to phase Henry out." Casey was blunt.

"I don't. But what the head honcho has seen of the Ghost Finders is their knack of showmanship. They have infrared cameras that can pick up distortions, EVP audio systems tied into all their cameras. We don't have a set up like that. If we were to do that the cost overruns would be too high. Our budget is getting cut this season as we failed to set the world on fire with the European trip."

"It's not our fault every ghost in Europe had been sent to the afterlife already. We were four hundred years too late on some of those." I was being honest; those episodes were a waste of time.

"No one is blaming anyone for the decline it is perfectly normal which is why we are bringing in the Ghost Finders. This will be a shot of patron at the end of the night. It gets you loose and you might get lucky."

"There is another side to that, you could puke your guts out and look like an idiot because you can't hold your liquor." Casey made a point.

"If you sign you get one more dance around the block. Then you can collect a check by making the occasional appearance. Then you collect a check by not being there at all." Peter shrugged his shoulders. "This is the best deal I could get you, other times it would happen behind your back, and you would be legally able to sue us. I didn't want that, so I took this route. It is more than fair, Henry, and

Casey. I like both of you. Let us end this ride happily." Peter was right. It was a business of show, and I wasn't even trained. I fell into it because of Detective Mullins and his rolodex.

"You've always been blunt and honest, Pete. You never steered me wrong. Let's do it. I am totally fine with this." I was pleased with the outcome. I never liked doing this show to begin with. It brought in a substantial income which is what I cared about it, let's face it, how was I ever going to make real money if I put Ghost Seeker on a resume?

11

My last season started like the first season, the first time out I saw a ghost. After six seasons and three specials I finally saw a ghost again. The Ghost Seeker allowed the Ghost Finders the glory of EVP appearance. I even gave them the direct dialogue to use, something like, *I FAILED IN MY LIFE, SO I WANDER SO LATE.* The boys loved it, the crew loved it. The real ghost was not pleased.

"I had a good life, my friend. I did not fail." He died in his early forties, a burgeoning millionaire real estate investment guru who was double crossed by his partner, Larry Kostrove.

"This isn't personal, Mike?" I asked the ghost his name, he insisted he told me, but ghosts have short term memory.

"Steve, God damn it. What is with you?" Steve, the burgeoning real estate millionaire was not pleased. If he wasn't murdered, I'm sure the stress of success would've killed him anyway.

"Sorry, Steve. Look for a door, do you see a door? One that shouldn't be there in any Earthly way?" I wanted to send this guy to the next life quickly, he was becoming annoying.

"Yes, usually it just hovers in the hallway daring me to open it, but it's not my time yet. I need to bust Larry." Steve phase shifted as he walked around me, the other crew was too busy shooting B Roll that they didn't notice my speaking under my breath. It had been a while since I had to do that, so I felt proud of myself that I didn't lose the skill. Minerva was a great teacher when I was ten.

"How do you intend to do that?" I asked checking to see if the crew was looking at me, they were too in awe of the three Ghost Finders, discussing the rooms affected by the ghostly phenomenon and taking staff testimonials. Something we never did on my version of the show. But now we had more money so we could hire actors if need be. Luckily this town had a local theater troupe opened to being on camera.

"My body is buried under the hallway leading to the back where the dumpsters are. Ass hole, Larry added a hallway because he didn't want the customers to see the garbage be taking out. I told him, it was a bar for the hotel, we had maybe three locals come in here in the five years we were open. No one gave two shits about a bar back throwing bags away." Steve was flustered, he seemed to exist in button up shirts, mostly cream colored with a sports coat. In all honesty, this phase shifting was the least jarring I had ever witnessed. "Just dig me up, boom, case closed."

"A little hard to do."

"Get Larry to confess on camera. Just trap him." Steve suggested, making motions with his hands against the row of glasses on the bar. "I saw this in a movie once, you just got to use your anger and gut power." He tried again nothing moved.

"Just save your energy for the door. I promise I will bring Larry down for you." I was being as honest as I could, I was going to call Detective Mullins as soon as I was done filming this segment. "The door? No thank you. I know this much, I am dead. I want my killer brought to justice. I want my name on this building. So, I can live on beyond this moment."

"What happens if someone buys this bar and renames it? And me, speaking to you, proves that you will live beyond this moment. You're already dead."

"Don't be a smart ass." Steven stopped at the edge of the bar. There was a protruding bulldog bronze statue near the bottom of the entrance. "I thought they would have gotten rid of this ugly thing. I used to trip on it daily when I was working late out here. Pour yourself a drink. then, bam, smash a toe, or fall to the ground headfirst into the concrete. A lawsuit just waiting to be had. Idiot, Larry."

"Hey, Henry?" Marc brought over a middle-aged man, handsome, suave in his dressing, he was a proud man who seem to carry himself with pride and success. A man you would look up to if you were a fledgling entrepreneur begging for advice up any ladder. "This is Larry Kostrove, he owns this place."

"Oh, this asshole even wears my shirts still." Steven lamented behind the bar as he swung his arms at any physical object he could.

I forced myself to concentrate on Larry who stood in front of the wailing madly Steven. "Ask him about his shirt?" Steven shouted trying to breach the plain of the living and dead with a flurry of windmill moves using both arms now.

"Pleasure, Mr. Kostrove." I extended my hand he gripped it with such strength I had to recoil momentarily.

"Forgive me, I always squeeze a little hard. I like to see a man's make with a shake. I have been doing that since I was banking six figure deals. Strength in a man's handshake is usually when I know I can sign off on the deal. Your hand seems strong for a television psychic." Larry Kostrove reminded me of Hershal. He looked to be bred from a young age to be successful.

"I see ghosts, Mr. Kostrove, not a psychic."

"Oh, much more interesting. You see any ghosts now?"

"If I used my gut, could I punch him?" Steven said to me alone, thrusting his pelvis toward Larry's back.

"Oh, Mr. Kostrove, this place is filled with ghosts or whatever you need it to be filled with."

"I know how this works. Marc didn't have to tell me. I knew

when I made the call to your producers. I want that tourism money. I need it. This place has been a hole. With you I could make this work out finally." Larry dropped an envelope on the bar. He poured himself a brandy and gulped it down.

"That had to burn." I never saw a man down brandy like a shot before.

"I am more man than most. Whiskey makes me sick; brandy never bothered me. When I was young, I drank it with milk. Grandmother fed it to me, said it would keep me healthy. She was one of those tonic believers. She lived to be ninety-five, so who knows, maybe she was right."

"You don't have to pay us." I wanted to see if this stirred anything in him.

"Oh?" Larry smiled. "I am sure Marc would disagree with you."

"He gets paid well enough Mr. Kostrove." I looked him in the eye, I was so close I could see the reflection of Steven in his contact lens. "What do you want me to tell you? That your bar is haunted?"

"Don't tell me, tell the audience." He laughed out loud picking up the envelope.

"That's a nice shirt, where did you get it?" I asked him point blank as Steven was standing to his left.

"I inherited it." Larry put the envelope in my pocket. "I don't tell, you don't tell. Have some fun at the bar on your last night here. My treat." He headed out shaking hands with Marc.

"I think the shirt angle might have been a bad idea. It wouldn't be my first." Steven said.

"It spooked him more than you ever could wailing your arms at him."

"I'm trying to deal with this stressful situation the best I can. What now?"

"Nothing I can think of."

"You are a terrible Ghost Seeker." Steven was a very honest ghost.

"Well then how did he do it? You said you are buried in the concrete? You realize that a human body would disrupt the foundation process?" I was losing my patience with Steve.

"Oh yes it did. That's why he had the pourers come in and redo it. They didn't take anything out, they just smoothed it out. Making the whole floor look as flat as it could. You notice the hump in the center?" Steven pointed out a slight raised portion in the center giving the hallway a slight hill on the way to the back.

"Yes."

"That's probably the last of my air flow. From all my cavities in my old physical body." Steven laid on the floor displaying how he was laying below. "This is me, two feet down. I'd be giving a middle finger, but I was already dead."

"How did he kill you?"

"Shot me in the back of the head." Steven pointed out a hole in the brick wall. "See that!"

I inspected the hole, looked like a bullet hit it. "And?"

"This is never going to court, kid. Look, he is a thinker. A plotter. He has angles already written out before he even begins to pick one to use. Larry is a snake and doesn't care what he must do to fix things. The way he looked you up and down just now. Know that he is coming up with a scheme. He didn't think you were real. But now he does. I wouldn't put it passed him to try and kill you."

"He just bribed me now."

"Exactly. He will use that against you. Maybe make that the motive for you to suddenly disappear. You are leaving the show, right?"

"How did you know that?" I was shocked a ghost was up on my business.

"Those idiots were talking about it. They were really excited to lose your dead weight. They think you're too honest."

"They're not wrong." I was lost as to what to do in this moment. I noticed a tremor through Steve as he shifted into another buttoned up high end tailored shirt of the same color morph over him. He shifted as if he noticed a swift change in the room itself.

"You just saw something." I knew that ghosts had a knack for seeing the future in glimpses, if you caught them in the right moment, you were able to peek into it. Much like how I made my money at the racetrack.

"It was plastic. The whole back of the hall over where I am buried was covered in heavy plastic, and the door was shut. A way to catch blood spray, maybe?" Steven was taken aback. "He would try to kill you."

"This was our last day here. No one will be around. No cameras. He could get away with it."

"Just don't come back. He might bring you here, somehow, he will try to bring you back here. Don't come." Steven resumed his practice, swinging at the bottles on the bar. "Damn it. I can do this; I know I can."

"You can only affect him if you use me. It has happened to me before. It doesn't last long but you can attack him if you go through me."

"Sounds awful."

"It doesn't feel great. But if we have a chance to stop him, we must take it."

"So, if I merge into you, I can merge into him and fuck him up?" Steven smiled. "Let's do it."

"He can't sense anything out of the ordinary. He must believe he has the upper hand. More than likely once I come into this room and see the plastic, he will lure me closer to it. You're going to have to be fast."

"I'll be fast, this is my deal."

Casey gaged over the image of Larry downing brandy. "He did that?"

"Said it made him more of a man."

"Weirdo."

"That's what you took away from this? The brandy thing?"

"Sorry. Just, damn. Wacky." Casey lifted a glass of wine to her lips. "I will miss this, buying wine I couldn't afford in hotel rooms I'll never check into again. Room service paid for by the production office. We got spoiled, didn't we?"

"Yeah, but it was fun. Now though I can't enjoy it because this ass hole is going to try and kill me."

"Maybe he won't." Casey shrugged her shoulders. "I mean, really, how is he going to kill you when we are all in town? Obviously, we would have questions if you suddenly disappeared."

"No body no crime. If I am wrapped in plastic and dumped in some concrete tomb somewhere else."

"I don't like this at all, Henry. You are putting yourself in danger for some guy you owe nothing to. This is the last show we are doing. Don't die for reality television."

"I can't let Steven down. This thing I can do sends people along the path to wherever they need to go. If I don't deliver on that, I feel like I would be killing him all over again. And I haven't saved any soul in over six seasons, for Christ's Sake. I am a fraud if I don't save him."

We shared a silent moment, hoping this would pass away. Hopefully there wasn't going to be a chance Larry could get me out of this hotel room. Maybe Steven was wrong.

A knock on the door ruptured the silence we were sharing. Casey opened the door to reveal Larry Kostrove, shaken. He looked tired, beat up, worn out. He was in the same shirt from earlier, but the booze stains were apparent.

"I didn't kill him if that's what you are thinking." Larry came in and sat in what the hotel said was the oldest wooden chair in the county. It creaked and popped forcing Larry to rise out of and sit on the couch, but not before he poured himself a glass of Casey's free wine. "Steven was a tough guy, tough. He was a loner for most of his life, raised by adoptive parents. I think that's where he built up his walls. Most people couldn't get close to him. I tried. I liked him. He was a mentor to me, and I always thought we would have been more than partners."

"Oh." Casey said that opening another bottle of wine from the supposed second oldest bar in the county according to the hotel.

"It didn't set in until I got to my closet. What you said to me about my shirt. It is Steven's shirt, absolutely. He had style. I could never figure out how to do that myself. He would be pissed to see me wearing it. I always raided his closet when he was out of town, and he would know it too. Even if I dry cleaned them. Why does he hate me?" Larry was holding back tears.

Casey and I both sat with him on the newest couch in the county according to the hotel. "You don't have to be upset. Ghosts don't have clear memory. They sometimes feel slighted in the moment of death then hold on to it. It's a comfort to them because the truth would be too much. I have come across a few like that. It taught me to let things go."

"What did he say to you?" Larry up close had lost all his tough exterior from earlier. I'm sure his handshake now would be a cold, limp fish.

"He didn't say anything other than he was buried in the concrete by the dumpsters. You two had a fight over it." I noticed the gears moving in Larry's head. All the memories were flashing beneath his eyes.

"He only ever mentioned that when…" Larry made the Eureka face. "That was the night I went to Detroit."

"Detroit?" Casey and I both asked.

"Yeah, cheap housing. City was falling apart and I though there could be a renaissance there. They wanted to make art centers or enclaves for artists. Cheap and free housing offered to anyone interested. Steven thought it was stupid. We got in a fight but that wasn't the only thing." Larry was playing this role well. He could've been an actor. I almost believed him too.

"You don't have to tell us anything." Casey said.

"Are they still shooting at the bar?" Larry asked.

"No, they're wrapped. Crew is coming in to clean up the catering set up. Shooting crew have two days off, so they are all out partying."

"Could you both come with me to the bar? Help me talk to Steve. Sort this out?" Larry was bringing Casey into this; I couldn't put her at risk.

"Casey has to meet up with Marc to go over the footage." This was the only excuse I could come up with.

"This late?" Larry lost his humbleness for a brief second, but his eyes went glassy then teared.

"It's the only time we can do it, we had a longer than expected shoot. So, we meet up late to cut out overtime fees. Since Marc and I are salaried, no overtime for us." Casey was quick and believable.

"I can see that." Larry being a businessman understood this language.

"If you need me to come along, I can go with you. Let's help Steve cross over."

"I'd like that very much." Larry gave a faint smile then stood up, opening the door for me. "We might as well do it now, huh?"

"No time like the present." I followed Larry out the door.

Casey couldn't say anything.

The drive was quick since the bar was six blocks away. The night life of the city was on a pause since the tourist season didn't hit until next month, why we chose to shoot there at this time. Larry seemed to cling to his performance, wiping his eyes while maintaining attention along his periphery checking to see if we were being followed or if they were any unwanted witness mulling about along the route. All the streets were washed in white light, but no people were around. We took an alternate route to get to the bar, one I realized had no cameras either building monitors or traffic light cameras. This was the ancient side of town where no modern technology existed.

"I never thought ghosts could be real." Larry started talking.

"Neither did I. I was ten when it all started."

"Wow. That must be unsettling."

"It wasn't that bad, honestly. Ghosts aren't anything new, they're people just removed from time. It's strange, they seem more akin to an older person with dementia than anything else. A lot of lost time and they either forget or know what they are. No two are alike I have found."

"Steven was a different breed of cat." Larry turned into the back of the bar. It's three-story brick edifice carried weight in the dark. No lights except for a large bulb above the back entrance. The parking lot had a sole van situated with its back door to the bar.

"Late deliveries?" I pointed at the van.

Larry smiled, "yeah, I unload tomorrow. I usually park it like that just in case some bum tries to rob me. And I got the camera in the corner right on it in case he does. So far, so good. No robberies." He led me to the side of the building to the side entrance. "How does he cross over? How do we push him into that?" Larry asked unlocking the door.

"It's simple. He must open a door. Projection only they can see. Most of the time they stay away from it out of fear. Or they just can't let go."

"A door? That's the big secret of life? A door?" Larry scoffed.

"Apparently. I didn't make this shit up. It's what they tell me."

"I didn't mean any disrespect. I believe you. That's both our problems." Larry went to the main bar entrance; it was a giant sliding door with a Master Lock on it. Simple security system.

Steve stood next to the lock as Larry stuck the key in.

"Plastic up all over the back. He's just going to shoot you once he gets behind the bar. That's where the gun is. By that stupid bronze dog."

"Super dark in here." I said it out loud trying to see if Larry reacted.

"No windows. This place was a hidden saloon in the 20's. That's the historical charm." Larry took the lock off then slid the doors into their groove. Darkness was created here. I couldn't see anything in there. No plastic, not even a bottle of booze. Larry went to the side panel and clicked one switch. The under lights of the bar came to life, emitting a soft glow barely illuminating the rest of the room.

"Main switch is behind the bar. You want a drink?" Larry asked as he began to move to the other end.

"Sure. Old fashioned?" I wondered if that would buy me time.

"I could do that." Larry was behind the bar.

Steve was shadowing him. "I see the pistol. He's not going for it, yet."

"Were you a bartender in a previous life?" I was stalling again.

"Yes. Ten years. I started here, oddly enough. This was always my second home. And when Steve wanted to sell it, I just couldn't let him do it." He finished making the drink then slid it to me as I sat on a stool, six feet away.

"Nice slide." I was impressed.

"I loved doing that to chicks. You know that old phrase about bartenders?"

"Everyone wants to fight or fuck the bartender?"

"Exactly."

Steven was coming up to me, "can I jump into you yet? He's going to shoot you soon."

"You can't shoot me from over there. Blood spray would be hard to clean up." I blurted out the truth to hurry up the game.

"I figured that's why you stood over there." Larry raised the gun.

"If we open up that cement floor we will find Steve, right?"

"Yep."

"Bullet in his brain?"

"No, I used the bronze dog. Popped Steve in the back of the head in case I had to bring up his corpse from under there."

"Oh shit, it was the damn dog. Sorry, Henry. I never really saw how he killed me."

"That's okay, Steve." I saw Larry freeze.

"Stop this bull shit. You don't see anything." Larry was anxious suddenly.

"I see him plain as day. He comes through the dark more than that plastic tarp tied all over the back." Larry kept his hand raised with the gun. "What are you going to do, Larry? Kill me? Wrap me in plastic? My sister knows what you were planning. I told her what Steve told me. Soon, they'll be cops raiding this place."

"Oh, I wasn't going to shoot you. This gun is in case I needed to wound you. I put so much money back into this place that burning this place down was the only way to come out of this unscathed financially. That's not plastic, it's fireproof blankets."

"How was I supposed to know that? I didn't even hear of such things." Steven was appalled over his mistake. This was a man in life who hated being wrong in life and this preceded him in death.

From beyond the sliding door, a pop echoed off the hallway. A blast of propane fumes hit my nostril as flame erupted from across the building. The fire ball sent me flying into Larry, catching my back coat on fire. I went for the gun but couldn't reach it. Then I felt my entire body go numb. It wasn't flame; it was Steve. He entered me as I was fighting against Larry.

"I can't believe you still wear my clothes. You never had any original thoughts did you, ass hole?" Steven was speaking through me, the distorted voice surprised Larry and myself.

"Steve?" Larry was fighting off my possessed body heading for the hanging blankets. "I hope the fire kills you again, you insufferable bitch." Larry took hold of his balance then swung a wicked right cross to my head. He connected easily. I went flying into the raised table and chairs as the flames rose around the wooden panels leading to the ceiling of the bar.

"Even as a ghost you're a pussy." Larry shouted heading for the bar. An array of one hundred proof booze lined the shelf. He proceeded to throw each one towards me.

"I can't believe you installed that wood paneling after I told you it was ugly." Steven, using me, dodged the bottles using my hands. It really hurt. I was trying to gain control of him inside of my mind, but nothing was working. I believe the smoke was affecting me more than Steve.

"Oh, I am so sorry, I got carried away." Steven immediately removed himself from my body allowing me to cough and spew phlegm rising in my throat. I was on the verge of vomiting. My dry heaving was making my eyes water, I blocked another bottle thrown at me.

"You couldn't walk into the light could you, Steve? Had to be able to watch mc fail even after I bashed your skull in."

Fire began to catch up with Larry having made his way to the middle of the bar tossing the rest of the flammable booze onto any piece of wood he could hit. Steve was trying to swing at Larry again, the display would be comical if I wasn't in the middle of suffocating.

"Sorry, Henry. I didn't want it to go this way, but you were too real. I didn't count on that." He was heading toward the fireproof blankets as his foot contacted the bronze bulldog that had been the bane of Steve's living existence. He launched into the air with a balletic grace, his face connecting to the corner of the opposite side of the bar. His nose shattered on impact landing face down with a thud.

I was able to get myself up, headed for the blankets covering the exit, I pulled Larry into them with me and with my backside hit the emergency exit door sounding off an alarm. I saw the van opened with a plethora of fire extinguishers inside all unlocked ready to be used in case Larry had caught fire.

"He never missed a beat." Steven said pointing at the van. "I wonder what his plan was. I couldn't see all his dealings. I guess it will come out in the investigation. So, I need to stick around for that."

"Just go to your fucking door." I was bruised, burnt, and coughing up black slime that was more than likely coating my lungs now. "I am sure you can see the outcome from beyond this world."

"You don't know that." Steven smugly suggested.

The last thing I heard before I passed out was the fire engines coming around the corner.

When I awoke in the hospital, Liz was seated asleep next to Casey. I smiled realizing this woman wanted to be here for me the moment I woke up. That means she had to hop on a plane literally the moment she was told what had happened. No one had ever rushed to see me ever, for anything. Granted this was a serious moment, which meant even more. I think Liz loved me. For real, loved me. I was hoping for something like this, but in Los Angeles, one can never be sure to meet your soul mate.

Liz sat up as she caught me smiling madly at her, as I coughed.

"He's up, you son of a bitch. You scared the shit out of me."

"You're here." Was all I could mutter.

"Of course, I am here. Casey called me once you went with that psycho."

"I love you." I smiled at her, lungs burning fiercely but I didn't want to close my eyes looking at her.

"Yeah?" Liz was holding back tears as Casey was dialing numbers on her phone.

"They arrested Larry at the scene. He gave it all up. He confessed as soon as he was in the police car." Casey hit me on the shoulder. "Why did you go anywhere with him, idiot?"

"Did I say I love you?" I held Liz's hand squeezing it hard, thinking maybe this was a dream. But when Casey hit me again, I cried out. "Stop that."

"That was your last hurrah, okay? You got to promise me this is the last time you bend over backwards for getting some dead idiot through the door." Casey put out her pinky.

"Pinky swears?" I asked.

"Your god damned right." Casey kept it out.

"Okay. I promise, I am done with doing anything like this again." I shook the pinky then coughed a giant phlegm projectile through the air, Liz had to duck.

"Can you say that again?" Liz had my other hand.

"I love you?"

"That's it."

"I love you." I meant it so much my pain subsided.

"You had to almost burn to death, but hey, I'll take the win when I can get it." Liz said kissing my forehead.

When all was said and done, Larry revealed his whole scheme, well his attempted one. He had learned about the show through one of his business partners in Detroit, we had done a few episodes out there in the third season. Larry was going to submit his location to the show as a hot spot for hauntings, even if it wasn't. It took Larry six months to garner the attention of Peter. Larry had known about the transferring the show over to the Ghost Finders, suggesting I would be hostile and needing money. Larry assumed it wasn't an amicable decision on my part. He knew of the cameras in the bar when he brought out the money, trying to bribe me for ghost sightings. He would've made this my motive for trying to extort more money out of him. Larry had known the catering service on the show provided food on the actual shooting location, using that, he turned on the propane tanks on the barbecues. He was going to blame that on me. The fire would erupt due to an electrical panel sparking as the automatic motion light came on for the alley. Why all the lights on the building were out making the entire block existing in a void. Larry had scheduled a maintenance check on it for the next day. He was going to shoot himself in the shoulder as the fire came closer to the bar then proclaim himself the victim of an insane charlatan television host losing his career. Bold plan, but he didn't realize Steve was hanging around.

Larry admitted to accidently killing Steve and in a stoke of madness, buried him in the concrete puddle he had maintenance pour. The trial would follow six months later, pushing us to reschedule the release of the episode. The executives loved it because it tied into real life crime story proving the best ratings of that episode two seasons later. When it was released, I was very happily married and had zero intention on coming back for a Halloween Special.

Steve found his door and decided to open it, finally. When they opened the concrete tomb, he gladly departed this world for the next one. I hope he was happily received and didn't complain too much. I was there to see him off as they did it, a favor to him and a fitting end for myself as I said goodbye to the reality show gig I fell into by accident. Liz was with me, so was Casey allowing me to focus on my next big adventure, living a real life without cameras and quizzical glances.

12

Ten Years of Living, Then Death Rebound 2008-2018

I will be honest with you, dear reader, I can't share this part of my life with anyone who wasn't there. This was my time with Liz, my love. I had ten years of just living with her and seeing Casey and my family grow tighter, finding those lost moments of peace. Not many ghosts among the memories here, which is why there isn't much need to go into detail. Besides, I lived these moments and I have no need to replay them for some one's curiosity. This was my decade. I don't share it. I can't because I don't want to cry anymore. Not out of sadness or grief, I understood that life was always precious, and I lived it every second of every day. I just didn't realize it would be such a short amount of time. Liz couldn't have children as we discovered early in our attempts for building a family. It was harder on her than me, she wanted to be a mom and she wanted me to be a dad. Life is always throwing monkey wrenches into the works, but they were manageable ones, After an initial year, Liz got over the pain. Eight years later she began to get tired. Exhaustive flashes belted her left and right at times, putting her down for a few days here and there. We dismissed it with the casual hand wave, *"stayed up too late, again." "Too much traveling, maybe not get too exotic with our trips."* It was getting worrisome after she fainted in the store one day. We had to go to the doctor at that point. And that was when everything changed for me again.

"Cervical cancer, stage three. We can fight that, but it will be tough. I know you are a tough woman. Treatment needs to start tomorrow, just to get a jump on this. I have scheduled a session in the morning." The doctor told us with such clinical calmness I wanted to smack him. Liz just sat silenced, taking it all in with nary a worry or raised eyebrow.

"How can you be so calm?" I was livid at her as we sat in the car under the shade of a tall Magnolia tree.

"It's my power. Calmness. I can be calm and collective even when all this shit happens. You can see ghosts I can be calm. You can't change things, Henry. Life teaches you that. We still have time and chance to fight it. Don't lose sight just yet." Liz had no tears only resolve in her eyes. She showed me what strength truly was as the months went on.

Watching the living slowly fade to the dead was destroying me. My love, being torn apart on the inside with this vicious destroyer that I couldn't fix. If I could find a spirit, maybe I could use them to pluck out the cancer cells. They could affect the living tissue inside the body I had seen it before. Instead of enflaming a beginning tumor it could burn out established ones. Chemo burnt everything in the system, with a spirit, I could focus on the area infected. It could save her, perhaps. I went from floor to floor in the hospital, looking for a roaming ghost. There were none to be found. I went for long walks like I used to do when I was a kid, stumbling upon lost souls brooding in their prisons. I guess they all found their doors without my consul.

After six months of treatment, the doctor could only shake his head. He didn't go into details with me, Liz made sure I wasn't in the room. I could see her through the glass doors of the office. She didn't hint at anything. My Liz just sat there and weakly smiled, weakly nodded, weakly spoke. I wanted to be next to her, but she knew I wasn't going to accept anything and besides she already knew what was in store for us, sitting with the doctor was a formality.

"You have to promise something." Liz was wrapped in her favorite blanket knitted by a long dead aunt from her childhood. "I need you to allow me to go through my door."

I couldn't answer her.

"You must promise me, Henry. God damn it, I am dead. I feel like I am already dead, living in this stupor of constant treatment. I don't want it anymore. I had my time and I had you. We had so much bliss, I know it because I have seen what others got. We were given a gift. You can't be pissed or sad over the inability to have more. We can't be selfish. We can't be children. My fear is I am not going to know I am dead. You will be able to keep me here if I began to question it. If I don't go to the door, I need you to lead me. That is your gift to the world, Henry. You're the ferry man for so many lost souls. So many needy people that were waiting for you. You must let me go. I know it will be hard, if not impossible, but you must let me go."

I had buried her three weeks ago. Liz would repeat this entire statement verbatim every week. Then she would stand up, phase shifting like the others did, then walk to the curtains.

"We need to open this place up. It's so dreary. When are we meeting your parents for dinner?" Liz smiled floating amongst the hard wood floor going beyond the living room where her hospital bed was. The square footage of our house was her entire world now. I kept every window closed, sealed off with thick curtains. Lights were on in every room and hallway. I had been locked in here with her for the last two weeks. Only using the phone to speak with anyone. It was easy with mom and dad retired in Florida as well as Casey living three blocks from them, I was able to be selfish and keep my love imprisoned.

"I want to watch our video from Naples. Remember when we were out there? The seafood?" I asked Liz, her focus lost in her door that would form up waiting for her exit. I couldn't see it, but I knew it was there because she would always shake herself out of the trance then immediately say, "weird, I think I had a dementia moment."

"You're old. When I start getting them, then you can be worried." I would respond back with a smile. Though as time went on, my smile began to fade. The repetition of it all was digging at me. I knew I was wrong. Then when she smiled and laughed it off, I was glad I did it. She was still there. She was still mine.

"You want to watch the video of Naples? Remember when we were out there? The seafood?" Liz would parrot what I had just said moments ago. I let her do it because she wouldn't doubt it was her idea to begin with. It would keep her from knowing she was dead.

"I love you." When I spoke those words, she always had the same reaction. A smile, a giggle, a bite of the bottom lip. I couldn't touch her. If I did, she would come to the realization that she was dead. I was keeping her here.

When the phone rang, I always rushed to answer it. I knew it was either mom, dad, or Casey. No one else ever bothered to check in on me. I was fine with that. This time, though, proved to be worse.

"You home? I'm out front." Casey reported.

I peeked out the curtains seeing her parked. I hung up the phone, Liz was standing at the kitchen sink.

"I was wanting to have some tea…" Liz was slowing down, as if she was a machine powered by gears ceasing.

"Liz, I need you to lay down on the couch. You need that nap before we head to treatment." I was using the past events to snare her back into the cage I built. More recent memories triggered something every time she slipped off into thought. More recent the event, the better response came out. The last one ended with us driving to an ice cream shop because for the first time in six months she felt like eating something sweet and cold. We drove to the King Cone and scarfed down a three-scoop sundae. It had all the fixings, peanuts, whipped cream, caramel, hot fudge, even gummy worms for the hell of it. When we finished, Liz put her head on my shoulder, looking up to me with sunken eyes.

"Now that's treatment."

As soon as we reached the car door, she puked it all up. It didn't faze her at all, she just laughed.

"The puke was cold." She giggled hysterically. *"I never had a better puke ever."*

Casey sat on the cement bench in the patio as I came out the front. I could tell she already knew everything. "You haven't spoken to me in ten days."

"So? I am mourning. It takes time."

"Why the curtains closed? You must have some light coming in." Casey was probing, she knew why they were closed. I knew her too well.

"Just ask me." I was standing with my back against the door. I wasn't willing to let Casey in. I don't know how much damage it would do to Liz.

"I didn't want to. But now I can see it's worse than I thought." Casey was keeping her anger down. I am sure she would've been hitting me if more time had passed.

"I am dealing with it."

"By keeping her here? She is gone."

"No, that's just it. She's not gone. Liz is still there. I can see it in her eyes."

"You of all people know this is wrong." Casey shook her head disappointment tremored through me. I felt dirty, I felt like a thief of life.

"I don't know how to let go. I am scared." I lost it.

Casey held me, my tears soaking through her shirt, being this close to a living person for the first time in weeks alerted me to my stench. I hadn't bathed, I didn't even realize it. Casey pushed me away with tenderness.

"You are ripe, big man." Casey was crying, but she forced a smile out of it, keeping me afloat when I was about to sink.

"I am sorry. I just didn't know what to do. You're right." I didn't want to admit it, but it was true. I was being a monster.

"What do you need from me?" Casey asked.

"Time."

"I am going to be at the Roosevelt in Hollywood. Suite 2."

"Suite 2?"

"I saved my money." Casey kissed my head like a good mother should. "Call me soon or else I'll come back. And you know I'll knock that door down next time. I love you."

"I love you too." Saying that to the living rang truer than repeating it to the dead.

I watched her drive away, I closed the door and stood in the foyer, seeing Liz looking down the hall at her invisible door.

"Was that Casey?" Liz asked in a daze.

"Yeah, she was dropping off tapes for the show."

"Season four triumphs!" Liz said as she lost sight of the door.

I was faced to face with her. Season four was fourteen years ago. We had been dating six months at that point. Liz kept me locked in her eyes. My mouth was dry, my head spun. It killed me to never kiss her again. To hold her and smell her. All this charade was growing slowly into a parody of life created by me.

"I want to watch that video of us in London. The Roman wall we saw? Remember that?"

"Sure do, you want to watch that video of us in London, where that Roman Wall was?" Liz went to the couch as I went to the rows of tapes. I didn't send her to the door. I couldn't let her go. I didn't care if I was a monster. I was secure in my selfishness. I was willing to be a warden keeping Liz imprisoned. I didn't care.

When Casey came back in the morning I didn't answer. I unhooked the house phone, turned off the mobiles, sealed off any openings in the curtains. I was expecting her to throw a fit. I was expecting rocks through the windows. Nothing happened, which was worse. Casey left crushed. She sobbed in the car as she drove off. I could see it from the upstairs bedroom. I felt so pathetic, but once I saw Liz standing next to the bed, I snapped out of it. I was losing myself to grief. I was losing myself to the gifts that were delivered onto me. I felt pangs from a distant God, warning shots, perhaps. But I rejected the slings. HE did this to me and now HE can reap what HE sowed.

"Who was at the door?" Liz asked as if this was just an ordinary day.

"Casey, she was dropping off a tape of the show." I brought up the past so she couldn't get confused.

"New episode? I know you hate watching yourself, but I am making popcorn and you can share the bowl." Liz smile wasn't the same in that moment. It was reflex. A pattern she was maintaining because her mind and spirit were flickering between two different plains. I was tethering her to mine. Most of the time she would brush it off as if it was a piece of random hair caught in the sunlight coming from a hairbrush. This time she hesitated, I thought she was about to figure it out then curse me for being her jailer.

None of that happened. As it always was and had been to that point, any new thought erupting in her floating psyche gave a tremor. Brief flash of truth but dismissed so fast because I knew she didn't want to accept it either. She told me to let her go, but I couldn't. I lied to her. I was lying to myself. I just couldn't allow myself to speak of her door to the other side. I wasn't ready. I didn't want to be alone again.

Seven weeks had come and gone. No one was calling me. They were giving me ample space and time. Casey on the other hand was just pissed, still leaving messages on the machine and on my cell. The last one was just an ultimatum.

"Let her go, God damn it. Henry, this isn't you. It's your heart. Let that go. Or else you won't be able to come back. Either in life or death. You will curse yourself and me because I won't even look for my door neither if I know you and Liz aren't on the other side waiting for me... Call me, I miss you."

Four days later an old friend was sitting on the porch. I took my coffee and sat right next to him. Charlie Hailey was squinting at the sun when I looked at him.

"When we get to come down here and do these little incursions, we get to taste what we missed out on. Not for a long time, mind you, but it's enough to make you realize what you don't miss." He pointed out at the summer sun. "Bright and hot out here, Southern California is no joke. But it's dry. Florida in August, it's hell. Literally, that's the temperature."

"I know why you are here." I told him never looking up to the sun.

"You saved my soul once. I am here to return the favor." Charlie was mature now, as if years had gone by in life. The awkward adolescent demeanor, if he ever had it, was gone. As if he lived a real life beyond his own death. I could feel him sitting next to me. The heat he exuded took me by surprise.

"I am as real as you are. I wasn't the one who came over. I had help." Charlie gave a coy grin. "Even kids can work off a debt, it seems. But I technically volunteered. Since I owed you anyway. So, here I am. Warning you. Let her go. Liz doesn't deserve this. Neither do you."

"I know why you were so mad. I got it the day she died. Your anger and hate were so comforting. It was like you left an imprint on me. But instead of rejecting it, I absorbed it. I couldn't let her go, Charlie. I just couldn't."

"I know. Both sides of it. Hate keeps you focused the misery gives you a false sense of righteousness. When the sadness creeps in, the anger rises, and you're allowed to bury it. That's when it festers. That's when you can't control the emotional power evolving into a true burst of physical energy. Remember the day I stopped your heart for a brief time?"

"Oh, I remember." I rubbed my chest as the memory cause a slight tremor in my heart.

"All that bottled energy, resentment from her, loss from you. Unholy combination. It can break time and space if not corrected. I almost did it too, but you saved me. You rescued a lonely, dead boy from his own hate. Hate destroys and love obliterates. Such power. Big Bang shit, when you think too much on it." Charlie smiled, giving me his inside forbidden knowledge.

"I never thought it would be this hard."

"Life is like that." Charlie stood up and fixed his tailored suit. "I always wanted a double-breasted suit. I finally got it, this go around."

As he stood, I saw the Death Birthers began their descent on the front porch. Their teeth gleamed in the sunlight, their claws ripping at the barks of the hundred-year-old oaks along the street. I could see their hunger. I could see their human eyes focused on me more than Charlie.

"My escort. If you spend time here after you already had your time, they tend to get hungrier. I am not going to be a meal for them. I am not going to be a trivial warning to you. Take this as the only warning. Fear is quite the tactic sometimes." Charlie swung a fist at them.

"They definitely serve a purpose." I was trying to see if I recognized any of them, this time no human face was recognizable. "I know I am wrong. I'm just sad."

"Understandable. Reason you get me and not them." Charlie

pointed at the Death Birthers they were beginning to retreat into the shadows of midday. "Get her to the door. I promise you, there will be a day when you see yours. You will hear murmurs on the other side. Know that it's Liz, know that it is you grandmother and grandfather, know that it is your parents. They will be waiting as if no time went by. A dinner will be served, all that you love will be there prepping the welcome party. It is up to you to take your place at that table."

"Is that what heaven is?" I never asked that before.

"Heaven is a human concept. You have no idea how wonderful eternity can be if you listen to life. Original sin isn't the only thing humanity is born with. Grace is something everyone has a chance for. We just fall deaf to it sometimes." Charlie smiled at me, he took my hand, lifting me up.

"Will she forgive me?"

"Up to her." Charlie waived to Liz at the window. She gave that warm smile that kept me up at night.

"She can see you?"

"Of course. We are both dead. We are both in a loop. And we both have the chance to move on. Sometimes death is a thief. Robs us of all we could've had. Wrath can be a logical step and it takes a chosen living human to provide another way back into the fold. Your curse was to be that way back. You just never lost true love before. Not many can. Just remember what I said. And I'll bring a pie for dessert." Charlie began to walk off down the empty street. Within twenty strides he dissipated into nothingness.

I stepped through the front door, facing Liz. She was oblivious to everything in the living world. She was existing in an aftershock. It was no way to exist.

"Death is not a thief. It is only nature. I stood in its way, and I know now that I have no more excuses. I must let you go."

Liz nodded, "you will always be with me. Even after I pass through that door."

"You see it?"

"I have always seen it. I couldn't leave you. You had to leave me."

"I know. I love you. I will see you later." I kept the tears at bay, I wanted her to see me strong. I didn't want to weep like a child.

And then she was gone.

13

Finding My Way to the Door 2019

This was my time of healing, my time with my parents. We had patched things up as best as we could, and now we were living with our truths more openly. When my mom got sick, Casey and I moved into the house to take care of her. That's when the headaches started. Slow at first, then frequent, almost daily. They were growing worse each time I had a spell. But I kept them to myself as my mother deteriorated in front of our eyes. Death was coming, anyone could see it. I was an expert in death, but Casey wasn't. Liz was traumatic but our mother was going to be devasting. I couldn't lose Casey to grief, even though I did the same to myself.

"I'm sorry I yelled at you, over Liz." Casey was brushing mom's hair, lightly, as mother muttered in a drug induced slumber. "I didn't understand true loss. I never thought it would be like this. Watching her go, like this." Casey kept her tears back, but her lip shook too much.

"It's okay, Casey." I held her tight, giving her permission to lose it. My shirt was soaked with her tears and snot within seconds. I didn't let her go.

"Have you talked to Steven lately?"

Casey had married Steven six years ago, Liz and I put up the money for the wedding, it was the best ten thousand I ever spent. A dream wedding for a dream couple. They were young but they had this charm that felt like an old-time movie. They were close and as my mother lay dying, they grew closer as Steven gave her the space and time to cope. I was happy and glad that she had found him. As the years grew on, I was spending more time thinking about mortality. When I am gone who will take care of Casey? I didn't have children, but she could. How I wanted to be an uncle, but something in the back of my mind kept me from getting too excited for that. Something was telling me my time was clicking slower and slower to a stop. I was on the edge now, not realizing in the moment, but understanding the possibility.

"I talked to him yesterday, he's coming out tomorrow. First plane ride out." Casey smiled, wiping her tears away. "I got lucky."

"You didn't get lucky. You just got what you deserved. I couldn't ask for a better sister, Casey."

"Don't say that yet. Mom is dying, not you."

I didn't respond to that.

"Have you been sleeping lately?" Casey flipped her worry on me again.

"No, have you?"

"I sleep enough. You look like a ghoul."

My appearance was revealing my health. Bags, deep and dark were under my eyes. My hair was thinning, I had lost thirty pounds since mom got sick. I tried to sit in the sun during the day, but the light blinded me as my eyes lost focus on what was in front of my face.

"Have you called the doctor?"

"One doctor at a time." I retreated to the armchair next to mom. My head suddenly fluttered in a tremor of pain. I almost vomited, but kept it in.

"You've been like this for the last three weeks. I'm making you an appointment tomorrow. And I am calling Dr. Murphy."

"He's still around?"

"He's been cashing in on you for twenty-eight years, he better be around."

I hadn't seen Dr. Murphy since I was eleven. His scans on my brain with the head trauma made the medical books and gave him a quick taste of celebrity. When I did the television show, his medical records were released again to correspond with the success of the show giving him that second fifteen minutes of fame. He gave me a hug as soon as he saw me.

"Henry, my dear boy." Dr. Murphy said coming off the hug, noticing my weakened state. "You're having headaches, severe migraines and vision loss."

"All of it and more."

"I thought this might happen. We need to get you into the MRI and take some pictures."

And here we go again, almost twenty-eight years later I was laying down in a tube, almost suffocating due to the extreme closeness of the walls. I was half expecting Minerva to pop her head in and smile. Looking to my feet, I only saw my toenails in need of maintenance. Listening to the hum of the machine gave me peace, I began to drift. I was feeling a pull on my being, jerked into opposing positions as if reality was beginning to bend. Trapped in a black hole, stretching me out amongst the infinite space. In this moment I began to see the past, present, and future take shape around me. I was seeing what the dead saw. Even sound and smells twisted, nature from the years before civilization blew into my nostrils. Cries of extinct animals, rivers flowing, rain dancing off the edges of overgrown leaves, tranquility one always wishes to discover towards the end of the journey. Even now, I was expecting the final drop. I was living on the last days of my life, and I didn't care too much.

"It's spreading, the tumor is beginning to wrap itself around the rest of your brain. Then it will embed itself. Then you will die." Dr. Murphy was upfront.

"I figured." Was all I could say looking at the readouts.

"I can do surgery, but it'll be tight. I think I can get most of it out. Though the danger to you is very high."

"It's up to me, isn't?"

"Everything is up to you." Dr. Murphy sat defeated. I could see his sadness stretching over his stoic clinical mask.

"How much longer do I have?"

"Six months, maybe a year. But it could take a turn either way."

"At least I know what the timetable might be. Better than most."

"What do you want me to do for you?" Dr. Murphy was asking more for himself.

"You have done what you could do. I was lucky enough this far. Let's not tempt fate any more than we must."

"You want me to tell Casey?"

"No, that's my job."

The dreams started to take more cohesion shape. I could see a room I had never stood in, basic, I was on a bed looking at a bookshelf, though I couldn't read the bindings on any of the books. A framed painting was hanging, a door stood leading to a bathroom. I was breathing, I could hear that. Whizzing and coughing, then silence, then another burst of whizzing. After a few moments of that I would hear a voice ask me, *"can I do anything more?"* Then I awoke.

Nothing about if made sense, but I knew it was the room I'd die in. The voice was a younger man. One I had never heard before. But I could have sworn I felt Casey's presence too. She was off to the side with the young man. I never turned to look at her. Maybe I will when I am there in the present. I hope so, anyway.

Casey didn't want to accept the news when I told her. She

thought it was stupid to deny the chance of operation. "You're being fucking difficult." She told me.

"I am just accepting it, Casey. A man who can talk to ghosts isn't allowed longevity. What more can I discover that most know nothing about?"

"You could discover your niece or nephew." She put her hands to her stomach. Two weeks into it she finally told me.

"If they're anything like you, I love them more for it."

"I've already lost dad, mom is on her way out too, now you telling me this. I don't want to go alone."

"You're not alone, Casey. And now you're telling me you got more life coming to you. That right there makes me even more happy and clearer in my decision."

"You're being an asshole."

"I've never had too many choices made by me in my life, let me have this one."

"Six months?"

"Maybe a year."

"That's nothing."

"It could be a lifetime for some."

"I love you."

"I always knew that. I can't wait to see what's coming."

Mom died a few weeks later. Her kidneys shut down, then her liver, then her lungs. A quick fall of the dominos. I was able to be with her and Casey as she approached the nine months. In that time, I stayed at home, writing all these words out. Going back and forth through them to make sure I didn't miss anything. I could only dream about Liz through most of it. Like I said before that time was for me. It made me welcoming of the knock death was about to send me. Casey and Stephen were loving parents, at once you saw it. They were destined to be parents, something I couldn't take part in. I was a conduit for the dead not the living. Destiny determined that. All I had now was the witness to new life, gurgling and spitting. They named him Stephen. I was able to change diapers, powder a butt, sing my grandmother's tune as my nephew stirred at night: *"I love you, a bushel, and a peck. A bushel and a peck. And a hug around the neck. With a barrel full of heap. And I am talking in my sleep, about you. About you."*

It was an honor to allow my sister and brother-in-law the chance to sleep and dream as their son, Stephen, my nephew, cried out in the middle of the night. All life was precious. And I got to see the most precious part of it firsthand. For a time, the dream about the room I never been in subsided. I saw no ghosts, just the living. And my God, I thank him for that. When Stephen was two months old, I hit the year mark. I had survived longer than expected with nary a headache or discomfort. I was alone in the house one night when my mind decided to send me walking. I packed a meager bag of spare clothes, socks, and underwear in a backpack along with some wrapped up snack foods and toothbrush and a razor. I opened the front door of my sister's house and stepped out never to return.

I was a missing person. Famous former reality star, Henry Claremont, is missing from his home September 23. I would catch the news promote my story every time I stopped in a bar or restaurant. I was living off my cash reserves I hid in my house. I always had this feeling that I would need a wad of cash down the road. Subconsciously, I put away rolls of hundreds in a shoe box in the safe hidden in my closet. It stacked up over twelve years of saving. Liz didn't even know about it. Honestly, neither did I. My mind was separating from myself even then it appears. Not many people ever gave me a second glance. It was as if I was being protected by the layer of shared reality with the dead. As I travelled, I was being guided by the dead, wherever I stopped, someone was there to point me in the direction of where I had to go.

"Who sent you?" I asked.

"You don't recognize me?"

"I am sorry, my mind isn't what it used to be."

"I was the veteran. I died from Spanish Flu, and you helped me get home. I must return the favor."

"When I was on tv?" I half remembered that time, flashes of the road, different locations, writing out fictional scenarios to secure audience viewership. A time so lost in my failing mind that I almost feel it was a dream. Another version of myself in some parallel universe that never truly existed.

"Yes. They'll be more. Returning the favor. Always be mindful of that." He smiled then disappeared.

Suddenly I would have the direction needed. I would move toward the next guidepost. It was an instinctual push at first, then my mind would fade, a fog corrupted my ability to see and think. Everything about me was fading, a slow slide into nothingness. I was lucky no one ever noticed because they could have easily robbed me of the thousands of dollars in cash I had. When I got tired, I checked into cheap hotels, one had a sticker plastered on the front window: HAUNTED ROOMS AVAILABLE!!!

In the moments I stayed still, the dream would come back as if it was a memory borrowed from a ghost I sent over. A simple closed door, but I knew it led to a bathroom. The bookshelf stacked with volumes I couldn't make out. The presence of Casey was felt and another man I had never known was there too, yet I knew him. I was seeing the future. I was skirting between life and death each passing day. I was running out of time. This night, another layer to the dream was revealed. Another door was at the foot of the bed I was laying in. Not the bathroom door, a free standing, almost Teutonic, as if carved out of a prehistoric tree. The knob was bronze, etched with glyphs I couldn't make out. Light was breaking through the gaps in the door sitting on an uneven invisible frame. I heard murmurs from behind. Familiar sounds, warm voices, family I could feel it. When I reached out to touch the handle I awoke.

Inside the cheap haunted hotel room. I saw a woman in the corner, her face against the wall. I knew she was of the dead.

"Did I frighten you?" I asked.

"Nothing scares me. I've seen it all." She answered keeping her face to the wall.

"Why are you here?"

"Waiting for you. To help you get to the next spot." Her back was phase shifting, within moments I saw what had happened to her. Knife wounds all over her back and lower body. Blood poured out of the slits in ghastly amounts. I fell back, missing the bed, hitting the hard floor covered in a shag carpet that hadn't been clean since 85.

"You don't want to see my face." She was crying.

"I am sorry. I've never seen a victim like you before."

"So many more out there. Where was your show? Where were you?"

"I didn't have much say in the decisions. I was just a host."

"You could've been answering your destiny instead of making money. You could have saved more souls if you weren't selfish." She kept to the wall, the phase shifting stopped, making me witness the viciousness of her attack.

"I am sorry. I am sorry. Can you see a door?" Was all I could give this woman. I didn't have answers for her. She was right, though. Why did I spend so much time being that dancing monkey on television? It was vanity. It was pride. It was all the deadly sins brought together making me feel important. I tried to ignore that rising arrogance. I denied the whole thing, feeling the shame. But what did I do to stop it? I just complained and moaned to my father. I was successful using forbidden knowledge. I had the snake from the tree of knowledge in my hotel room now, looking for satisfaction.

"So much money for so little." She kept her face to the wall. The puddles of blood forming beneath her started to churn. Dozens of snakes began to move across the floor, forcing me to leap to the bed.

The woman walked to the windows, lifting the curtains to reveal dozens of Death Birthers roaming the parking lot of the hotel. Snot and steam streaked across the windows as they began to lick the glass. Minimal inches of cheap glass kept them at bay.

"All they have to do is push." She laughed, suddenly her body took on another shape. Tattoos began to etch across her bare skin, revealing a labyrinthian design of ink on flesh. She finally turned I was face to face with Maggie Bantam. Her intricate tattoos and evil eyes filled me with such dread I almost puked.

"You ever see a sinner turn into the sin?" Maggie had no eye lids her lips were cut off too. "I did this to myself in the hospital. Then I stabbed myself in the heart. It takes force to do that to oneself. I had to slam myself against a brick wall to force it through my rib cage. It took a few slams. But the blade finally broke off as it sliced open that black sack of blood. Then I woke up here. With you." She fell to her knees.

Four Death Birthers were filling the window now, watching Maggie shape shift into one of them. The metamorphosis was grizzly, her legs and arms filled up with heavy diseased blood, splitting the flesh along her tattoo lines. Blood gushed through the tears all the while her arms blew up like a flesh balloon.

"You must go to Nevada, Missouri. That's where he is waiting for you. That's where you must die." Maggie spoke with bloody clenched teeth, then threw herself against the brick wall rolling behind the cheap motel couch. Her Death Birther arms ripped through the couch as she jumped at me.

I awoke in sweat, screaming. I was on the floor, rolled right off the bed, my bare feet landed in the left-over pizza I ordered the night before.

"Nevada, Missouri." I said to myself, knowing that was where

I had to get to. I rushed for the phone to call Casey. I was frantic because I knew if I waited, I would lose this moment. I would lose this memory and Casey would never be able to find me. I fumbled for the phone, then a piece of paper and pen. I scribbled out Nevada, Missouri as Casey picked up the phone.

"Casey!" I shouted, already beginning to forget what I was doing.

"Henry! Where are you?" She was as frantic as I was.

"You have to meet me in Nevada, Missouri." I shouted as my head began to split as a migraine ripped through it like an ice pick.

"Nevada, Missouri? Where? Henry?" Casey was fading on the receiver. I was blacking out. "That's where I have to go, I have to go there…" I dropped the phone, drool dripping from my agape mouth then darkness.

Ten hours had drifted, my legs were cramped being in a sitting up position on the edge of the queen-sized bed. My stomach in knots as my blood flow begin to shift back to my legs. I looked to the window and saw the curtain was closed the night had taken over. The window had no streaks of slime or grease. The Death Birthers were not among me. I was alone. And I felt it.

I went to the phone, dialing the front desk.

"Is there a way I can secure a bus ticket to Nevada, Missouri? Thank you, I'll hold."

With a direct route to the city, made the trip easier. It was a long bus ride which did not help my fading mind. I had my cell phone always charging, I was trying to remember certain moments accessing the myriad of pictures I had. As the hours wore off the clock, my recall faded. I was looking at pictures of my life with diminishing returns. The Ghost Seeker show, Liz, mom, and dad and then even Casey were fading away. I was crying without knowing why as the bus stopped in Nevada, Missouri. A town smaller than the one I grew up in. Not without its charm, the recent snow dusting left a miraculous winter scene for me to lose myself in. Suddenly, my fear of lose was replaced with the severe cold surrounding me. I hadn't dressed appropriately for this season. I was in jeans and a sweater, the backpack filled with my extra underwear and socks didn't help the need for layers. I sped of to the local thrift store and purchased the proper winter apparel. Being in the state I was, most just ignored me, thankfully. I bought a black peacoat, long sleeve thick flannel, Long Johns to wear under my jeans and a pack of thicker socks. Within moments I was felt better allowing me to wallow in the sense of fear not knowing where I was supposed to go within the borders of this town.

I spent the first hours aimlessly traversing the city blocks. Finding a little coffee shop, I stopped in to eat. The menu was simple, the coffee was hot, the service thankfully disinterested in the new person showing up in their quiet burg. I scanned the interior in the booth. Nothing was revealing itself. I smelled the cooking as the denizens were dressed in mostly red for the football team was nearing the play offs again. The giant televisions were blasting the sport channels prognostications of the future of the team. The entrance of the diner led to two different sections, a bar and the second dinning room. I made my way to the bar entrance, noticing a board with local flyers of businesses peddling their services, guitar lessons, play auditions for local productions, college rooms for rent and in the center was an advertisement for the McMahon House. For some reason I locked eyes with this flyer, address and phone number printed in bold. I reached for my phone and dialed the number frantically.

"McMahon house, this is Robert." The voice on the other end sounded familiar. As if I had just heard the words of a long lost relative, long estranged.

"My name is Henry Claremont. I think you have a room for me?" I spat out the words so clearly, I surprised myself.

"Yes, indeed we do have a room ready for you, Mr. Claremont. Your journey is nearing its end."

"How do you know that?"

"I always knew. They have been speaking your name for a few years now. I have just been waiting for your call." The voice was soft, not one bit of insanity in it. A warm voice that reminded me of my grandmother, as if she planned this the day, she last saw me in my room as a ten-year-old child.

"Should I take the bus?"

"There's a stop outside the restaurant. Take it. It will bring you to Delivered Road. It's the three-story Victorian. You can't miss it." He hung up the phone, leaving me to a frantic state of writing down the information delivered.

I was approached by a stranger outside the diner, he remembered me from the show. One of my last celebrity appearances. I told him to contact Casey, then gave him a wad of cash I didn't need anymore. He seemed like a man I could give a last request to before I lost what was left of me. My mind was shifting constantly against the black cloud forming around it. Swallowing whatever I had left in me, removing the power I used to have, replacing it with stabs of pain. Each headache grew more and more intolerable as I trekked across the states. All I could do was close my eyes, focus on what I used to have, only to lose it once it began to take shape. Maybe I was a sinner after all. I deserved this pain for reasons I couldn't understand. God never spoke to me when I had this power, or maybe he did, and I misunderstood. I don't think the All Mighty who usually called himself The Word would have a problem communicating plainly but here we are.

It was a short bus drive to the Victorian home. It was a beautiful example of its period. The wrap around porch, the stained glass third floor windows gave it the holy glow often lost in this new world. A man stood on the front step hand raised signaling me to come forward.

"Robert?" I asked coming face to face with the man I heard in my dream.

"Henry Clearmont. It is an honor." Robert was a younger man, twenty-three if a day over. He had a stern look, a serious nature as if he was charged with duties above those of normal humans. It wasn't arrogance, it was a humble, stoic demeanor more likely dismissed as bravado.

"I don't understand how I got here. Or why?" I was still in control of my facilities. I could listen and remember in this moment but feared what would happen once I sat down on that porch.

"Let me make you a stiff drink, then I will tell you about myself." Robert led the way up the steps.

Whiskey from a crystal tumbler was always welcomed especially when it was freezing outside. Robert didn't drink, he just sat behind an ornate desk with stacks of paper and a state-of-the-art computer in between us. Shelves of books lined the walls, portraits hung displaying the history of the house itself.

"The McMahon House was designed to help people like yourself. In the beginning we were dismissed as Spiritualist frauds seeking people's monies through the grift of Spiritualism. We never made a dime off the people who stayed here, we knew what they were going through. We knew about the brain's trauma, the ability to communicate with the dead often leads to a mental break down. Sometimes a human being can go fifty years with this power, others ten years. The sadder cases we see madness and death within six months. It depends on the mind."

"Some of the ones I send over helped me get here. Was that real? Or was that something I did?"

"I don't know. I was born with this gift. You inherited it through a head injury. Many differences when you compare the two."

"You were born with this?" I was stunned, I couldn't imagine being s toddler running in diapers looking up at lost souls.

"I had parents who understood the gift. In my family it seemed to move about generationally. Though, the gift is different to us all. My ability to speak to them was more oral, I couldn't see them. I can close my eyes and hear chatter when I concentrate. This ability has allowed me to suffer no ill side effects. My brain is not clouded like yours. I have a much smaller cloud floating around my grey material."

"They tell you about me?"

"Oh yes. All the souls you saved spoke out into the either of the universe and I was able to pick them up. Like messages in bottles, I was able to unroll the parchment they tossed out never realizing they would be answered."

"What did they say?"

"Save this man. Save Henry Clearmont. He is coming."

"They ever speak of the Death Birthers?"

"Oh yes. I have seen those in my dreams, warnings not to abuse my gifts. Much the way you saw them, I take it?"

"They make sure you understand what is at stake, I'll give the universe that one."

"Not God?"

"I am I wrong to say it like that?"

"God and the universe are tantamount. But you hesitate to mention God directly? You never questioned Him?"

"I tried. I just never received an answer."

"You were visited by your grandmother, correct?"

"How did you know that?"

"Like I said, I hear what they say."

"Am I fool to question?"

"Never. God is the ultimate question, so much so, most don't care if there is an answer. You being questionable, you even thinking of asking air itself, displays more faith than most these days." Robert smiled.

"I guess that makes me feel better but doesn't answer anything."

"I can not answer your questions. I can just give my opinion being based on my experiences and research and knowledge. And I have quite the insight, as do you."

"Is that why I am here? To admit to my guilt over this gift?"

"Certainly. You need to let the guilt go. You didn't do anything wrong. The television show, Lauren, RC, Charlie Hailey, Liz, all of it done with the fullest of hearts."

"I was selfish for most of it."

"You stumbled into most of it. There was no plan. You just continued. Never asking for more or a way out. Selfishness takes planning and cunning, you never showed one iota of that trait."

"How do you know that? You weren't there."

"I was told. I was told by the ones who were there and are now in the beyond. That is my gift. I am here to make it comfortable for you. I am here to allow you to let it go. You don't have to be afraid or ashamed anymore. You have earned your peace. You have earned your place back home." Robert used the phrase, back home, as I would've.

"I need to call my sister, Casey…" I was losing myself again, ringing thunderstorms were attacking my inner earlobe. I could feel every ping of the drops of the invisible storm inside my brain. Now that I was here, I began to lose more of myself to the idea of slowing down. Robert took me to the room I saw from the dreams, same bookshelf, same bed, same window, same door to the bathroom. In some strange way, I was happy to be here. I wasn't crazy, I was just projecting the future. It must have dusted off on me along the way. Being a conduit for the dead gives you the capacity to exist in multiple dimensions of reality. Past, present, future is all on the same spectrum if you look close enough. I was smacked in the center of it all now and my brain was feeling the effects. I realized then that the black clouds over my brain were the fragments of different time periods all playing out in the same movement. It was going to crescendo in this final act of the opera of my life. Soon, I would be dead. Soon, I hope the door is presented. Soon, I hope I hear Liz's voice behind it. Soon, I will be home, and the rest will be silence.

Epilogue
Goodbye, Casey. Robert Will Give the Details.

C asey dressed herself as quickly as she could after the strange phone call. A man from Nevada, Missouri left her a message about Henry. The man seemed nice in the message but alarmed at the appearance of Henry. Her brother had been missing for three weeks. Many different calls came in from the hotline number Peter Roy was wonderful about getting out to help with the search. Casey hoped he was able to function still, she knew the brain inflammation was beginning to take the toll, Henry had three months tops at this stage in the game and that was a estimate. Casey packed a light travel bag and had Steven, her husband of the last nine years to take her to the airport. They bought the ticket online, surprisingly nobody seemed to be buying up last minute tickets to Missouri. Within an hour she was in the terminal waiting for the plane to dock and to board.

All the while, she was remembering all those years with him. The good ones, the bad, the ones where he royally screwed up. She smiled, cried, laughed all at once. She kept her head down low, but no one seemed to notice. At this time of night, the red eye sneak flight into Nevada, Missouri yielded ten passengers all of whom were either asleep or on the their phones losing themselves. Casey wanted that ability at this moment. She wanted to turn off the world and yield to simplicity of a phone screen. Henry kept popping up in her mind, she hoped she had time left to see him before he was lost. His gifts forced her to know one day they would all be together, but that was not the same as seeing him alive in this time, in this world.

Once the plane landed, she rented a car and headed out to Nevada from the airport, it was a three-hour drive. Small towns in middle America had the knack of being tucked away from any true metropolitan vista. Casey didn't have the time to be casual, she sped through most of the highways with nary a Highway Patrol car in sight, a blessed event as she knew she was breaking speed limits. Time was a luxury she didn't have in this journey every hour was a stab in the back, a punch to the kidneys. Driving like an expert due to the memorization of the map directions printed out from the internet, Casey was not going to rely on her cellular phone speaking its monotone artificial voice. It took her two hours twenty minutes to arrive at the front of the house, decent record breaker.

Robert was on the front steps; Casey had spoken to him on the phone she was shocked to see that he was not what he sounded like. He looked young robust and quite handsome he waved her welcoming, "Casey, we have been expecting you."

The house was a time capsule filled with antiques a family dynasty laid out like a museum. Casey couldn't believe the amount of antique books lining the shelves along the hallway leading to a staircase she was shocked to realize that this was just one section of the library. The connecting room was the actual library filled with shelves built by the Amish the woods skills apparent in its design making the room a showcase for manual handiwork. An entire row of books featured titles such as *Spiritualism, Speaking with the dead, Spirits and their needs, Listening to the words of the dead,* along with many others. Casey felt like she was in the right place this is where Henry would be. Robert led her up the stairs and open the door to Henry's room. he was lying in his bed she teared up seeing him broken lane like an old man approaching his last hour. His youth and vitality were no longer present all the life in him seemed to be already gone. She rushed to the side of his bed and on her knees kissed his forehead.

"Henry I'm here, I made it like I promised. You better be awake damn it."

Henry slowly opened his eyes a smile erupted from his sunken in face, his lips moved but no words came out. He brought his hand to her face caressed it feeling the tears roll down his fingers.

"Don't cry for me, no need. This is what must happen. I had to wait this long for you to let you know that everything is alright. It's time to let me go, my door keeps showing itself to me. I never listened to them before, you know there's voices behind it only the dead can hear them. They are familiar voices all the voices of the people I loved they're out there waiting for me and I don't want to keep them waiting. One day you'll be sitting in bed or standing in a room or dying in a hospital you'll see the door and you will hear my voice telling you to open it. Don't be afraid of it, the door comes for us all. You want to know a secret, there's no such thing as time, we're all connected. When we see each other again it would be like time never existed. The banquet will be served, your chair will be open waiting for you. The toast will be raised, and we will celebrate life in death forever... Blessed be God forever; grandpa will say that… I love you…" Henry sunk into the bed then was gone.

"You better save three more spots for my husband and the kids." Casey laughed, and let out the rest of the tears, soaking into the quilt she put her face in.

"He's made it through. I can no longer hear him." Robert said putting his hand on Casey's shoulder. "This is my gift, the ability to bring people together before the end. I am a life seeker, in a sense. Born to listen and bring forth what the living need to finish before they depart. The dead whisper to me, who to bring forward and protect. I abide. Your brother was powerful, he did so much for the forgotten. And you were his rock in the times of tempest." Robert went to a cart loaded with an assortment of alcoholic beverages. "I think you like bourbon straight up?"

"He tell you that?"

"I think it was your mother."

"She would know."

They both shared a toast to the dead even though Robert didn't drink.

They both saw the mortician come to take Henry's body away.

It was just the practicality of it all now. Peace washed over Casey, as she accepted the loss of her last family member. Now she was alone. Now she was able to embrace the present with her own children. Her own life could be hers. Henry was at the table waiting for them all. Casey knew it would be a long time before she would see her door. When it would come for her, she will smile, she will listen to the other side, laugh then open it. All of life is a gift, even if it is short or unfair. One must simply live to understand anything. The only true reality is that death is a door waiting for us all to open it so we can all go home again.